One of the most original and accomplished science fiction writers
working today.
NINA ALLAN, AUTHOR OF *THE RIFT*

A singular, uncompromising achievement.
WARREN ELLIS

A haunting, beautifully written tale of edgelands and edgelives.
ROGER LEVY, AUTHOR OF *THE RIG*

Fearsome, tender, witty and weird, *The Smoke* is a searingly
inventive, sumptuously written novel about love and grief in the
Yorkshire space age. A masterful vision of another past – or future.
M.T. HILL, AUTHOR OF *ZERO BOMB*

As weird and jittery as a caffeine overdose, and possibly the most
heartbreakingly evocative book you will read this year.
GARETH L. POWELL, AUTHOR OF *EMBERS OF WAR*

Compelling and beautifully realized.
LOCUS

Fulfilling and thought provoking.
BRITISH FANTASY SOCIETY

An intense meditation on loneliness, capital and cognition.
RISING SHADOW

Simon Ings has created a distinctive world and style that captures
the weirdness of what might have been.
SFCROWS

From Simon Ings and Titan Books

The Smoke
Wolves (January 2020)

THE SMOKE
SIMON INGS

TITAN BOOKS

The Smoke
Print edition ISBN: 9781785659225
E-book edition ISBN: 9781785659232

Published by Titan Books
A division of Titan Publishing Group Ltd
144 Southwark Street, London SE1 0UP
titanbooks.com

First Titan edition: January 2019
10 9 8 7 6 5 4 3 2 1

Copyright © 2018, 2019 Simon Ings. All rights reserved.
First published by Gollancz, an imprint of the Orion Publishing Group,
London, 2018

A CIP catalogue record for this title is available from the British Library.

Printed and bound in the United States of America

For Michelle

ONE

This desert, stretching in every direction visible to the observer, is not smooth. Its topology is in fact absurdly disordered. Yet the observing eye, unable to parse its complexity, flattens everything. Simply to comprehend it, the eye must reduce its thousand thousand defiles and dried riverbeds, stands of silver gidgee trees and banks of Mitchell grass, to a flat monotony.

This desert is made of stones and sand and indeterminate things which, alive or not, have found little use for the living state. Anyway they are so coated with dust that they are already halfway mineral.

The sun has risen too far to reveal, by way of shadows, Woomera's natural topography: how the ground rises to the north; the geological remnants of an ancient coastline to the west; to the south-east, the rubbed-out, filled-in sketch of an archaic meteor strike. The blast pits, on the other hand, are as clear as an artist's first marks with charcoal upon an orange paper. The lips of three, four, half a dozen arcs of pitch-black shadow are distinguishable by plain sight, with a suggestion of further, similar pits stretching as far as the horizon.

The pits are all the same size, curvature and depth. The

nearest of them may stand for all: a great scorched hole in the fractured ground, suggesting not so much a massive blast as a caving-in and blackening, as if, in this diseased zone, the rocks themselves have shrivelled.

Between the pits run lines of finer, whiter stuff that might be roads, though they are in fact just the crushed marks left by heavy vehicles rolling from one pit to another. Not roads, then; only desire lines. (Desire lines: a strange expression to apply in a place like this.)

The wall is made of glass. The observer – your own brother – looks down through the wall and sees, reflected there, the white rubber boots encasing his feet, the white tiled floor on which he stands, the grey-green grout between the tiles. Focusing past this Pepper's Ghost, he sees, in an oblique and foreshortened fashion, the lip of the pit in which this structure stands. High as this eyrie seems – twenty storeys at least – the whole structure must be even bigger, to rise so high from so deep and sharp-sided a bowl cut in the sickened earth.

Around the pit he spies little vehicles, and little men, wielding white hoses that from this vantage point resemble nothing so much as strands of spaghetti, trailing across the ground and down into the pit. Your brother leans his head against the glass wall, straining for the angle. He glimpses a ring of small, windowless towers – units threaded like beads around a great metal girdle which curves out of sight to left and right.

These are the shock absorbers. The angle of observation is too steep, the pit too dark, for your brother to see more, but he knows that below them there is a shallow domed plate weighing a thousand tons, built of steel and coated on its underside with a rubberised concrete. And above that, in a hermetically sealed *zone, there is a pipe, and down this pipe the bombs are meant to fall: bombs that are held in magazines arranged within the ring of massive shock absorbers.*

The bombs, each weighing half a ton, will drop at a variable rate, sometimes once a second, sometimes much less frequently, their speed matched to – indeed, dictated by – the resonant frequency of the shock absorbers. Once they have fallen a precise distance through the small bomb-shaped hole in the centre of the curved plate, the hole will clam shut and the bomb will detonate with the force of five kilotons of TNT – an atomic blast about half as powerful as that which devastated the city of Berlin in 1916, ending, at the cost of some 40,000 lives, the bloody farrago of the world's Great War.

The bombs boast virtually no propellant; a smear of tungsten paint. Material just enough to spread a hydrostatic wave across the surface of the plate. The heat generated by each explosion is immense – ten times the temperature of the visible surface of the sun – but very short-lived, so that the inner surface of the plate is hardly ablated. It will survive this treatment for years.

The pressure exerted by the blast pushes the plate. The shock absorbers dissipate the kick, spreading the acceleration along the length of the tower. By the time the shocks reach that part of the structure where your brother is now standing, he and his fellows will hardly feel them.

In this manner, the whole ungainly structure will rise from the ground and through the air and, at an altitude of around 300 miles, be serviceably clear of Earth's gravity well. From this comfortably high orbit, the stars beckon. The Moon. Mars. Even Jupiter is not beyond this ship's projected range.

Whether your brother will see Jupiter, and explore its rings with an unaided eye, remains a secret. *Before Jupiter, before Mars even, there is a necessary duty he and his fellows must perform, a mission only the captain knows about – and your brother is not the captain. He is a midshipman (first class, mind) and his name is Jim. Jim steps away from the window. (There is plenty of room to manoeuvre – the economics of this kind of propulsion favour big craft over small, and this vessel is as big as a frigate.) He reads his name, backwards, reflected in the blast-proof, heat-proof, cold-proof, pressurised and tinted glass of the wall. James Lanyon. Over his name, a Union Jack. Over that, stitched to the breast of his white leather flight jacket in gold thread, the name of his vessel.*

HMS Victory.

1

Troy has fallen. The belly of the wooden horse has splintered open in the town square, vomiting forth Greek elites. The gates are torn open and the city, gaping, lost, runs with blood. Priam, King of Troy, is dead, slaughtered on his throne; his lieutenant Aeneas saw it happen. Now all the heartsick warrior can do is try to save his family. His wife Creusa. Ascanius, his son. His father Anchises.

Anchises, that Venus-lover, that lame old goat – you're put in mind of Billy Marsden the fitter chasing after the barmaid of the Three Oaks, out Halifax way three winters past, and laugh.

Two men you do not know look up from their game of cards and stare at you. Their eyes, carrying no hostile intent, are nonetheless like crossed staves barring your path. No overtures. No gambits. Stranger, keep to yourself. Four years in London have made you a foreigner here, who grew up in streets not three miles from this spot.

Helplessly irritated, you feather the onion-skin pages of your mother's *Aeneid*, turn and read on.

Aeneas's other half, Creusa, she's no slouch. She's set, little Ascanius upon her hip, sandwiches packed, water bottled, tickets in her purse, scarf tight around her chin, *Let's go! Bus leaves in ten!* Ancient Anchises feels all his years and wants to stay put, *Here I was born! Here I will die!* Not a shred of Billy Marsden now, and much more like your own drear dad.

It is a relief to you – if only for a moment – that by tomorrow you will be free of Yorkshire and back in London for a while. For a moment (only a moment) you wish you were already embarked on the long, rickety journey back to the capital. There is very little left for you to do. In this home that has forgotten you, all you can do is wait. Weather the afternoon. Weather another Friday night fish-and-chip supper with your dad, self-stoppered Bob Lanyon (who, according to persistent rumour, nonetheless slapped Billy silly once, for grabbing at your mother). Weather another sleepless sleep in that garret bedroom you know as well as the cavity of your own mouth. The room's absurd: it is too small to accommodate a grown man, and the truckle bed is even more ridiculous, your feet hang over the end of it at night. At one and the same moment, however, that room feels too big for you to bear. When you were little, you used to share it with your brother Jim. But you are on your own now, and Jim is off to outer space, by Woomera.

You drink off your pint and set the jar down a good distance from you. The tabletop, black with varnish, is getting wet from your beer, and you do not want to damage the book.

Ascanius's head bursts into harmless flame. Aeneas, resourceful, grabs a water jug from under the sink and chucks its contents at his son's head. Creusa meantime chides the dripping boy, *How many times must I tell you with the matches?* Clueless, the lot of them; deep in defeat's addlement, they don't even realise that these harmless flames around their infant's head are a sign from the heavens.

So the Gods, feeling generous, provide the family with yet another hint that all may be well, if only they'd get a bloody move on. Aeneas sees it first, scudding the heavens outside their door. It is an asteroid: a chunk of rock, about half a mile on its longest axis, white hot and shedding gobs of flaming stuff into the superheated air. It streaks over the dying city. This signal is unmistakable.

Time to go, says Aeneas, and loads his chumbling father on his back.

You leave the pub to catch the last of the daylight. October: the air is restless, the clouds intermittent and dirty against a sun that still thinks it's summer. There's rain on the other side of the valley, and a band of low blue cloud sweeping along like a curtain, so you take a short cut and turn off the road down a paved gutter, still wet from the morning and treacherous with dropped leaves, to a path above allotments. This is a route you found as a boy, cheating on a school run. It leads to the wooded cut where the remains of old engines founder among the roots of trees that only pretend to be ancient, and stone basins send fingers of rusty water rushing hither and thither, from terrace to terrace, to power the ghosts of freshly rotted wheels.

The local coal diggings were exhausted a generation ago,

so the town regrouped on the valley floor to feed off coke that's hauled up daily by railway from the strip-mines of Nottingham and Derbyshire. These days the town is busier than ever. New works, great mechanical mouths agape, belch smoke through stacks built tall as cathedral spires, taller, all to protect the lungs of the town, but it doesn't make any difference. Smoke dribbles out of the chimneys, dribbles down and around them, especially on a day like this, and gathers in the streets and smuts the washing.

The old brick donkey path weaves behind a moss-green outcrop. As you follow it, you catch a brief glimpse of the town, steeped in its lake of smog like blue milk. The town is arranged as a series of terraces spreading like ripples from the big brute facts of spaceship factories. The town drowns in waves of smoke while up here, where the town's story began – the first fires lit, the first iron smelted, sweet waters of the peat bogs blasted into screaming steam, and the region's future literally forged – here the air is as sweet and rotten and brambly as any untouched hollow out by Byland or Rievaulx.

A cart rail hidden under dead leaves proves as slippery as black ice, and down you go. You pick yourself up, mouldy, cursing, and pat your coat pocket to check that your mother's book is secure. Your hand meets your hip. You cast around. The *Aeneid* lies open in a muck of twigs. You pincer it up with forefinger and thumb and blow dead leaf fragments from its blue cloth covers and its frayed and faded spine. Not much damage done. You shake the thing, not hard, to free a leaf that's stuck to an open page. A slip of paper falls from the back of the book. You put the book in your pocket and pick up the paper. It is folded once and you open it.

The paper is headed 'Gurwitsch Subscription Hospital' with an address in Queen Square in Holborn, London. It is the hospital your mother attended when she first took the rays. The letterhead is fancifully antique, but below, the details of an upcoming appointment – B–P 'therapy' and a date nine months old – have been dashed off by an ink-starved dot-matrix printer.

The 'BP' in *BP therapy* stands for biophotonics. The biophotonic ray is a cytological phenomenon discovered by the embryologist Alexander Gurwitsch. For that reason, it's often called the 'Gurwitsch ray' or G-ray.

Gurwitsch, a Munich graduate and a Russian Jew, was born towards the end of 1874, the year of the Yellowstone Eruption. So far as biographers can ascertain, young Gurwitsch was the only member of his family to survive the global ten-year winter which followed North America's fiery end. And thanks to the quick and generous actions of the family's lawyer, he thrived.

Contemporary memoirs describe a bright boy, obsessed with colour. This was no uncommon obsession back then. Yellowstone's profound effect on the atmosphere of Northern Europe, especially at dawn and dusk, fuelled a short-lived generation of consumptive and hungry artists. Gurwitsch's first ambition was to join their starving ranks, and this, unusually, met no opposition from his patron. But he was no good, and after two busy yet barren years, Gurwitsch returned from the soup kitchens of Paris, his paintings and diaries consigned (ritually, and with a certain amount of drinking) to his friends' fireplaces. He later quipped that his art had served the essential function of warming hands more talented than his own.

In starving Saint Petersburg, where a ban on domestic cats had brought forth rats the size of dogs, in rooms heavy with the smoke from burning furniture and even floorboards, the young Gurwitsch set about his second career. He became, of all things, an embryologist, fascinated by the mysteries of development.

Why do things grow the way they do? Why is growth such an orderly business? Especially: how does every part of the expanding foetus know at what rate to grow? At every stage of life, the foetus is exquisitely symmetrical, its internal organs developed in a manner perfectly suited to support its periphery. How is this possible? What constrains and encourages this roiling ball of fast-dividing cells to fashion itself into so intricate a form?

There were at the time two broad answers to this question. Gurwitsch's lecturers were wont to throw up their hands and talk about the existence of pre-existing 'templates'. But Gurwitsch, a young liberal, radicalised in Paris and hiding seditious German pamphlets behind his stove, preferred the more radical alternative. This hypothesised that the cells of the foetus actually communicate.

Gurwitsch's militant materialism and powerful, disci-plined imagination marked him out as a radical. He was arrested, served out a short period of exile, and maintained a secret correspondence with political and scientific figures in Vienna, London and Berlin. There was a revolution going on in the life sciences quite as profound as the revolution brewing among the trades unions of Paris and London, and Gurwitsch's letters offer a fascinating, if bewildering, glimpse into years during which scientific and political questions were virtually indistinguishable.

The trouble was, Gurwitsch couldn't get the painterly monkey off his back. He had all the makings of a liberal martyr, a Duma minister, a scientific entrepreneur like Koltsov or Vavilov, but, one by one, all the key public moments passed him by. His time became entirely absorbed by the conundrums of colour. Pigments and spectra. Constructed colour. Colour mixes. Colour wheels. Goethe's anti-Newtonian maunderings. John Clerk Maxwell's mistakes. The nonsense of the primaries. The tapestries of Le Blon. Canvases of Signac and Seurat. He wasn't, by a long chalk, the only Russian intellectual to succumb to the temptations of 'internal exile', using personal study as a shelter from the political chaos outside. Read any short story by Turgenev. Attend any play by Chekhov. And so his tale might have ended: another one of Russia's lost generation of Francophile pantaloons.

It was in the Collège de France, working down the corridor from Pierre and Marie Curie, that Gurwitsch achieved the breakthrough that would, for better and for worse, immortalise his name: *the Gurwitsch ray*.

A colour all his own!

What he had in fact found was a weak ultraviolet pulse, passing from cell to cell. *Living tissues emit light*. This was a significant finding, but not unexpected. What was unexpected – indeed, revolutionary – was Gurwitsch's leap of faith: that it was this self-generated light, this 'biophotonic ray', that was orchestrating development. Why do birds give birth to birds, and dogs to dogs, and cats to cats? *Because*, said Gurwitsch, *every species emits its own special ray.*

Easy to say; harder to prove. Anyway, Gurwitsch's discovery had to join the queue. There were altogether too many newfangled rays abroad. Every ambitious physicist in middle Europe was touting a ray of some kind. X-rays, N-rays. It took time to sort the wheat from all this hopeful chaff.

But in the end—!

At an international conference held at the Ukrainian animal breeding station at Askania-Nova, on the eve of the war that would consume a generation and irradiate a continent, Alexander Gurwitsch was ready to declare, not only that the biophotonic ray was real, but that he had already taken the first steps to control it. Biophotonics, he declared, would give the next generation the ability 'to sculpt organic forms at will' – no small promise to make to men and women scarred, as Gurwitsch was scarred, by memories of the ten-year Yellowstone Winter.

'In the near future, man will expose foetal material to a finely tuned and targeted ultraviolet ray, synthesising such forms as are entirely unknown in nature,' he declared. 'Biological synthesis is becoming as much a reality as chemical.'

This was Gurwitsch's promise – nothing less than 'the planned and rational utilisation of the living resources of the terrestrial globe'.

No one standing and applauding him that day had the slightest idea how badly this was going to go. The speciation of mankind. The Great War and its battlefields. The all-too-many undead.

*

So the whole sorry history of the twentieth century un-packs itself, leaving the appointment slip, wilted, crumpled in your hand.

When you think about it (and you do think about it, all the way down the wooded valley and in under the filthy milk-waves, past factories of cold smoke and the shop-floor smell of suds and hot metal, through the town's smutted streets to your father's front door), who's to say, with medical science being what it is these days, that cancer will not turn out to be the product of some virulent biophotonic ray?

Of course, there's no earthly way you can talk to your father about this.

You enter the house without knocking. Bob is having his weekly wash in a tin bath by the fire. Bob: a man made of sticks, reduced by age to the gawkiness of a teenager. Strong, but somehow ... *whittled*. You go through to the kitchen, giving him his privacy. You fill a kettle and boil it on the hob, and while the tea mashes you fish around in the bread tin, fetch out a stale nub and try to turn it to good account; damned thing near snaps a tooth. Through the half-closed door you ask your father how his day has gone. He replies, 'A thousand turned.' His voice, full of pieceworker's pride, now admits a new and discordant note: the defensive vocal tremor of an ageing man pitted against the young.

And they are so young! Many of them cannot remember a time before the spaceships. When Bob started there, his factory was making frames for ladies' bicycles.

'We need bread, Dad.'

'Chippie'll have some.'

You hear him clamber from the bath. The quick thwacking of a thin towel over tight, hard limbs. His footsteps on the stairs, surprisingly fleet as the weekend approaches. This has been Bob's life: cares tumble off him on a Friday night only to pile redoubled upon his thick and aching head come Sunday morning. A few hours' fishing in the beck above the old wheels will put his mood right by Sunday afternoon and ready for the week ahead: a week of numbing, repetitive labour in the factory. Fishing, though, is a summer occupation. The rest of the time, or kept indoors by the weather, he can only mope.

You bring out his tea and your own and set the mugs on the mantelpiece. Two tall cones of condensation form on the mirror behind, apparitions rising to occupy the room that lies beyond the glass. When your dad comes down he's wearing his suit, a grey shirt with a collar and shoes bought in Leeds less than a year ago. Around his wrist is the watch Jim left him for safe-keeping two Christmases past: the one from the flight school in Peenemünde, with the logo from *Frau im Mond* surfing starlight on its engraved underside.

'Christ, Dad.'

His face falls a little. You have embarrassed him, and well may you want to kick yourself. Now you are going to have to talk him, stage by painful stage, back into whatever holiday mood overtook him, that he has put on his best clothes for an evening of fish and chips by the canal. He dressed hardly finer the day he and your mum first waved you off to London, a scholarship under your arm and a promise of digs at your aunt's house in Islington. What is there for Bob to celebrate now?

It is not impossible that he's simply glad to see the back of you for a few days. These have been trying months, the pair of you without companions. Abandoned Lanyon and his singleton son have been hanging out their washing in the yard on a Wednesday night when any housewife, sensitive to the changing currents of the town, could have told them the Wednesday air runs foul from the shipyards.

Fish is brought on ice from Whitby twice a week to Hebden Bridge, and from there it is carried across the valleys of the Calder, from Mankinholes to Hipperholme, by cart and lorry and bike, even to the very ends of Jerusalem (or at any rate to Jerusalem Avenue, where it intersects with Dry Cart Lane). Were you able to map this distribution of wet fish on a screen such as the wizards of the Bund employ, you might say, in something approaching wonderment, that this is a great transmigration of sorts: how the corpses of fish move through the upper air, and up, and up, even to the giddy heights of Mount Tabor, three miles north-west of Halifax. There, on that busy, deceiving (and for you, incomprehensible) handheld device, would be evidence of the land's invasion by the sea.

'With chips.'

'Right you are, Mr Lanyon.'

'Twice.'

Bob's futile *noblesse oblige* has him ordering, in nice detail, the only dish the shop can possibly serve, since fresh pies won't be delivered before the morning and they're out of pickled eggs. Bob has a weak man's habit of standing on his dignity. 'We'll sit here by the window.'

'Right you are.'

Bob wants you to tell him what things you plan to bring back from London: how much in hand luggage and how much by the van. Hard to imagine that you'll need a van at all, unless you were to ship your drawing table home. 'Which,' you explain, 'what with petrol and the hire, would make it the most expensive drawing table in the whole of Yorkshire.'

'But if you need it, lad—'

Now here's a question. Do you need your drawing table? Do you need any of the appurtenances of your vocation? Life in London, with all its little disappointments and petty humiliations, came damned close to convincing you otherwise. There you were, pitting your poor, bare, unforked drawings, your set squares and putty rubber, against the generative gambollings of the Bund's machine-brains. How could you fail to fail?

To Yorkshire, however, no Gurwitsched superbrain will ever come. No Bund-made architectural projection will ever flicker in hologram over the waxed tabletops of local council rooms in Halifax, because even if they did – the speciation of the human race being what it is – no one in Halifax, however handsomely educated, would be able to understand it. Your skills, however crude, however outdated, are still valid here. Here the pencil and the slide rule, rule.

How long, once you set your mind to it, will it take you to turn your skills to account here? How long to learn to wall a furnace, or calculate canteen space for a factory? Not long. Never mind for a moment the accelerated lives of others: in this part of the world, your talents still count. And you have to do something. Anything. You can't always be freeloading off your dad. Puffing your way up the valley to the pub and back. Poring through your mum's old Everyman Pocket editions. It won't be long before your savings run out.

'Wherever I find work will have a drawing table for me.'

Your father is disappointed. 'But your books. Your clothes. That chest of drawers—'

You try not to show a smile. Bob once visited the flat you and Fel shared near Cripplegate. He might have been visiting a fairy's castle. The place astounded him: its size, its light. It was only a flat on the Barbican Estate. A self-igniting hob. An electric piano. Tablets. A phone without a cord. Nobody he knew owned such things as he saw there. Furniture from Fel's family. A chest of drawers, meticulously painted in the Moldovan folk style.

'That was Fel's, Dad. Not mine. Anyway, it'll be long gone. She'll have cleared out her things by now. I'll get to the flat and probably find just a couple of suitcases' worth of textbooks.'

Bob wants there to be more for you to ferry back. He wants you to fill his house. He wants to come downstairs of a morning and find his living room cluttered with someone else's clothes, someone else's furniture, the tools of someone else's trade. He wants his home filled with the signs of life.

You sense your father's hunger so suddenly, and with such lurching clarity, that you're finding it hard to swallow down your fish, and there is a moment, not long, but real enough, in which, unable to breathe, you reach for your teacup only to discover that there may be not enough tea there to clear the batter clagging your throat.

Now that you know how lonely your father is, you also

know that you absolutely must not carry on living with him.

'You want another tea?'

'No. Ta.'

The way your feet dangle absurdly over the edge of your little truckle bed is surely evidence that moving back in with your dad was only ever a stopgap: a chance to breathe free air again, out of the Smoke. It is time you found your own place. Earning enough to afford it is another reason to pick up your trade. No more paper bridges, no more fancy permeable-walled pavilions on the Bartlett forecourt. It is time for some serious application. Workers' housing for the spaceship yards and bomb manufactories of Huddersfield (an upwind location would be best, in light of recent reports from the Ministry of Health). Planning meetings to be scheduled with the users of Greenhead Park. Written objections anticipated from the parents of children attending the adjacent grammar school. You read the papers, you talk to people, you even know which firms to approach. You know what the work will be like. You believe it will be worthwhile. The prospect might even excite you, were it not that London has poisoned your love of building things.

Hasn't it?

Since January you have been breathing Yorkshire air, air you grew up in, air that made you. All year you have been walking these valleys, eating this fish, drinking this beer, rubbing blood and feeling back into your night-frozen feet of a morning. This has been your solid, ordinary life.

Now, again: the Bund. It floods back. It fills you like a tide.

London, and all you have seen there, as street by street, investment by investment, handshake by soft handshake, the Bund's enclave in London has spread. Not that anyone talks about 'enclaves' any longer, far less 'ghettos'. The Bund has grown synonymous with its constructions – its great shining towers of plastic stuff, all glass curtain walls and weather-responsive bricks – and 'Bund' has come to stand for both. Today the Bund stretches from Fenchurch Street to Spitalfields, while on the other side of the river it has turned South London, in the space of a few years, into Medicine City: an incomprehensible medical theme park, a macabre sort of Blackpool for Georgy Chernoy's undead. (Or pick your term, as the papers do. The nigh-on-dead – the *Telegraph*. The better-off-dead – *The Times*. The might-as-well-be-dead – the *Sunday Express*) All this building done at a cost so high that most nation-states would break before they had accomplished nearly so much – and done with hardly more effort than it took to push a button on one of those confounded, impossible, incomprehensible keyboards of theirs.

'Come on, lad,' says Bob, clapping you on the shoulder, 'let's get a jar.' He's already up and shrugging on his coat.

Flowing yourself into bed, five pints the worse, you pull back the curtains in your room. This is the plan: that even through a fug of Friday ale, the morning light will wake you in time to catch the milk train to London.

Five hours later and light wakes you all right: not sunlight, but light from the furnaces. Even at this early hour, the town's chimneys are belching sparks.

The air in your room is so cold that for a while you lie

in bed, pinned under the blankets, watching your breath rising like smoke from a stubble-field. It pinks in the light of a distant steelworks.

Now you stand, hunching in the cold, before the window. The street lamps are out and the road surface, hidden from the furnace-pink predawn, is a river running silently and forcefully under your window, down the hill, towards the beck, and the mill wheels, and the weirs. This is the current taking you away today, back to confront those things that lost you your love and ruined your nerve. This is the river you have no name for, bearing you back into the Smoke.

On the surface the matter could not be simpler, and setting it out, in terms both clear and pleasant, took no more than four lines of standard type on a sheet of legal-sized paper headed 'Hotblack Desiato'. The letter arrived through the door a couple of weeks ago from the estate agent that manages the flat in the Barbican you'd shared with Fel.

The flat has been lying idle and the lease is finally up. Any remaining personal property must be removed. You had six weeks from the date of the letter so there is still a month to go. There is a number to call in case of problems, and the letter ends, for no especial reason, 'Warmest regards'.

A gloomy metaphysical river you cannot name is dragging you helplessly off into the difficult past, but here's a comfort: at least your papers are in order.

You put on travelling clothes. Your best shirt is crisp, and in the minimal, industrial light of belching chimneys, the cotton does not show the stains you know are there: indelible smuts the fabric acquired within days of your coming back home. (Do you remember the look Bob gave you when you asked him if there was a dry cleaner's nearby? The strangled mess he made of the word 'Halifax'?)

It pleases you to be fastening the cuffs on a shirt so new-looking, so apparently white. But are you not saddened, too, to find time rewinding so easily? You must look very much the same as when you stepped down off the train in the New Year: a returning, not-so-very-prodigal son. You thread your tie. Close your throat against the room's cold. Think of your father's face as you glimpsed it from the train that day in January: a face framed in the spray-can snow still adorning the station café window. On it was a loneliness you could not then begin to measure, but instantly reckoned with your own.

Bob is downstairs in the parlour now, raking out the fire. The almost-musical scrape of that tiny shovel in the grate. Robert Lanyon, third-generation lathe-man. He has proved too firmly rooted to ever leave this valley, as the rest of you have left, one after another.

Stella – your mother's sister, ten years younger and a looker – was the first to leave Yorkshire, leading the family's diaspora. No one was surprised to see her go, least of all the teachers at that miserable school you went to, slumping along in her footsteps. Your headmistress had been a probationary English teacher when Stella was at school, and imagined people admired the way she and her staff held to their original, dismal view of Sue (as she was back then), stiffly ignoring her subsequent successes on stage, in film and, most recently, in the Bund. It is an attitude that has only made the institution appear more petty.

The next emigrant? Uncle Michael, Bob's older and

reputedly much smarter brother. Michael upped sticks to Canada. Fleeing the bombs, he said. The rocketship yards and reactors. The radiological toll. The 'greens': government-issued radiogardase pills. 'The whole country is committing slow suicide,' he wrote, in the only letter he ever sent home: you found it years ago in the back of your dad's clothes drawer. Whatever the reasons for his emigration (along with the stick of plutonium, there came the carrot of a sizeable tax break), the upshot is a whole slew of barely-heard-of relations are earning quick fortunes and hard knocks in the shale fields of Alberta.

Jim was next, your brother: straight from school into the army. You have no idea where his fascination with the Space Force began. At home, the nearest he ever got to rockets was the percussion caps he persuaded you to steal from a nearby quarry. The pair of you spent a whole summer blasting them, trying to reroute the course of the brook below Heptonstall. You were never caught; the police were baffled. Since joining the Force Jim has written to the family with decreasing frequency, his stories becoming ever more bland, their details more and more thoroughly redacted. Last month he recommended your dad buy government bonds. That had to have been dictated by somebody else.

Finally Betty, your mother. Three years go she moved in with Aunt Stella to attend outpatient chemotherapy appointments and, in so doing, took her first, fatal sips of Georgy Chernoy's magic medicine.

Sue/Stella. Michael. Jim. Betty. All of them have been blown down the valley, one way or another, onto the rails and away. Bob alone remains.

Your jacket pockets are full of unnecessary things. You sort them out in the half-light. A penknife and a tube of mints. A scrip for 'greens' and a packet of them, half-gone but still more than enough to see you back to the city.

You pause for a second, the cold prickling you under your clothes. Below you, in the sitting room, you can hear your father cracking kindling.

You go to the mantelpiece and pick up the two objects you always take with you when you travel. Jim grins from out of his cheap brass-effect frame. On his army dress uniform are pinned the black, white and desaturated blue colours of the Space Force. (They didn't have separate uniforms when he joined, only colours; the service is very new.)

Into one pocket goes the photograph. Into the other goes the dolly. It's a chickie-made thing: a figurine of woven straw, faceless and shapeless; a frayed bundle of knotted stalks. You found it one day while walking the peat moors high above the town. It was lying, not even in the grass, but somehow on top of the grass, not hidden, not settled, but almost as if it were balancing on the tips of the grass blades, as an Indian *sadhu* might distribute the weight of his body harmlessly across a bed of nails. You were skirting a small, anomalous island of earth maybe a foot above the surrounding ground. Old peat workings, you assumed. Only later did you let your imagination run riot. That table of earth: *might it have been an ancient altar?*

Making up grandiose stories about your find became a kind of habit with you; a game you played with yourself. The stories enjoyed a bizarre resurgence when you went to architecture school. Chatting up young women in student bars on the banks of the Thames, you found it tempting, though wildly dishonest, to ascribe to this foundational moment the beginnings of your fascination with the built environment. ('And there it was, this tip of a buried ziggurat, the whole plan of the place laid itself out before me, I found myself able to read the earth,' and so on and so forth. Some well-inclined women will fall for this kind of thing.)

In truth, you did experience a kind of revelation that day. Though you knew there were chickies living in the hills above your town (why not there? There are chickies everywhere), the dolly in your trembling hand was solid evidence of their presence.

You showed it to Jim and he grunted and you said, 'Is this a chickie thing?' His shrug said, *Whose else would it be?* You wished his response had not been so casual, so unsurprised.

Clutching the abandoned dolly, not understanding it, or what there was about it that needed your understanding (was it a toy? A votive figure? A mislaid household god?), you felt suddenly at odds with everything, divorced from the whole accepting world. You hadn't even seen a chickie in the flesh by that point. Only pictures.

Pockets full for no reason – Jim an awkward, sharp-cornered slab in one, the dolly a solid lump in the other – you work your way around that absurd child's bed you still sleep in. As you leave the room, the loose board creaks as usual beneath the thin oatmeal rug.

You clatter down uncarpeted stairs to the parlour. It is darker down here. At street level the windows, lace-curtained, are shielded from the furnace light of the valley, and Bob is a shadow among shadows, a heavier-than-life blocking of the darkness. Bowls scrape and spoons rattle as he lays the table for breakfast. The blocks of him turn and swivel: 'Morning,' the word less of a greeting than a statement of raw fact.

Back at him: 'Morning.' You feel your way into a chair. The blocks of your father move to the chimney breast, and in the light of the few flames there, shrink and slenderise and gather into human form. 'Ready, then?' He brings the tin jug from the hearth and, his hand gloved in a thin towel, pours the coffee. You sip at it; as always, it is watery and tannic. Bob goes back and forth, bringing each part of your breakfast out of the galley kitchen one item at a time: bacon, butter, bread, a tiresome ritual, something to do with love, and though it renders you a child – a little pasha perched upon his wooden throne, waiting to be fed – you know better than to spoil the moment by helping.

The salt and fat filling your mouth are a more effective alarm than any bell, any cold. Fully awake at last, you gaze around the room. Its sparse but heavy furniture – bureau, rocking chair and sideboard – float more than stand in the dark room, as if only habit and old expectation maintain them in this cramped space. Photographs in heavy frames on the walls contain dim but well-remembered scenes: holidays, school photographs, newspaper portraits of Jim. Jim is a celebrity now, the toast of the valley, first Yorkshireman in space, for all that (a local joke, this) he has only had to follow in the van of his valley's own steel.

Once back from this trip, you will be moving out, finding a room, and Bob will be on his own again. Surely he knows this? It surely will not come as a surprise to him?

No point saying anything yet, since you have no particular

idea where you will go. (Not far, if you can help it. There are rooms to let near the station, you could rent something there, though the noise bears thinking about, and the filth kicked up by the wagons, the soot.)

What will life be like, with you there (wherever 'there' turns out to be) and Bob here? You imagine meeting him in the station café, in the blue hour before his shift begins. You imagine buying him breakfast. You would like to do that, after years of him bringing your breakfast to you, one item at a time. (A foible of his. A joke, even. Something he picked up at the cinema. How food is served in grand houses. How the other half live.) Though if you're going to buy him breakfast every day you had better get on looking for that job. A practice in Halifax might pay you something while you learn how to supervise the construction of kilns and presses and production lines. It will be a change from what you are used to. The profundities drilled into you at the Bartlett will not cut it here.

Bob is already clearing the plates. You stand to help him but he waves you back into your chair. He is smiling; you catch the shape of his mouth as he turns briefly through the light of the hearth. Not much of a smile: a rictus made of embarrassment and a desire not to speak. It took a while for you to understand this expression, which has become habitual.

It is to do with Jim, and the awkward transferred celebrity Bob has had to bear: father of a famous son. Bob's smile acknowledges the good fortune that everyone imagines must be his lot: his fellows on the shop floor, the neighbours around him at the bar, the scarved wives nodding at him in the street. How proud he must be, with a son gone off to conquer outer space! Strange, given the enormity of that project – a quarter-mile-high spaceship raised on the shock wave of atomic explosions – how no one realises how afraid Bob must be.

You cross to the fire, reach under the bench and pull out your boots. A needless and heavy affectation, these, as you knew full well when you bought them, shortly after returning to the Riding. Steel toe and heel: honestly, it's not as though you're lugging rebar about all day long. These heavy boots will mark you out in London. Is this the idea? That they should be your armour? Your constant, dragging reminder that life is changed, changed *back*, rewound? As you draw these thick laces tight, you find yourself wondering – bitterly, suddenly – if this is to be the pattern of your life: a series of tactical withdrawals.

Bob comes and sits beside you and draws his own boots out from under the bench.

'You don't—' you begin.

He leans against you, gently, and maybe he is trying to communicate something to you. On the other hand, he could simply be toppling over while trying to get his boots on. Either way it doesn't matter, don't say anything, let him come with you to the station if he wants.

In silence, the pair of you pull on your coats. You lift the wire-mesh fireguard into place across the hearth; Bob unfastens the front door. Cold floods the room as surely as the vacuum of outer space floods an airlock, and the fire in the grate is all light and no heat, bidding you both a chemical farewell.

The porch step gives directly onto a narrow pavement. The street, unlit, flows around you both, tugging you to the right, and down its little gradient to the great black flow of the main street, also unlit. You navigate by long practice, lifting heavy feet over the stones. The clopping of your boots suggests the passage of pit ponies.

Ahead, over rooftops and glimpsed between yard walls, pink towers of steam and dun smoke spill into the air. These inexpert washes colour the half-darkness, forcing in the idea of a new day.

The pavement is broader here, so that you and your dad may walk side by side. Bob links his arm with yours. It is an intimate and ordinary courtesy that the men of London long ago lost. (In Keighley, men hold hands.) Ahead of you, in a smutted sky without stars, one light hangs like a planet. For a moment, you think it might be Mars. Then a second, smaller light appears, a red light, blinking at the very edge of the white. Then, to the left, a steadier green light. You stare, mesmerised, as the white light's red and green companions clarify themselves. They separate from their white parent and the central light grows oblate so that the planet is transformed, in an instant of perception, from a world into an artificial thing. The red and green lights move in a tilting orbit around the white light as the aircraft banks towards a distant airfield: first of the day and herald of the morning.

'One from the Bund,' says Bob, without bitterness.

You admire that. You wish your own heart did not pucker at the sight of that impossible, incomprehensible aeroplane. But it does. The stuff of the Bund feeds a resentment you have to acknowledge, if only to tell yourself, over and over, how shameful that resentment is. Does the horse resent its rider? Does the dog resent its master?

Sometimes. Perhaps. It has been known. And the speciations brought about by Gurwitsch's ray are recent: little more than a generation old. The wounds are still sore and bloody where the human family has pulled itself apart into cognitive haves and have-nots.

You know what aeroplanes are. Obviously. As does your father, who has gone in his working life from chamfering the holes in the frames of ladies' bicycles to checking the tolerances on pressure rings bound for rocketship propulsion systems in Woomera.

But these are crude mechanisms, set against the creations of the Bund. In a few short decades, the Bund's minds have somehow fused engineering, architecture and design into an alchemical *son et lumière* that, at the touch of a secret button, transforms entire cities overnight. The Bund's aeroplanes are not even planes any more. They have no wings. Or the whole plane is a wing. And even if that makes a kind of aeronautical sense, how is it possible that this same vehicle can plunge vertically, like a ball, then spread like a flower, disgorging its human cargo, not remotely discommoded, onto any square of even ground?

The aeroplanes you know are the aeroplanes your dad knows: rivet-and-sheet-metal concoctions, prayers to the Bernoulli principle, ungainly as storks. Dependent on runways. Dependent on air speed. Dependent on *fuel.* They are machines like the army airvan that carried Jim into the clouds over Croydon Airport, two Christmases ago. And how you all cheered that day (the last time you saw him; he's not been back since), first Yorkshireman in space, kangarooing his way to Woomera by Tripoli, Cairo, Calcutta, Singapore!

This thing ahead of you, above you, wheeling around you, this red-green-and-white fairy galleon of aerogel and costly china, might have sprung from a different world. And if a world is only what we understand and handle and possess – then another world is *precisely* from where this thing has sprung.

'One from the Bund.'

Like James's shrug, the day you found your corn dolly on the moors, your father's words leave you hanging at an uncomfortable angle to the world, as though everyone else knows some simple, small, obvious thing that only you have to puzzle over.

It ought to be your father seething with untutored resentment. It should be him shaking his gnarled and oily fist at the sky – 'This sky no longer mine!' – while you, with all your knowledge, all your education, all your experience (once the lover of a Bundist's child), say nothing, for what is to be said? Perhaps a shrug, perhaps a smile.

Instead you scowl at the cobbles, feeling like an idiot – and this is bad, because from the Bund's point of view, that is exactly what you are. Do you remember that card game you used to play with Fel? 'Set', it was called. Its cards were printed with different designs, each assembled from four pictorial components: one of three colours, one of three shapes, one of three fills, one of three numbers, maybe there were other components, you can't remember, and you had to make tricks of three cards, all cards the same or all cards different in every component category, and just trying to rehearse the rules to yourself is itself a mental stair-climb, a breathless stagger-run to the very bounds of your cognitive capacity, but she never had that problem, did she? She could explain the rules to your friends in seconds. And she beat them, that goes without saying. She always won.

You cannot hear the Bundist aeroplane. There is the thumping syncopation of the mills to consider: not loud, but deep, arterial, the molten blood of the town stirring into slow life. Also the fact that Bundist planes make absolutely no sound.

At the bottom of the slope the buildings of the town rise around you, and darkness and silence make a final sally. Arm-in-arm, you pass shopfronts. A memorial of the Great War. The street gives onto a square, grey in the slow, thick light that comes before the dawn, and you let go of each other to cross hobble-footed over cobbles to an alley between warehouses.

Night-time folds itself away while you're in the alley, and you come out among brick warehouses and wide, bruise-blue cobbled lanes as if into a foreign town that bears an uncanny but only surface similarity to home. The furnaces that appeared to be sitting directly ahead of you now belch far to your right, as though they had contrived to evade you.

The railway station is a series of low-slung brick buildings erected in the midst of a complex network of tracks, most of which are used to shunt heavy goods and fuel between the town's furnaces and factories. Few passenger trains actually stop here. With practised caution, the two of you step over the rails. Stairs made of sleeper wood take you up onto the island platform and its shuttered tea house. You stand together under its portico and shelter from the day's grey nothing.

Beyond the rails, a motor truck rolls past, its headlights on, and then another, and a handful of men pick their way across the ribboned steel to join you; they are here for the same train. Cheap smutted suits and hats; they look drowned in their clothes.

A light appears, far up the line, and you hear a squeal of wheels on curving rail.

'Be well,' says Bob.

You shake hands as the train takes form, bearing down upon you. The locomotive has the clean, swept-back lines and deep-green livery of the national service. It is as big as a steamship. The rolling stock it draws is tawdry by comparison. Matchwood.

Bob opens a door for you and you lumber into the carriage in your heavy boots, encumbered as a spaceman. Bob swings the door shut behind you. You pull down the window to talk to him: 'Next week.'

'No rush.' There is a studied casualness to these words, as though to say, *London has a claim on you no less than my own.*

A great horn sounds pointlessly. The train does not move. Behind Bob, on the wall of the tea house, hangs a government poster: Hattie Jacques urges you to eat your 'greens'.

You take a seat. Your father raises his hand and wanders off. The rail service is a law unto itself this early in the morning; heaven knows how long you will be sat here. You stand and push the window up, pull the coat around your throat, sit back in your seat and try to doze. Your feet in their heavy boots feel as though they have taken root in the ground, drawing you down into slumber, but there is something in your trouser pocket, the lining of your pocket has twisted around and made an uncomfortable ball at your groin, so that you have to stand and fish it out, whatever this is that has caught in the lining.

It is the dolly. It is even more misshapen now: a knotted handful of straw waste that once resembled a man.

The doll was in excellent nick when you first found it. It can't have been lying on the ground for long.

There was a bulge for a head, legs shaped with clever little knots to suggest knee and ankle joints, and arms bound to the torso – part of the torso in fact, but extra knots created the illusion of arms pressed to the sides of the figure, lending it a faintly military cast: a straw soldier standing to attention. The corn stalks were dry and crisp and tied firmly in place, smooth when you ran your thumb along the grain, ridged and resistant when you ran your thumb crossways.

'Hey!' James's voice came from a surprising distance away – he had just that moment noticed your absence. 'Where are you?'

You looked up and could not see him. Hunkered down like this, examining the figure, the tall grass of the moors surrounded you.

'Here.' You waved, hoping that would suffice.

'Where?'

You stood up.

Jim was more worried than you realised. He ran back to you. 'For crying out loud, I thought you'd fallen down a hole.'

Yes, there are holes. Old mine-workings. Some of them

are ancient: pre-Steam Age. And there are odd dips and ridges where the peat-diggers have been. There is no way at all to tell how old the peat-workings are. People have found flints near some of them, arrowheads, scrapers. And near others, Mars wrappers, the foil off Tunnock's teacakes, prophylactics, wet filters from spent cigarettes.

You held the dolly out to him. But when he reached for it, you withdrew your hand. You did not want to let go of the dolly. Anyway, he was not particularly interested. You asked him: 'Is it a chickie thing?'

Jim shrugged a yes to your question and walked away.

These moors, so barren, so deserted, just so much waste ground to play in: for the first time they became a populated place, and you wondered if you were, after all, welcome there. Across the tawny land before you, mile after mile of it, a thousand pairs of unseen eyes blinked at you.

You followed Jim, unsettled, wanting to be beside him, yet at the same time keeping your distance, a studied ten, twenty steps behind, clutching the dolly, jealous of it, guarding it. Jim paid it and you no mind. Every once in a while he would pause, head raised, the waxed paper kite rolled up in his fist, scenting the air. But it was hopeless. Even here the breezes lasted no more than a minute. They were idle things: God leaning out over his cloud and stirring the air like a girl trailing her fingers through the waters of a boating lake. You hugged the dolly to yourself and a warm-bread smell came from the hot straw. As you walked you felt, between your legs, a dampness, a swelling you didn't know what to do with, and you had to adjust yourself. You felt clumsy and delicious at the same moment, and you knew you shouldn't clutch yourself there, that you would only make it worse.

Jim walked. You hobbled behind. You entered a stand of thin trees, and the ground grew damp and green, the moors falling behind. There were rocks to catch the foot and sheep paths to follow, and Jim glanced back at you more often, as you came off the heights, to see that you were following. The path dropped down a narrow stone staircase and Jim was waiting for you at the bottom and he said, 'Throw that thing away.'

You stared at him.

'People will see,' he said. You could tell from his eyes, and the contempt there, that he didn't mean the dolly. He meant the other thing: what the dolly brought on. You scowled, hunching forward a little, inexpertly trying to hide the swell tenting your pants. You went ahead of him so he could not see. You held the dolly carefully in one hand, by your side, where you could not smell it, its bread smell, its milk smell; you wondered if it had been left there for you.

You entered woods, a clear path zigzagging down the side of the valley, and came at last to a road. You had overshot. You turned in the direction of town. By the time you got back to the house, Bob was already home and Betty had the fish he had caught gutted and floured. You ran upstairs, hid the dolly under your pillow, washed, came down again, and ate. Everything was normal. Everything was as it had been.

You shared a room with Jim. That night you waited and waited, hands cupped around your privates, waiting for him to fall asleep. The smell of the dolly was rising through the pillow. A warm-milk smell. A baking smell. You thought of a girl trailing her fingers through the waters of a lake. A little girl. No taller than a chickie. The thing in your hand gave a kick.

You did not trust Jim to be asleep. You shifted in bed, turning to face the wall, moving the pillow so the scent flooded you. You stroked yourself. You thought of its mouth. Its sharp teeth. You had only seen pictures. The complex entrances between its legs. Its enormous phallus. You did not know what to imagine, and you did not know what to do with what you imagined. Your own modest cock was hard in your hand and you were seized with fear: what if it wouldn't go down? You wanted to look at it, to reassure yourself. You wondered if doing this turned you into a chickie. It felt as if it might. You tried to remember the pictures you had seen and the feeling in your groin overtook you and something hot spilled into the palm of your hand. This had never happened before; you wondered what was wrong with you.

You lay still. Jim was silent. It was not a silence you trusted. Only when he started to snore did you ease yourself from the bed. You didn't know what was in your hand. You thought it might be blood. You were afraid of getting blood on the sheets so you cupped it in your hand and cupped your groin with the other hand and hobbled to the door. The floorboard squeaked. You closed your eyes. Jim did not stir. You wondered how you were going to get the door open without smearing blood on the doorknob. You wiped your hand dry over your belly, opened the door and tiptoed onto the landing. You went downstairs and fetched your coat and went through the kitchen to the back door and into the yard. In the privy there was a nub of candle and a box of matches. You lit the candle and held it near yourself. There was nothing to see. Whatever it was that had come out of you, it was not blood. The fear went away, leaving you hollow inside. There was water in the jug. You soaped and towelled yourself. You tried to pee but couldn't. You went back to bed.

In the morning, you lay under the blankets until Jim had dressed and left the room. You fished out the dolly from under your pillow. It was clean and tightly woven, but in the course of the night its smell had changed. There was a sharp note like cat pee running through it, and something damp-smelling: moss and musty washing.

You took it into the kitchen and poured cold water into the sink and shook the dolly about in the water to clean it. It came apart immediately. There were things living inside it. Insects. They fled up your hands. They crawled about in the water. You slapped and splashed, balled the mess of straw in your hands and took it through the back door into the yard. You screwed up the dolly and dropped it into the bin.

For twenty minutes the train sits without moving. Then, with a great gush of steam, the mechanism gathers itself and with a painful, squealing slowness, the locomotive tugs at its matchwood burden, nursing you over so many meshing rails, into the narrowing mouth of the valley and out again on a broad embankment, east and bending slowly south, past sodden pastures and the silver smears that recent floods have made of rivers, past so many flocks of indeterminate black birds, and mill towns, and the backs of terraces.

The dolly in your hands is a new thing. Now: how can that be?

It must be a replacement.

From where, though? They none of them last more than a few months.

Let's say you bought this one in London from a shop east of Charing Cross Road.

You have no memory of this.

And then (I'm good at this) you do.

2

You come up out of the Underground into Aldersgate Street, at the junction with Long Lane. There are banks and clothing shops. Office workers on lunchtime errands jostle you towards the road. The traffic on the dual carriageway is heavy and unaccommodating.

Everything here is motion, business and the constant shuffle of people, information and goods. It is hard to imagine that anyone could live around here. Were you to lift your eyes, you would see, rising above the faceless brick wall impending over the opposite pavement, the accommodation towers of the Barbican Estate. But the pavement is too busy, the road too dangerous, so people do not look up. The street keeps their attention. Up this close, the Barbican becomes a kind of secret, a region made invisible by strategy, known but disregarded. Your private kingdom.

When the lights change, you cross the road and follow Beech Street to where it becomes an underpass, and up a white-painted concrete spiral stair to raised brick-paved walkways. Though the estate follows a rough grid plan, routes between its multiple levels, its towers and terraces and gardens, are confusing for the visitor, so routes to the main towers and the arts centre have been marked out on the ground with durable coloured tape. You follow a yellow line to a view over the ponds. The flat you shared with Fel is directly above you, hidden by a concrete canopy. You are summoning the energy to turn and enter the tower through a door controlled by a keypad. Inside there are stairs and a single elevator. You lived on the eleventh floor and often took the stairs, a late convert to exercise, working off the weight your unathletic college years had piled on. Today you have been awake too long, you have been sitting on the train too long, you are tired and unhappy and you just want to be done; you call for the lift.

The elevator is clean and cold. A notice behind clear plastic mounted on a mirrored wall reminds tenants of the rules governing sublets. Beside it are an advertisement for a dance performance and advance warning of the annual residents' AGM. The elevator is painfully slow.

On the eleventh floor there are two flats. Outside your neighbour's door there's still that thin red welcome mat which was always tripping you up when you passed it on your way to the stairwell. The door sports a non-regulation brass-effect knocker that belongs on a house. Not that you expected changes. You haven't been away long. Anyway, most of the residents are old; they're settled here for the duration.

The door to your flat is secured with an Ingersoll and two mortise locks. You did not bother with the mortises when you lived here, so it takes a second to remember which way around the keys go. Inside there is a burglar alarm, disarmed by typing 1-2-3-4 on a keypad near the door. The hall smells exactly the way it used to smell. You had expected to walk into an empty shell. But no: this still feels like home.

The lounge is an airy room, though the ceiling is low, with generous windows all down the longest side. Nothing appears to have been removed since you were last here. The shelves are stacked with books, and there is Fel's piano against the wall beside the kitchen door; you're surprised she hasn't taken that. She must have a better instrument now. A real one. A grand. What kind of life does she live now? Money will not be an issue inside the Bund. What friends does she have? No one you know has heard from her since the pair of you split up, nearly a year ago. This is one of those times when losing a lover has been like losing a world.

Weary of your ruminations, you go to sprawl on the couch, but first you have to empty your pockets. The dolly. The frame. What on earth made you bring these things along? The dolly goes back in your pocket. It's a wonder that the glass wafer in Jim's photo frame hasn't snapped. You set it up on the table beside the sofa and sit there idly tapping it. You move the photo frame around the table, pointing it to face the hall, the kitchen, the long window. As though you are showing him your home. As though the photo were a screen, and your brother really were looking out of it. Tap tap tap.

He never did visit the flat. The timing was never right, and then he was gone to Woomera. You wonder how he is. You wonder how long it will be before he can write his own letters again. It occurs to you that this whole block must be roughly the size and weight of the army's new spaceship.

You never played the piano much while you were here, though you know enough to pick out chords and follow a melody, accompanying drinkers in the pubs you and your father frequent back home.

Fel was the pianist. Compared to hers, your efforts sounded ugly and lumpen. She said she liked listening to you, but you would not be encouraged.

The piano is electric and you are surprised to find it plugged in and the power still on. The stand holds a book of cocktail-bar arrangements. Frederic Curzon, Ronald Binge: if you substitute octaves for chords in the left hand you can just about follow the line.

The work boots you're wearing are no use on the pedals and will scratch them, so you take them off. It's good, shedding these great heavy boots, but at the same time you're left feeling naked. You are making yourself at home in a place that no longer belongs to you.

There's a three-against-two syncopation in this piece you've lost the knack of. A run of minor sevenths, tangling under your fingers, is so pretty you try it again and again but you don't make much progress. Run after run, the music falls away, becomes an athletic thing, a banging about. You wish you had practised more while you were here, but at the time the piano had been of a piece with the card games you and Fel used to play together, and the dinners you used to try and cook together for your friends. Ordinary shared activities, they could not help but remind you how far you lagged behind her in understanding, accomplishment, even the plain brute capacity for living. Fel didn't just think faster than you. She felt faster. She felt more. Until in the end you acted more like her pet than her lover. Until, in the end, you realised that was exactly what you were.

Too loud. Enough. You close the lid over the keys.

Has Fel even moved out? It doesn't look as though she has. Heavy items like the piano: with money no longer an object, you can understand her leaving such things behind. But her sheet music is still here, and her books. All the countless ordinary little things that add up to a person. Did she even pack a bag?

You need the toilet. In the bathroom, you find that she has left her perfumes gathering dust. This is doubly strange: it's not a collection anyone would want to just abandon. Blood, moss, wet rope, tobacco, cat urine, ash. In her whole collection there is not one floral note. The business of scent was one of those many subjects Fel had absorbed and mastered, enthused about, obsessed over, and to stand close to her in her weaponised state was to fall down a rabbit-hole of queer associations.

Your hands are shaking. Are you afraid to try these scents? They will bring you to the edge of places and times you know you will never be able to revisit. The nostalgia they wield is a threat. Let them go!

But like an agoraphobic drawn to the edge of a high place, you take down a bottle and open the cap. You spray your wrist, shake the alcohol into the air, and once your skin is dry, lean into the scent.

It is for all the world like being strangled in a damp cellar.

According to the estate agent's letter, there are just a few weeks to go until new tenants move in to this flat. You can clear your stuff in hours, but what about the rest of it? Is she really going to abandon Chopin, Debussy, York Bowen, all these well-thumbed scores scribbled over with her own fingering? You imagine her coming here to pack, scraping through the door with a rucksack full of bags. (This is, remember, how you moved in here, carrying gear on the Underground from the shared house in Tooting.)

More likely, Fel's belongings will be packed carefully away into boxes and crates by men hired by her father. They could turn up at any time.

In the kitchen, you dig out a blister-pack of greens and thumb two tablets onto the granite-effect counter. You run yourself a glass of water. And think about it: the power is on, the water is on ... Try the hob – yes, the gas is on, too: seriously, did you forget to turn the gas off when you left?

You open the kitchen cupboards and there are some tins and dried goods but all the perishables and opened packets have been cleared out. The kitchen bin by the pantry door is empty, and there isn't a liner in it. The fridge door is closed. A mistake: it's been emptied and turned off and the door should have been left open; there are lines of black mould and a bad smell inside; it'll need disinfecting.

So here's a possibility. (You neck your greens – a silly name for little pills of radiogardase, common name 'Prussian Blue'.) *What if she's coming back?* What if she's moving back in?

The painted chest of drawers is still in the bedroom: an heirloom from Moldova, and Fel's favourite object. 'It used to stand in my nursery. When my grandmother was a baby, they put her down for the night in the bottom drawer.' The frame and the edges of the drawers are a yellowish green, the drawer panels off-white decorated with carnations. Fel's underwear is here. Her tights. Her hairdryer.

She's entitled to come back, obviously. To carry on living here, if that's what she wants. Thanks to her father's generosity with the rent, this was always more her flat than yours. You work through the drawers, pulling out your things, the few clothes you left here. Are they even worth taking back with you? If you're not going to take them with you, you ought to throw them away. Imagine leaving them for her. Imagine her coming back in here, sorting through these drawers and finding your belongings, your socks, your T-shirts. Imagine her throwing you away.

This is no good, you're going to drive yourself mad, you have to stop thinking, you have to find something that will stop you having to think. The power is on, the gas, the water; you go into the bathroom and run the shower over the bath. You undress, and halfway through you remember the fictional removal men you dreamt up, muscling in with their crates and their boxes. Half-naked, you cross the hall to the door and deadlock the Ingersoll.

The water is running hot when you get back. You adjust it a little, keeping the heat as high as you can bear, and step in under the flow. For a while you stand there, willing on catatonia. The shower does not numb you, but it does refresh you until, to hell with it, you might as well wash and be done. Maybe there is coffee somewhere in the cupboards; you could make yourself a cup.

You squeeze soap from a bottle: expensive stuff you remember Fel got from a *parfumerie* on Wigmore Street.

Rosemary leaf, cedar-wood bark, juniper berry. On the side of the bottle there's this absurd, humourless sales screed, to convince you the purchase was worth it. Why on earth should reading this again bring on tears? Maybe it's the smell. The associations. Something, at any rate, is drawing out tears you have never been able to shed before.

Ridiculous. You turn off the shower, pull the curtain aside and step out of the bathtub. You dry off. Finding some toilet paper, you blow your nose. Then, out of habit – because you could as easily have flushed the tissue away – you pedal open the bin which stands under the sink.

This bin has a liner and it's full – so full, the tissue you've dropped in there has rolled onto the floor. So you bend down and pick it up and poke it into the bin, and lying on top of the screwed-up tissues, a used-up toothpaste tube, flossing sticks and cotton wool, there is a pregnancy-testing wand.

You pick it out of the bin. The little screen is blank, though it's doubtful whether this means anything one way or another; there's no telling how long the wand has been lying here. You stare at it, waiting for you know not what to overwhelm you. But loss is not like that. Loss is not some pain you can steal yourself against.

You sit up against the side of the bath, slowly, numbly rehearsing the way the world is now. It is different from what you thought it was, and at first only the words make sense, so that you have to repeat them, over and over, to bring this new world into being.

She got her child, or is trying for one.

She got the life she wanted, which you would not give her.

She's with someone else now.

She's with someone else now.

That's the hardest part to come clear, the part that needs the most rehearsal, not because you resent this newcomer, but because you genuinely do not know how to imagine this. *Someone else.* Who? You think of your old friends, people you shared a house with in Tooting. You've spoken to them, it's none of them, it's someone entirely new, probably a Bundist like Fel, someone with whom you have absolutely nothing in common.

You feel like your heart's just been ripped out of your chest and you wish that felt as dramatic as it sounds. You wish you could bleed. You wish you could be sick. But no. Without a heart, you feel absolutely fine, the way a doll must feel, absolutely fine, all of the time.

And because you want to feel something, anything, you allow yourself, for a split-second, to think of the life you could have had – and, *Christ*, you pull back immediately, of course you do, *there's* the cut, *there's* the wound, not going there, not going there again.

Fel must still be staying here. This is still her flat. She could come through the door at any moment – only your gut tells you she won't. If this were her usual home, there would be a liner in the kitchen bin and the refrigerator would be stocked and there would be open packets in the cupboards.

No: she has held on to this place for occasional visits. Her pad in the city. This is where she stays when she wants to be alone.

3

The Kaiser Wilhelm Society meant well. The idea was to save lives. To treat wounded soldiers from the air. In the winter of 1916–1917, during an extraordinary and extended hiatus in the conflict, Zeppelin-mounted floodlights raked the dead and dying of the Somme with healing Gurwitsch rays.

A bubbling in the winter mud. '*A fantastical mulch,*' *Punch* burbled; *The Strand* was likewise mightily intrigued. On both sides of this ever more evidently insane conflict, a great hope arose: that the freshly killed might be squeezed and pummelled back into order by Gurwitsch rays. If it worked, then (argued some) war itself would become meaningless. On the contrary (argued others), war would become infinitely more heartless and mechanical. It didn't matter whether your heart was filled with dread or with longing; everyone, in those few quiet weeks, believed they had glimpsed the world of the future.

But the future was of a sort no one could have imagined,

and the spring of 1917 brought forth strange fruit. Where the name 'chickie' came from, no one now remembers, and it's a strangely innocuous name to have stuck given the bloody nature of their arrival, rising, diminutive and needle-toothed, from the mudblood of the Somme.

They feasted upon the dead, dragged gangrenous limbs into their hives, prospered and, after their fashion, bred, while all around them, the heavily armed constituencies of Europe succumbed to existential horror. Nothing budged the chickies. Not flamethrowers. Not gas. Attempts at pogrom further complicated an already impossibly complicated conflict, and attacks against this bizarre new threat very quickly deteriorated into campaigns against the usual: Gypsies, students, Czechs perished by the hundreds of thousands. Jews came in for special persecution, as it got into people's heads that Gurwitsch's biophotonic technology was the weapon of choice of a cosmopolitan Jewish conspiracy.

Young leftist Jews had for many years been torn between two competing political camps: the Zionists, who sought a political homeland in Palestine; and the Bundists who, rejecting the old 'obscurantism' and embracing Marx, sought integration in a new, humanist future. The pogroms of 1917 polarised that struggle. The Bundists, seizing Gurwitsch as their secular saint (who would be strung from a lamp post in Prague in 1920), fled to Moscow and Saint Petersburg.

It should have been the end of them. Reduced to a pitiful few hundred radicals, they were flying right into the jaws of yet another Russian famine, even as every other intellectual was trying to get the hell out. Lenin, grateful and canny, offered them Birobidzhan in Siberia as their homeland and, singing hymns to the New Soviet Man, they leapt aboard the carriages of the Trans-Siberian. No one expected to hear from them again.

Within a year, Birobidzhan had become the engine of Bolshevik atheism: industrious, innovative, positively American in its embrace of new technology. Still no one foresaw its rise: how the Bund should, in the course of thirty bloody years, overtake and surpass its Bolshevik paymasters. But how could it have turned out otherwise? The Bund had the Gurwitsch ray, and with the ray they transformed everything, just as Gurwitsch had predicted. Gurwitsched wheat averted the '21 famine, saving Saint Petersburg. Gurwitsched horses twenty-five hands high pulled rocks out of the path of the White Sea Canal, connecting the Arctic to the Baltic. All Europe fed on Gurwitsched pigs, Gurwitsched apples, Gurwitsched lemons. Until at last their mastery was such, the Bundists dared to try again, and in a much more careful, targeted fashion, what had been tried in 1917. They turned the rays upon themselves.

The Barbican: two towers, and seven storeys of maisonettes upon a rectangular podium, grouped around lakes and green squares. Its architects were your teachers: German war refugees with strong ideas about simplicity and utility. Men who, with their past ripped from them, embraced the future. They were men whose self-idea was constructed entirely of new materials. They were old when you met them, stood in lecture halls and applauded them, and they are long gone now. They surfed the wave of the future, and it swallowed them up. The flat you shared with Fel looks inwards, over the lakes, the greens, the lines of trees, and it is easy, standing at the living-room window, to imagine that nothing has changed. Ironic, that a building conceived with an eye focused so fiercely on the future should already be feeding your nostalgia.

Meanwhile the Bund races ahead, overtopping everything, swamping everything. This wave your teachers surfed has grown so big, all you can do now is run from it. Head for the hills, the mills, the moors! There is not much dry land left above the Bundists' liquid way of building. Walls that shift to accommodate the occupant. Roads that move. Aircraft that unfurl from the sky.

The Bund's in every country now, with enclaves in all big cities. The obvious metaphor for this process – a tumour, metastasising – fails because of its unkindness. The Bund's enclaves offer the Old World much, and almost all were welcomed. Good regulation helps, as London proves. Founded in the city's financial heart, London's Bund may overtop the Barbican all it likes, but it is here, on this line, that its deluge ceases and its wave is frozen. It has been agreed and signed into statute that the Bund's glass and LED glitter will come no further west. And after all, the Bundists are men and women, not without feeling, not without judgement. Even if it were in their jurisdiction, the Barbican Estate would probably survive as, within the purlieus of the Bund, traces of London's Roman wall survive, and local wells and rivers under stone, Bazalgette's pump house, and the foot-tunnel under the Thames at Greenwich. The Bundists are kinder to the past than your precious émigrés ever were.

Remember those pictures: how thoroughly they erased the ruins of Cripplegate to bring the Barbican into being?

In your first year (such was the city's desire to keep up with the Bund) the Bartlett assigned you some ruined land of your own. It lay within a stone's throw of this estate. It was yours to survey, yours to refashion on paper and in balsa, and in your second year, assuming your vision was not hopelessly inept, you got to see it built. You read and reread your commission, unable to believe your luck. The Corporation of the City of London was giving you a whole block of the city to play in: a huge, weedy lot, bombed out in the Great War and neglected since, running south from Roscoe Street as far as Fortune Street, and bounded east and west by Whitecross Street and Golden Lane. You imagined yourself another Geoffry Powell, another Christoph Bon. You imagined great Brutalist towers rising. You didn't have nearly the amount of money needed for such grandiloquence (nor, indeed, the freedom; your tutor was constantly breathing down your neck). Undeterred, you traced the borders of your playpen on maps both old and new, in council offices and in libraries, struggling to encompass your fortune. Fortune, Whitecross, Roscoe, Golden Lane . . .

You picked through the stones so gingerly. What were you expecting to find in that choked and rubble-strewn quarter? Another corn dolly? Superstition kept you hesitating at the outskirts of the bomb field for a long time. Street by overgrown street, garden by garden, cellar by flooded cellar you crept forth, timidly occupying your very own zone of council-approved redevelopment. Theodolite over your shoulder. Cheap camera. Notebook. Sandwiches in a tin box.

Over the course of spring term, you came to know every ruin, broken arch and orphaned doorway. Every exposed interior. The papered walls of everted reception rooms. The absurdity of sanitaryware under a blue sky. You found a fox nesting inside a toppled wardrobe, a spindle of buddleia taking root inside a shoe.

You worked hard, long into the night, and gradually that square of streets – Fortune, Whitecross, Roscoe, Golden Lane – became your private kingdom. And why not? This was the zone assigned to you. This was yours to transform. Yours to improve. The clearance operation was scheduled for the summer break. Before then, you had to bring your friends here. You wanted them to appreciate the scale of the work ahead, and see the shabby Before to your carefully drafted After.

You brought Jill here, with whom you acted once or twice in college plays. She was very stiff, her fingers always playing at her throat, and you imagined she was a bomb just waiting to go off. Which, as it turned out, she was, though not in the way you had hoped. You spent an entire spring day trying to seduce her. Mind this drop, that spar, an unprotected hole! She wasn't dressed for it. A yellow frock. Strappy sandals. You took these as good omens. *Listen*, you said, *hear the water, running just beneath our feet!* Here, there's shade and a seat, someone's abandoned sofa, not too damp, behind this abandoned car. Here – *shush* – look at the pretty little foxes!

Until, in the ruins of a bomb-hollowed church where you led her by the hand (you had got that far) down an aisle filled with coloured light filtering from a great west window still unaccountably intact and there, butterflied in green and red and blue, she let go of your hand and knelt, fingers clawing at her neck for the little gold cross you had imagined was no more than an ornament. Then tears, and the hysteria that (you learned) invariably accompanies a religious visitation. 'The light! Such light!'

So that tore it.

Who else did you bring here? More college friends. Stan and Robyn. In their third year of music studies they had decided to get married and had moved into rooms absurdly far from the campus.

Towards the end of your first year your scholarship monies had all run dry, and you were making ends meet playing lounge piano in a dive north of Soho. One Saturday night, Stan and Robyn turned up there. They paid you hardly any mind, they were too busy screaming at each other, throwing wine at each other, throwing plates. It was the sort of place that appreciated character. You were more likely to get hustled out than they were: your plodding arpeggiations were the definition of dismal.

They showed up the following Saturday, and the Saturday after that, and the one after that. They told you they were co-writing a musical review. It was all about the art of the English murder and the impossible airlessness of the garden suburbs. You didn't take them at all seriously, until their faces were in the papers. Your Aunt Stella bankrolled the show's move to the West End, where it won instant acclaim.

As a favour to Stella, you led Stan and Robyn through your soon-to-be-flattened wilderness – Fortune, Whitecross, Roscoe, Golden Lane. The earthmovers were already trundling into position as you sat the pair on piles of broken masonry and took moody publicity shots of them with a very complicated large-format camera. Stan was wearing a lounge suit and Robyn was in a cocktail dress and they were constantly brushing the plaster off each other, picking off burrs and thorns and seeds and stray grasses. 'We've got to return these clothes.' They couldn't take their hands off each other.

Six months later and with the baby beginning to show, they parked up on a bridle path in the Lee Valley and piped exhaust fumes into the cabin of their car. The papers, in a frenzy, rang you up for more photographs. 'Anything unpublished will do.' You dug out the portfolio. You gazed at them. They looked so very happy. So very unworldly. You burned everything, even the negatives.

Stanislaw Lesniak – another 'Stan' – was no celebrity, but of all your visitors, he was the one who most publicly identified with the place. Early one summer vacation, so as to fill a gap in his little magazine *Responses* ('Poetry, Politics, Gardening'), he took a tour of Cripplegate ('The foxes here are riddled with rabies: what has the council to say?'), casting you as that region's native guide ('Surly, incommunicative, venal, but a match for the wildlife'). Stanislaw was in love with you, and you must have felt you owed him something because you spent four whole days leading him up and over banks of broken masonry, through thickets of bramble and self-seeded foxglove. It was a stop–start affair as he was constantly having to peer at, pick and identify the surrounding plant life, cross-referencing diligently between three heavy field guides. 'It must be fat hen after all. I've never seen a specimen so tall.' Buddleiae were just buddleiae to you until he taught you to distinguish between Lochinch and summer lilac. 'I have also come across wall lettuce and hedge mustard here, among the usual smooth sow thistle, nipplewort and coltsfoot, all with yellow flowers.' You appear in his exhaustive account of his Cripplegate explorations often, and always through the lens of incredulity. 'The rubble banks to the west of the site are "a sea of bluebells" in March, Lanyon tells me: a convenient claim to make in July.'

Responses withered but Stanislaw Lesniak's account of unrepaired Cripplegate has never been out of print. The Penguin edition has woodcuts for each chapter head. You still hear him on the BBC sometimes, explicating difficult ideas to do with soil radiobiology.

Felicine Chernoy.

Last and not least.

When you led Fel through Cripplegate, she drank in everything you showed her so passively, it was impossible to know whether she was having a good time or not. She was not equipped, mentally, for an unaccommodated world. She had no idea what to do with it. If you led her to a vantage point, she would follow. If you sat her down in the shade behind a wrecked car, she would sit. She said almost nothing. She more or less ignored the picnic you had brought. You had no idea, back then, how little she ate. She was a vacuum into which you had been pouring all your hopes for weeks. She was, at that time, still a simple object of desire, absurdly too beautiful for you.

In the night that followed your explorations of Cripplegate, you took her back to the house in Tooting where you rented a room. She let you make love to her again.

In the middle of the night, the faulty central heating clanged you awake and you found her sitting up beside you in the bed, sketching with a biro on lined paper. She had tweaked the curtain aside to illuminate her page by street light. You sat up and turned the light on. She had your likeness down in all its gawky preposterousness. Her portraits never tipped into caricature; they were crueller than that. The plants at your feet were identifiable. Mercury, lamb's ear, black bryony. You told her the names of the plants she had drawn. She blinked at you, half-smiling, and you began to understand what the vacuum inside her signified. She was built to absorb everything. Nothing escaped her notice. Nothing was beneath her regard. Not even you.

Somewhere there must still be the drawings Fel made of the construction site when, in the autumn term of your second year, your paper buildings were given planning permission and began to rise upon the plane of levelled rubbish separating Fortune Street and Roscoe Street. She caught details with her pen onsite, and when you were alone together you explained the things she had drawn. That the sill-plate bolted to the crawl-space wall is made of pressure-treated lumber. That the lintel carries the load from the roof to the trimmer studs, so the door does not burst open under the weight of the roof. Your careful explanations were completely pointless. You surely realised this. A tribesman patiently explaining to an anthropologist how to work a flint into a scraper.

Bringing Fel to the building site strained your relations with the foreman, who already had little interest in anything you had to say. He knew what houses were. Again and again you had to drag him back to the plans. Answering the builders' objections became an exhausting and nightmarish version of the fairground game in which hammering the head of a mole into its hole causes three other moles to pop out. You had to fight for every off-width stair, every pricey curtain wall, every non-standard sheet of glass. What you did not know at the time was that construction of this sort was already redundant. In fact, your houses were the last the foreman would ever oversee, or his workers build. The Bund's constructions stop east of City Road, but its construction crews are available for hire by any cash-strapped city council. The homes you and your construction crew so painfully conjured into being, turning pencil strokes to timber and nights of careful calculations into so many tons of mixed cement: for the Bund, these are merely printing jobs.

Your work survives, though much of it has suffered after being passed rapidly from owner to owner and from use to use. On Banner Street someone has tacked faux-Elizabethan timbering over your brick frontages. Flats that impend over the pavement on cantilevered beams have been propped up with massive and unnecessary concrete pillars. Carpet shops and convenience stores fill the small, uniform retail units you had meant for artists' studios, rehearsal spaces and left-wing bookshops. Where Banner Street meets Golden Lane, the Foresters pub remains true to your vision: a rectilinear shell of yellow brick, hardly different in its proportions from the houses surrounding it. The architectural suggestion here – that the pub might have been made later, by knocking through two ordinary residences – was, if you recall, deliberate: one of many knowing nods to the idea of a manufactured past. It is an embarrassingly bad building but this is where you find yourself: a criminal returning to the scene of his crime.

The inside of the pub is carpeted throughout with worn red industrial stuff. The balustrades around the little raised dining areas are made of wood, as are the chairs, though they are slathered over with such a layer of thick and shiny varnish that they may as well be made of plastic. Plastic drip-trays line the long bar. Tall electric pumps offer a narrow selection of beers. A Heineken will do. You carry it over to a round table set out for eating. Not that you plan to eat, but there's a television blaring away in the taproom.

The channel it is tuned to is fixating, not for the first or even the fifth time, on the construction of HMS *Victory*, a British spaceship, powered by atom bombs, that is your world's best hope for reaching the Moon, and Mars, and other stars. Ever since the end of the war, politicians have been promising to use atoms for peace, and the *Victory* is the flagship of that effort.

Unfortunately, it has also come to stand for all the frustrations, delays and broken promises of the Atoms for Peace movement. It is taking far too long to build.

The TV is regurgitating information films and animations and interviews that everyone has seen several times over. It is all old material. So far as you can tell, there is no actual news.

Cynics say this state of affairs is likely to last indefinitely: a ship always about to launch, a new era of discovery always just around the corner. This dark joke rankles with you, since it casts your brother and his fellow crew members into perpetual purdah: always ready, hands on the hatch doors; always, and for ever, just a klaxon's blast away from boarding.

Since its inception, the project has hung in a queer no-man's-land, part military project, part national festivity. Politically, keeping the entire project dangling makes a queer kind of sense. Never mind the real possibility of failure (after all, no one has ever tried this before), success will be expensive, in an instant turning investment into expenditure.

Even sat with your back to it, the flickering screen is hard to ignore: dramatic current affairs-style music, all bombast and synthesised brass in a 5/4 rhythm, shakes the little set so that the casing buzzes. The only distraction to hand is a crammed tin dish of ketchups and sauces and individual servings of sugar and low-calorie sweetener. Why on earth didn't you bring a book?

The door opens, admitting the sound of traffic, a man in a pork pie hat, and a chickie on a lead. The man leads the chickie up to the bar. The chickie may as well be a dog he has led in, for all that anyone here seems bothered by it. It squats at its master's feet. With small, stubby, nailless fingers, it scratches at its neck where the collar has raised a mild red line. The collar is black leather, about an inch wide, and studded with small, rounded stainless steel studs. The chickie yawns, lips peeling back to reveal purplish gums and long, stained teeth. Its incisors are filed to points.

The chickie is big for its kind, though it is wearing a puffy powder-blue nylon one-piece that adds much to its apparent bulk. Its feet are laced up in strappy black high-heeled sandals. Its toes are long and delicate and end in thick nails, lacquered a glossy black.

The man in the hat is someone you recognise, though it takes you a minute to place him. He has on a black leather blazer, dull and greasy with use, baggy jeans and tasselled tan loafers. It is the foreman of the construction crew that built your houses. The man who knew what houses were and, worse, knew that he knew. The man you ignored when he told you that you couldn't bring your girlfriend onto a building site.

You can't remember his name. He has lost weight since you last saw him and much of it from his face, which is lined and cadaverous with an ashy forty-a-day cast. You watch as he deftly crushes the filter of his cigarette prior to popping it in his mouth. This is a man with a taste for tarry goodness. He used to be defined by his drinking, his pot belly neat and protuberant and virtually liver-shaped, a cartoon of cirrhosis. Now he has become a man defined by his smoking. The hat is new. At least, you have only ever seen him before in the fluorescent yellow hard-hat of his profession.

You wonder (because for some reason this does not seem to be in your power to decide) whether you are going to stand up and go over to the bar and say hello to him, though you know full well he will not remember you, and even if he does he will make a business of not remembering, because architecture students with their fancy ideas, their timber decks and neutral facades, are a dime a dozen to him.

The TV sparks and gutters out and from the taproom comes the soft, hollow sound of tables being dragged across thin carpet. You turn and watch through the rails of your snug. There are a dozen or so men pulling tables together to make an impromptu stage. The barman – a young man with acne and plastered-down hair – disappears out the back and a moment later the stage is bathed in a blood-red glow from small spotlights mounted on the ceiling's fake rafters.

Someone sets a glass down heavily on your table. You turn, take in the glass – it is dry, there is money inside – and the fist and the arm and the pork pie hat and the foreman's eyes. You remember his eyes very well: how they packed and focused and delivered everything he knew not to say. Wilkes. His name was – is – Wilkes.

'Fiver.'

Had it been anyone else you would have simply stood up and left. Instead: 'Thank you, Mr Wilkes.' And in goes money you can ill afford to waste like this. Wilkes, indifferent to his name, moves off. You wonder where his charge has gone.

The barman is back. He is walking around the lounge, bar towel in hand, wiping tables now that they have been vacated. It occurs to you that what is happening here cannot be legal, and this realisation, coupled with the charge emitted from Wilkes's eyes, lifts you to your feet and propels you along a line of least resistance into the taproom.

There are people following you in, nudging you closer to the makeshift stage, and it's a puzzle to know where they've come from, the pub wasn't this busy before. The stage, made of slippery, highly varnished tables pushed together, a rickety platform full of gaps and raised edges, blears red under the spotlights. You know what is coming and it amazes you they think they can get away with this. The council is not kind to these kinds of infractions, the pub could lose its licence. To cover your nervousness, you try swallowing the rest of your pint. (No? No. It absolutely refuses to go down. Its gassiness has defeated you.)

The man in the pork pie hat is no longer around. He

doesn't even introduce his act: a thin cheer greets me as I mince through the crowd. With a muscled grunt, I push myself up on my knuckles and swing into a sitting position on top of the tables. I have been here before. Not in this particular pub, as it happens, but on stages like these, in front of crowds like these. I'm surprised there are so many men here; it's normally a mixed crowd.

There's some applause, a couple of wolf whistles. I reply with an expression I know will get you all going: something midway between a yawn and a threat, exposing my sharpened teeth. You all think this is a natural thing for me: feral. You have no idea of the hours I have spent in front of the mirror. You cannot imagine the tedium of all those facial exercises. But that is where the art is, thankless as this sounds. It takes work, making this look easy. I stretch my bowed and rickety legs and part them a little, scraping the table varnish with the pointed heels of my sandals, then get to my feet (such tiny feet! I am proud of them, I take a lot of care of them, can you tell?) and parade slowly over the tables, testing them, marking my space. I bring my hands to my throat, feeling for the zip, and because my eyes are as black as a bear's, with no whites visible, everyone here thinks I am looking at them as I pull the zip down.

Is no one going to put on any music? I have played some dives before but this takes the biscuit. Not that I need music. I am more than capable of setting my own rhythm. I know what I'm doing. Let us be clear who is in charge here, shall we?

Shucking this bloody blue nylon coverall is a relief. You may cheer to see what's underneath but your pleasure is nothing compared to my own. What was Wilkes thinking, dressing me up in that sweatsuit? I run my nailless fingers through the spangled glitter of my skirt (*yes*, it hurt; *yes*, it was Wilkes's idea; *yes*, with pliers; into each life a little rain will sometimes fall) and once I shed my bolero shirt I find that half my carefully applied paint job is coming off on my fingers. I can feel it, it's just slopping off me, I'm *drenched*. I run my hands around my belly and my breasts, finger-painting myself. Always, if you can, turn a mishap into a number. I remember I once slipped arse-first between two tables in a place hardly better than this and you should have heard the laughter, oh, they thought I was done for. But I came up through that crack like the devil himself and all his little demons. Spitting. Snarling. Dripping. Tonguing. They laughed on the other side of their faces that day. They climaxed with terror. The landlord literally so, the gropy bugger. Which is why Wilkes decided that night to see to my claws.

I need a moment for my skin to breathe and for the glitter spray to tack and harden: a slow, sashaying process around and around my little 'stage' gets the audience clapping in time. I'm gathering up the threaded stuff of my skirt as I go, revealing the junctions between buttock and thigh, between buttock and buttock. And stop. And – *bend*. These heels are at the absolute outer envelope of what I can manage. Bend. *Bend*, damn it. The bed last night, if you can call it a bed, the foam pallet Wilkes tossed down for me in the back of his garage, has stiffened me like a board. *Bend*. Good grief, it's a long way down . . .

The money shot. Are you looking? You are looking. Sex

means very different things to me, which is why I can make it so powerfully personal for you. This is anything but nature expressing itself, let me assure you: how I reach behind, and spread. What on earth you find of paradise in those complex and inutile folds and swelling, hairy lumps beats me, but I'm not complaining. I like being looked at. Can't you tell? I like being seen and studied. I like being recognised. For me . . .

Ah, but what's the point? You don't even know I can think, and I'm certainly not going to blow the gaffe now. Not here. Not yet.

Still bent, I part the threaded stuff covering my breasts and cup and squeeze and pull. Milk drips from my fingers. And I am off again, tripping to my internal rhythm, orbiting the stage. My tongue is swelling, the way it does, and without my meaning it, it rolls out of my mouth. Every slip becomes a gesture, every fault an element: I lick the curve of my clavicle and the smooth knob of my shoulder, writhe my slim, long neck against the restriction of my studded collar and – *there*.

What you have come to see. Or, at any rate, are going to get. This big, bifurcated member of mine rises of its own will through the silver grasses of my skirt. Honestly, just *look* at the bloody great thing; it's hard sometimes to say which of us is in charge. Clear mucosal oil gathers in its bowl-shaped tip, and from it rises a scent as powerful and penetrating as any incense, a human ambergris to set your blood on fire, so gather round, boys, girls, gather round and breathe it in, now that I have you under my spell.

It says something about your state of mind that Wilkes's absence from the scene distracts you from my presence. Frankly, I am somewhat hurt. But I have to hand it to you:

you're quick on the uptake. You're wondering what it is that lets Wilkes sit there quietly at the bar, supping his gaseous bitter, when the air is turned all golden with my milk-and-fresh-bread smell.

Wilkes glances at you. He says: 'You'll av to zerve yourzelf.'

There. The secret is revealed.

'Barman'z gone to wodge.'

You shrug, aping the other man's indifference.

'What'z de madder wid you, den?'

'What?'

'You don't lige de show?'

You have no answer to that. You neither like nor dislike my show. You understand that it is a thing beyond liking and not liking. Still, you want to say something.

Wilkes's face is as belligerent as his question, and you struggle to right yourself under the power of his pale blue gaze. You fancy that our close association – talent and agent, slave and master – has lent him some of his living property's power, though none of its charm.

'I know you,' you tell him. 'We worked together. On these houses. You had charge of the site.'

Wilkes looks at you without even trying to recognise you. He shrugs. 'Worked all over,' he says.

'But here. These houses—'

'Shid houses.'

'Are they?'

'Bund do better dan dese in an afdernoon.'

Wilkes breaks off his stare, snaps upright as though heaved on a wire and begins paddling the pockets of his trousers. He tilts his head back, his mouth stretching in a rictus that reveals the browned nubs of never-shed milk teeth. His sneeze, coming after so theatrical a delay, is explosive, escaping his rapidly cupped hands. Spit flecks your cheek; you take a step backwards.

'Shid.'

You have no handkerchief to offer him.

'Fug.' Wilkes wipes his nose with a bare hand. 'Shid.'

The break in transmission encourages you to try again. Why you should want to attempt communication with this oaf beats me. But try you must.

'How do you—?'

Then his eyes are upon you again, and you stop.

'Whad?'

'The chickie. How do you—?'

Absently, Wilkes runs his hand down the front of his shirt. 'Rezizt?' The man snorts phlegm and, swallowing a bark of laughter, taps the side of his nose. 'Oh, I gan rezizt. No broblem. I don av none of dis, mate. None of your zense of zmell.'

The show is over. Chickies bring you on, goes the old joke, but they cannot bring you off. Now my striptease is done, we have a room here full of men and women with no idea – none – what to do with themselves. All this spangle and glitter is but the delivery system for a state of mind you lot cannot resist and can never find a name for, suckers that you are. And since no one wants to meet each other's eye, it makes logical sense that the entire audience repair en masse to the bar, clamouring and shouting, waving damp banknotes in the air. It is thirsty work, being worked on the way I work on you.

Glasses clash and tinkle, in and out of the bottle-washing

machine. Beer gushes. Slops puddle the bar. The barman reappears, disappears, reappears. Now there are two of him. Seriously: they are as alike as twins. Someone nearby lights a cigarette. You fish in your pocket for change. There's only enough for a half. What time is it?

'Bollogs.' Wilkes leans away from the bar. He wobbles a moment, a boat casting off, and by the pitch of his gaze you can only assume he is looking for me, for while I am many things, I am not what you would call tall, even in these ridiculous heels. 'Mate,' he says to you, 'wodge my pint.'

One glance at the cloudy muck Wilkes has made of his drink is one glance too many. Anyone making off with that yeasty backwash gets what they deserve.

Half a pint of IPA in hand, you squeeze through to a narrow space to the right of the bar, and at a small table you sit, only to find yourself tourniqueted by that damned twist in your trousers again. You stand up and turn out your pockets, and what should turn up but that corn dolly of yours? Odd: you could have sworn you left it behind at the flat. It's somewhat the worse for its escapade. One arm is mushed beyond saving and there are loose stands of straw around its neck: a makeshift ruff.

You shove the dolly back in your pocket and sit down abruptly. You feel embarrassed, though there's no very good reason why. Such trinkets are common enough. Dollies. Arrowheads. Little baskets ('Fairy baskets', they call them). Felt shoes. Crude clay figurines of animals, no bigger than your thumb.

Every village in England has a store peddling the leavings of its local chickies. They sit happily enough in the window display, nestled among the other tat those places sell. Stuffed mice dressed up in doll's clothes. Hand-drawn maps of local walks suitable for the halt and the lame. Pamphlets anatomising the local church. There were a couple of shops of that sort in Hebden Bridge, do you remember? One was a post office, the other a riot of incense, posters, semi-precious stones, pendulums, tarot cards, runes, wands.

Do you remember the summer Jim came home on furlough and brought along mates of his, rough army lads from Sheffield and Penistone? How excited you were! How much you wanted to be a part of their games! You were just about old enough to drink by then, and Jim let you tag along after them up to Heptonstall for a boozy lunch of curries and crumbles, and then to the pub for more pints. They were friendly lads after their fashion. They teased you for your glasses and your weak frame. You were too excited to let anything they said hurt you.

Do you remember afterwards, what you got up to together on the moors?

Do you remember stumbling upon my hive, and what you did with it?

If you had bothered to clear it out instead of burning it, you could have sold my things to that shop. It sold all manner of rubbish, that place, like Mayan Music Balls which came with a note that read, 'Because they are handmade, no two balls ring alike.' Most didn't ring at all.

What would you have found to sell, had you bothered to dig me out? A brooch made of hammered tin. Some horn buttons. A few long-stemmed pipes. A clay oil lamp. You could have earned a few bob from that lot.

But no. Jim and his mates were far too drunk by then. Liquored up, they were, and they even had you lugging a crafty keg after them onto the moors. Big army louts, your brother's mates. Clumsy and vicious, and you no better, leaping up at them, wagging your tail: Jimmy's kid brother, eager to be joining in with the older boys.

Pathetic.

It was your match, Stu. Remember that.

Do you remember the dance you did? Of course you do. Ululating and farting, how you hopped and skipped around the blaze. Such brave young braves. Shirts shed and feathers in your hair. (And I got the last laugh there, didn't I? What did you think I saved feathers *for*? How could it not occur to you, to any of you, that I might want something soft with which to wipe my arse?)

You didn't hear my mewling, and this I guess is just as well, because it saves us having to explore the vexed business of what you would have done, or not done, or egged each other on to do, if you had realised what was choking to death under your feet. A dozen eyes not opened. Half a dozen mouths not weaned. Does anything so young feel pain? Oh, trust me.

A peculiar ululation, distant but very loud, cuts through the pub and silences its banter. The noise is impossible to place: it sounds hardly human. Something horrible must have happened, but beyond that the cry gives nothing away.

In a silence so total it is almost comical, you stand and walk to the door. For some reason you are the only one in motion. No one else thinks to follow you and investigate the sound. This, apparently, is your moment, though you would feel more the man of the hour were you able to walk in a straight line. Your early start this morning (did today really start in the West Riding?), a few mouthfuls of lager and those ridiculous work boots of yours have robbed your legs of their power; you might be tottering from a sickbed.

The door isn't nearly as heavy as its thick varnish and bottle-glass panels suggest: when you pull it towards you, you practically hit yourself with it. The roadside air, though far from fresh, washes over you like water. You don't have to go far to identify the source of the commotion. Bent over the pavement, his hat gone, his thin hair disarrayed, Wilkes dribbles blood into the gutter.

You catch him by the shoulders and ease him away from the road where the traffic is barrelling by. He has his hands over his face. You take hold of his arms to steady him and his hands come away. His nose is half-off, his left cheek horseshoed by neat triangular punctures. His chickie must have attacked him. He sinks to the pavement, his feet stuck out wide, like a toddler lost in a mall, and pats spastically at his jacket. He finds his cigarettes. The lighter's in the packet but his fingers are bloody, the flint wheel will not catch. You bend down to help him. He kicks at you like a child.

You ask him: 'Do you want me to call someone?' Where is his chickie? Where has it gone? How long will it last, scampering back and forth across these busy roads?

Wilkes is still struggling with the lighter. You force it away from him and snatch the cigarette packet from his lap and stay out the way of his drumming feet while you light him a fag. He won't even take it when you offer it to him. Some punters from the pub have joined you now. You throw the lit cigarette in the gutter, hand the pack and the lighter to the barman – one of the barmen, seriously, they must be twins – and, heading south, you take City Road back to the Barbican, trying very hard not to let the misery in.

Shit. He pronounced your houses shit.

You look about you. Yes, shit by any measure, though they might still be thought well of in the West Riding. You wish very much that you were home already, back in the valley, back in your father's house, feet dangling off the end of your little truckle bed and freezing in the cold air. And, come to think of it, why not return tonight?

There is a sleeper service. If you're not sticking around in town you could afford the ticket for that. Is there anything in the flat so very precious that you really need to fetch it? For a second, you pause, and the foot-traffic of City Road barges about you: secretaries and clerks are tottering sore-eyed from a day's work in the Bund; shop assistants stride along in determined pursuit of happy hours.

Thinking to leave it all behind, you look around for a bus stop. Then you remember James's picture in its frame. That's a problem. You can't leave that behind, can you? And once you are walking again, a dozen other vital articles spring to mind, things you simply cannot do without, though you've managed perfectly well without them for months.

You take a meandering route back to the flat, hoping to clear your head a little after this haywire afternoon. City Road is the line along which original London abuts the Bund. It is the civil boundary beyond which Bundist land purchases cease. The contrast between the two halves of the city – the unaccommodated West and the Bundist East – is stark. It is as though the city has been divided by war, rather than by the conscientious and passionate avoidance of it.

The border between old and new is clear, but it is not brutal. Finsbury Circus, which happens to lie on the Bundist side of the road, is hardly changed. Quality will out, and nothing has been allowed to interfere with the lines of Edwin Lutyens' Britannic House. There is still a ring of limes around the park, though otherwise the planting is much improved, and the Bund have introduced lemurs to play about its stand of preternaturally matured baobab. Office workers sprawl exhausted on blue lawns, watching as the lemurs chase each other through the branches. Sometimes a lemur comes to ground, steals someone's phone, settles on a high branch to study its blank screen, disappointed, then drops it in fright the moment it rings.

You sidle through the crowd waiting to enter Moorgate Tube Station. These are unaccommodated workers who have spent the day working in the Bund. Serving coffee. Sweeping offices. Operating phones and reception desks. They are quiet and slow to move, each nursing the mild headache induced by hours spent on the Bundist side. Many unaccommodated men and women work in the Bund. The pay is good, though the jobs are menial. The Bundists' treatment of their unaccommodated guest workers is always civil, and when you slip up, or seize up, or panic (it's inevitable, sooner or later), passers-by are kind, though some of them sigh a little. Where is it you are trying to get to? What is it you are trying to do? Here, let me open this for you. Come over here. Have a sit down. Can I get you some water? Is there anyone I can call?

You turn right along London Wall. Where the Barbican estate overtops the road, making a tunnel, you turn right again on Wood Street, past maisonettes above green-painted garages, and left, into the estate by Saint Giles.

A scrabbling sound to your left startles you. You see a concrete spiral stair near a sign for 'Gilbert Bridge'. Over the top of the curved pebble-dash wall, you catch a glimpse of something grey. A pork pie hat. Whoever is wearing it is no taller than a child, but (trust me on this) it moves much more quickly.

Slowly, cautiously, you take the stairs up to podium level. There is no one about, just a view across the ponds, and the maisonettes on the far side of the rectangle are half-hidden behind the foliage spilling from planters and window boxes.

Behind you, you hear a door click shut. You turn. Nothing moves. A few yards away there's the entrance to a stairwell. You go over to the door. It's locked, and access is gained by typing a code into a stainless-steel keypad. The code has not changed since you lived here. You pull the door open, take the stairs back down to street level, and in the crawl space under the last flight of stairs you find me crouching, clutching Wilkes's pork pie hat in my nailless hands.

I stare back at you with blind-black eyes, giving nothing away.

You're waiting for me to move, but you'll never win that game. I can outstare suns. Slowly, carefully, you pull the corn dolly from your trouser pocket and hunker down, so that you are on a level with me.

I have shed my skirt of silver grass and my spangled bolero shirt, but there is still that black leather collar round my neck. You would help me take it off, but you are afraid to approach. The mess I made of Wilkes's face is not something you're going to find easy to forget.

You speak to me as to a dog of unsure temperament: 'How did you get in here?'

Because you told me the code for the door. Dummy. I lick my teeth at you.

'Hmm?'

Impasse.

'Here.' You hold the dolly out to me. 'You like this?'

I lean forward a little, sniffing. I'll play along.

'You like it?'

I lean back into the shadows and nictitating membranes flash sideways over my black eyes. I paw the hat closer to myself, hiding my groin.

'Was he a bad man? Was the man bad to you?'

I take the hat from my groin, straighten it out and place it at a jaunty angle on my head.

So that is that. What are you going to do? You mull the options. The council exterminator is just a call away.

Carefully, so as not to startle me (as if!), you stand. You go to the door, palm the green exit button to unlock it and push it open. 'Out you go, little one.'

I hunker further into my corner.

'Come on, now.'

I draw the whole business out for an age – I need you to think that I'm frightened – but as I sidle past, I can't resist tugging the corner of my new hat in salute. Courtesy ought to beget courtesy. You laugh.

Back up the stairs, then, to the podium – and what

now? A drink in the Barbican Centre beckons but you can't afford it. There's still plenty of time to grab some essentials and head for the sleeper train, but can you face more travel after today?

Wearily, you cast about, getting your bearings. Orientating yourself is surprisingly hard; you don't normally approach the flat from this direction. You finally settle on a route that leads you around Speed Garden. It's not direct, but it's dusk now and you want to catch the last of the light. The corn dolly is still in your hand, or what's left of it; you look for a bin, but when you get back to the flat the dolly is still in your hand.

Standing at the door, fishing for your keys, it occurs to you that maybe you should knock first. What if Fel's removal men have arrived? What if Fel is here?

Oh, to hell with the whole situation! Savagely, you wrestle the key into the lock.

There's no one inside.

Unlacing your boots takes the usual age, then you head into the bedroom. You can barely keep your eyes open. You figure that if you steal a nap, you'll wake up just in time to buy something to eat at a convenience store. But if you sleep on, does it matter? This day has gone on too long already.

You'll at least leave the blinds open. You take off your trousers and dump them in a heap in front of the wardrobe. The duvet is folded, without a cover, at the foot of the bed. You pull it up over yourself as you lie down. You close your eyes.

Wilkes's ruined face looms at you behind your eyelids. The shock of finding him bleeding on the pavement, never mind your potentially risky confrontation with the chickie just now, has left you trembling. You turn over, away from the window, willing on oblivion.

When you came off the moors behind Jim and his friends, you could still smell the smoke. It was in your clothes and stuck to your skin. You ran sooted hands through your hair and wished you could get away with shaving your head, the way Jim shaved his. You wanted, above all things, to be like your brother. It's why you lit the match in the first place. It's why you torched my nest.

You sit up in the half-light, confused.

A warm-milk smell is rising in the room.

You turn the pillow over to its cool side and something falls off the end of the bed onto the floor. You look over the edge. It is the corn dolly. You should get up and throw it away once and for all, but the kitchen bin has no liner, remember; anyway, you are far too tired.

You close your eyes, letting the smell rise and set around you. A fresh smell. Flour and milk and heat and sugar. You imagine afternoons with Fel. Cooking with her, listening to music with her, listening to her play. You imagine her warmth against yours in the night. As you drift off, you are dimly aware of your tears, and your hand, as if of its own volition, moves to cradle your erection.

*

You wanted to be like Jim in every way. You wanted to be a soldier like him. You wanted to leave home with him when his furlough ended. You didn't want to be left in the valley with your maundering dad, your fading mum.

At the point where the path made its first, marked descent off the moors, Jim and his friends broke into a whooping run. They had forgotten about you. You paused a second, glancing back. The smoke rising from your fire was white at last. You figured that it had gone out, that it was just smouldering. Satisfied, you turned on the path and scampered after your brother and his friends.

Jim's brothers-in-arms were gone the next day and Jim himself returned to his regiment at the weekend. Left on your own, you told yourself you would explore the moors, dig for treasure, practise the physical exercises James's friends had taught you – their lunges and presses and thrusts – and intersperse these activities with long, punishing runs. That way, you would be in training. That way, even as you remained where you were, you would be beginning your escape. But, what with one thing and another, you did not set foot on the moors again that summer.

Jim came home for Christmas. On Boxing Day Betty, feeling as well as she would ever feel again, suggested a walk up the valley to the pub at Heptonstall. You begged her not to tire herself. You grew insistent. Bob, shying away from confrontation as usual, weighed in on your side, so that your mum never did climb the valley, but sat listening to the radio all day long, fidgeting and disappointed.

Jim came home again, but only briefly, the following summer. He asked you if you wanted to take a walk with him over the moors and you said no. Jim asked you why not, and you had no answer. He asked you what the matter was. You looked at him, quite blank: wrong? There was nothing wrong. You just didn't want to.

'I'll buy you a pint in Heptonstall,' he said.

'You can buy me a pint here,' you said.

'If we're staying here, then you're buying.'

'All right,' you said.

Over your second pint, you asked him: 'When do you think Mum will come home?'

Shortly after Christmas she had decamped to her sister's in Islington, north London. There were treatments there she could not get locally. You had begun to wonder whether she was, after all, dying.

Jim finished his beer. 'Honestly? I don't think she's coming home. I think she prefers it in the Smoke. Can you blame her?'

Naturally you blamed her. She was your mother and she had deserted you. Whatever was wrong with her, however serious it was, she had no business using it as an excuse to avoid you.

Another Christmas. Betty was still away at Stella's.

'Dad, when is Mum coming home?'

Bob told you to dubbin your boots. Tomorrow you and he and Jim and Billy Marsden and his new girlfriend were going for a Boxing Day tramp about the moors.

Somehow you contrived to stay at home.

Come Easter, your dad found your walking boots under the stairs and they were in a terrible state, all dry and cracking; you hadn't been up on the moors for over a year.

Did your boots even fit you any more? They did not. And so it went on. Until at last you matriculated and it was time for you to leave for London: an exhibition scholar, bound for the Bartlett School of Architecture!

'Can't keep him out of his books,' Bob used to say to strangers, his voice always more puzzled than proud. 'Can hardly get him out of the house, this one.'

It was true. Since burning my nest, you had found yourself unwilling to return to the moors. It was as if, beyond a certain altitude, all the oxygen left your lungs. You spent your days indoors, inventing playgrounds of your own with pencil and ruler and protractor. You grew monomaniacal. You grew proficient. The people you thought of as friends at school began to laugh at you, began to shun you, but you did not care. You built and built. And such a fortress you raised around yourself! Palaces of tracing paper. Moat-loads of Indian ink.

You weren't much to look at when you left for London. Pasty, fat, stooped, white as a sheet. You looked self-buried. But what a fuss everyone made! Betty came back for a week or two to help get you ready. At night you had to lie there listening to her and Bob arguing.

To you she said, 'We'll be living in the same city soon!'

You managed a thin smile. Her friendliness was coming far too late. You'd needed her here, at home. You'd needed her to be your mum. Now that you were leaving, you did not need her any more. She was just one more part of the past you wanted to put behind you.

It took weeks to get you ready: days spent in and out of shops and the barber's and rail stations and council offices in Halifax, in Bradford, and once as far as Leeds, all to outfit you for London. From up on the moors, on top of the barrow where once I had worked away with flint and wooden shovel, preparing and burying my dead, I could see you all rushing around, gathering and dispersing across the valley: what a carry-on!

You looked like so many ants plundering a heap of grain. Here they come, a dark column of Lanyons: cousins, aunts, family hangers-on, hauling their spoils along a narrow track through the grass! Some heave with their shoulders against a large seed. Some push. Others tighten the ranks and punish delay. A whole river of expectation flows down the Calder, pouring you east and south, through the irradiated country's strip-mined middle into London: *Do us proud, son!*

It was all you could do to stop your mum from marching all the housewives of the terrace to the station to wave you off. As usual, the train sat there for ages, but no one moved, no one left. They wouldn't leave you alone.

'Get some fresh air, lad, if you can.' Your father's sound advice.

At last you were away. Beneath you, the wheels squealed and rattled over a set of points. You closed your eyes, relieved, took a breath, then stood up and leaned out of the window to wave goodbye.

Do you remember it?

Your mother, your father, the people of your street are tiny swatches of cloth, twitching and shivering in the morning cold. High above the station the valley wall impends, and above that, rising into the clouds, clear as soft pencil on tracing paper, runs a line of thick black smoke.

TWO

4

Felicine's father, the celebrated surgeon Georgy Chernoy, had no more time for chickies than any other Bundist. At a public dinner, one warm night in May, he made his views plain. Memories of the dinner have stayed with me, partly because this was the first time I met him in the flesh; mostly because this was the night I met his daughter.

The dinner was held in a corner of Windsor Castle. It was one of those uneasy cultural gatherings meant to preserve backchannels between London as it had been, and the Bund which was effectively colonising its eastern part.

I was still in the first year of my studies at the Bartlett and absurdly underqualified for this gathering. But I was not alone: scattered among the dignitaries – and, come dinner, sat one to a table, as a sort of mascot – London's young 'creatives' (choreographers, actors, comic book designers, musicians) found themselves being told how they might, by their civic engagement, 'foster dialogue' between the two ever-separating halves of the city. We were also here (according to my invitation, embossed on heavy card) to celebrate our 'promise', which in my case consisted of a paper plan for a park-like green bridge across the Brentford arm of the Grand Union Canal. I looked forward to an evening spent representing Architecture. When I explained my evening's mission to him, Stan Lesniak suggested I arrive dressed as a wall.

I caught the train from Waterloo to Windsor at dusk, read a while, then glanced up and stared in mild disbelief as the floodlit castle came into view, perfectly symmetrical, perched above the lamp-lit town on its conical and lonely hill. This imposing yet straightforward structure conformed so exactly to my picture-book idea of what a castle should be, I wondered if every childhood castle might not be traced, through influences both trained and untrained, conscious and unconscious, back to this one foundation.

The climb to the castle, past shuttered shops and cheery pubs, was taxing. I am not fond of physical exercise. A soldier examined my invitation and let me through the wicket gate.

Electric lights bedded in the lawn marked a discreet but clear path across the inner court of the castle. I doglegged around a cloister, passed through a gift shop (which took some of the shine off the adventure) and came to the back of a short queue. A man older than my father offered to take my coat. Entering a timbered, book-lined room, I was handed a glass of British *méthode champenoise* and an earnest woman in flat shoes eagerly introduced me to represent-atives of Dance, Literature and the Plastic Arts. We had absolutely nothing in common, and – aside from money, or rather the lack of it – absolutely nothing to talk about.

The Bund as a culture is not famous for its cultivation of dialogue. In place of a nuanced give-and-take, its members tend to substitute power or, in a softer setting, volume. Georgy Chernoy's voice, neither deep nor shrill, nonetheless cut through lesser conversations as though tuned to a wavelength unused by anyone else. 'It is,' he announced, 'simply a matter of limits.'

An opinion, expressed with patrician self-confidence, has a seductiveness of its own, unconnected with its content.

'These limits are real. They are not imaginary, and they are not theoretical.'

Wrapping my fingers inexpertly around my glass, warming it, I worked my way through the growing knot of listeners while, away from the throng, men and women in kitchen whites entered through disguised doors in the bookcases to gather abandoned glassware and arrange the supper tables.

'At what point – this is what we have to ask ourselves – at what point do we assign a painful pejorative like "pollution" to a living thing? Oh no—'

(Impossible, at this distance, to tell whether Georgy Chernoy was responding to a genuine interjection or to a rhetorical one of his own devising.)

'—I do not dispute for a second that chickies are living things, with as much "right" (as you might say) to life as any other ordinarily evolved thing: a horse or a house plant or a human being. Though the Bundist interpretation of some terms here have wider philosophical implications than the definitions we find operating elsewhere. Terms like "rights". And "life".'

'He talks as if he just stepped off the boat.'

Surprised, I turned to my right. The young woman standing next to me came barely up to my shoulder. She had expensively cropped blue-black hair and so many bright studs in her ear, it had at a glance the appearance of a single jewel. I had assumed her words were meant for me, but she was not looking at me. She did not seem aware of my presence at all. Words burst from her, softly but with an extraordinary intensity, as though she were drawing little knives and hurling them in Chernoy's direction. 'He was born in Beckton, for crying out loud.'

'Yet when it comes to the beings you call "chickies"—'

'Oh, for crying out loud.'

'—we find ourselves struggling for an appropriate vocabulary. Their human provenance – the way they bubbled up from the blasted earth of the War's greatest and most terrible battlefield – inflicted upon all parties in that wasteful conflict a trauma that has yet to be fully appreciated, let alone understood, and not at all healed. I would go so far as to say that historians of the future will dub our present age as the Great Shock. If one considers – as we almost never do – that these creatures emerged from the death-throes of doomed soldiers, what does one feel, what *can* one feel, but a great numb pressure, such was the enormity of the German mistake? Meaning to bring the dead back to life, they brought something new into the world. And in an attempt to contain that mistake, they then tried to put the new thing to use. The industrial utility of the chickie is beyond dispute: our economy thrives and our culture is fed and watered on an infrastructure built by these easily regulated sub-men. But this easy regimentation veiled from us the other half of their nature, what I might call the Dionysian half of their nature, which ultimately brought an end to the German industrial project and led to our current, uneasy stand-off.'

This was Chernoy's circumlocutory way of referencing the way the Ruhr Valley's entire industrial workforce, who by 1937 had been labouring alongside chickies day in, day out for years, were finally overcome by an insatiable lust, downed tools and spent the entire summer and most of the autumn of that year frolicking with these so-called 'sub-men' in an orgy that all but broke the nation's economy. Similar, sometimes grotesquely violent 'outbreaks' across Europe brought an end to all grand experiments at the industrial regulation of the chickie population. Left alone at last, the chickies simply melted away. And as Chernoy charmingly put it, 'Who can say how many of these oh-so-easily-organised work animals conduct affairs of which we know nothing, in places hidden from us: the crannies of our derelict spaces, our edgelands, our abandoned outhouses?

'Their numbers matter, you see. And on this very island, in this great nation, a great unplanned experiment is under way. Let me say it. Someone has to say it: as a species, regarded as a species, chickies impute a so-far-unmeasured pressure upon this island's ecosystems. It is not a matter of what they might intend. Such concepts are wholly irrelevant. It is, simply, a question of what the chickies *are*.'

I leaned towards the girl beside me and said, under my breath: 'He doesn't know what "impute" means.'

She shot me a flat glance and looked away. Her rejection

was total, as though I had poked my head around a door into a room in which I was not welcome.

On the other side of me, a hand shot out and gripped my own. I turned, and was confronted by magnificent breasts and a freckled décolletage adorned with a single silver medallion on which an aeroplane rose above a stand of palms.

I raised my eyes. 'Stella.'

'Naughty boy. Why haven't you said hello?' This in a much louder, gayer voice than the girl had employed; it put even Chernoy off his tracks.

'So that, erm, we might consider them – the chickies, I mean. I mean, how should we regard them? As we attempt, for instance, to control the spread in our southern waterways of American signal crayfish—?'

'Good God,' a man in a dinner jacket exclaimed, sliding his hand around Georgy Chernoy's shoulders, 'in my local restaurant we *eat* them.'

Georgy Chernoy blinked at the interruption, before smoothly joining in the general laughter. 'Well, that isn't quite—'

'Happily,' the man in the dinner jacket went on, assuming control of the party – I think he was a junior minister, something to do with the Arts, or Sport – 'we have no culinary plans for the chickie race this evening. I have just been informed that our somewhat more conventional menu is ready for serving. Friends, would you take your seats?'

Aunt Stella, her hand tight around my own, led me along the room to where about a dozen round tables had been laid for dinner. 'Come with me.'

Bootless to point out that there was already a seating

plan. Stella placed me firmly in the seat to her left and brushed off the small confusions this generated with a charm she had learned years before on the stage, steering repertory performances in which she alone had properly learned her lines.

'So come along,' she cried, settling herself beside me. 'How on earth are you?'

'Well.' I was in love with her; so were most people, irrespective of gender. As is often the case with actors whose power resides in declaiming their lines as though they were poetry (a dying and undervalued art), she was magnificently sexual. Putting everything into every line tends to leave everything on show afterwards. 'Well,' I said, 'I think I'm here to represent Architecture. I feel a complete fraud.'

'I think it's rather sweet,' Stella said, picking up and examining the tableware with a critical eye. 'The government hasn't a clue about what any of us do and thinks we all subsist on air and sunlight. Come a crisis, though, they gather us up and rally us over the top like the good little foot soldiers we secretly long to be. Oh, to belong to society! Imagine! The vanguard of soft power. Good God.' She peered more closely at her fork. '"John Lewis". Really?'

Her clipped delivery was hard to parse. Painfully, I ascended the ladder of her logic. 'Crisis?'

'What?'

'You said there was a crisis. That we were here because of a crisis.'

'Oh. That. The spaceships, I mean. The whole Woomera effort.'

'That is a crisis?'

'Not for us, dear. For us it's a red-letter day. But for the Bund ...' Her eyes widened. 'For the Bund, well ...'

'Well what?'

'If the *Victory* reaches the Moon and the Bund are already there ...'

I shook my head. 'The *Victory* is not even built yet,' I told her. 'And even the Bund aren't on the Moon yet.'

'Their machines are.'

'Exactly. Their machines.'

Stella pulled one of her little-girl-lost faces. 'Well, I don't pretend to understand the details,' she said.

'And you?' I asked her, backtracking. I wasn't equipped for a political conversation, and not in the mood to be bested in it.

'Me?'

'What are you doing here? You're hardly "a young person of promise".'

'Well, thank you for that.'

'More a woman of glamour and accomplishment.'

'You stepped around that hole very neatly, dear.'

'Thank you.'

'But if I hear you utter the word "mature" I will stick this fork in your eye.'

'So?'

'So, what?'

'So what brings you here? Presumably there's a production on the way I should have heard about?'

Stella laughed and patted my hand. 'Dear Stuart, don't you ever read the papers?'

'Not really, no,' I said. I didn't want to say that I had

taught myself to read a better sort of newspaper these days than the ones in which she regularly featured.

'Well, if you *had*, you silly boy, you would know I am your hostess this evening.'

I frowned.

'In a manner of speaking.' She gave me a big false grin. 'In that I'm Georgy's fuck.'

Over the years, Stella's promiscuity had likely earned her more column inches than her acting. How plain Sue Cosgrave had escaped the confining expectations of Yorkshire's West Riding in the first place was the stuff of a dozen gushing articles in a dozen different magazines, to the point where she had reduced the entire saga (Pye Nest Methodist Church, the Halifax Victoria, Leeds Rep, Birmingham Rep, Liverpool, Bristol, the Manchester Tivoli) to one of her pithier one-liners: 'I owe my career to three things: a gift for mimicry, a vice-like memory and an inability to conceive.'

She saw nothing salacious in the way she had arranged and rearranged her domestic circumstances over the years, and as for the men she had supposedly exploited, well, she never approached the role of muse with anything other than perfect seriousness. This had made her one of theatre's more notorious *femmes* and, until the recent decline of the West End, one of its more powerful players. Only the youngest commentators ever took her to task: earnest, unattractive young people from provincial stage schools, sharpening their wits on Stella in between, say, a casual catering job and a devised theatre production in the basement of an Islington pub. Newcomers imagine theatre runs on talent. Stella learned early on that it runs on morale.

'I can't imagine there are many theatres in the Bund.'

'Stuart, don't be an anti-Semite.'

'Are there?'

'There's *television*, you silly boy.' She let me mull over that as the waiters brought the soup course. Then: 'Georgy's very interested in a concept I have for a show about unidentified flying objects. They get a lot of them in Wales.'

'You've lost me.'

'They come from a dying planet. They are genetically spent. Their germline is exhausted.'

'The Welsh?'

'The *aliens*. I'm calling it "DARE". They have come for our organs.'

'Really?'

'In the first episode, DARE's flight commander downs an alien craft over Theydon Bois, only to discover that its occupant's heart belonged to his abducted sister.'

'Dare—'

'D. A. R. E. Only I don't know yet what it stands for. What do you think?'

'How old is Chernoy?' (When Stella was in this garrulous a mood, one's only line of defence was attack.)

Stella affected weariness: 'How would I know? How old are any of them? Good Christ, pea and ham.' She picked up a spoon and stirred it experimentally through her soup. She gave a squeal as bullet-headed tadpoles of pancetta flocked and nibbled at her spoon.

This playful demonstration of Chernoy's mastery of

biophotonics elicited some scattered laughter but no one knew whether to eat the soup or not. The effect wore off soon enough, the cubes losing their motility as they cooked in the hot broth. The stuff, once I got up the nerve to try it, was far too salty.

'If we can find match-funding from Germany then *DARE* goes into production early next year.'

'So this is real.'

Stella pursed her lips at me. 'Of course it's real.'

'I'm sorry, as a pitch it just sounded a bit ... unformed.'

'We're talking about the Bund, Stuart. Things happen quickly there.'

Stella had always maintained that once she reached the age of fifty-five she would retire, fit out some attic rooms and gather together a small salon ('It's how all the real business in this town is done'). But, as I learned later when I caught up with the gossip columns, Georgy Chernoy's antics outside Wyndham's Theatre – nightly deliveries of flowers and chocolates; light but swingeingly expensive suppers; incomprehensibly pretentious cocktails in the bars of so-exclusive-as-to-be-invisible hotels; taxis to friends' country houses – all this had turned her from her purpose. She was still acting, too – in television.

She had found a man at last. Not a boy, uncertain of sex and in need of a guide and a mother, God knows there'd been plenty of them in the last few years, but a man of accomplishment, ready to fuck her, riotously (she wanted the yellow press to know that, for some reason) and well. I wondered what Chernoy thought of that.

It amused her to cast herself as Chernoy's plaything. She

had always enjoyed pulling the puritan tiger by the tail, but 'Georgy's fuck' – was there not an element of the abject here? 'A fuck and nothing more'?

The waiting staff entered once again through hidden doors to gather up empty plates. The rest of the meal was conventional, even stolid. The Bundists were served slabs of pinkish stuff on a bed of spiralised radish. The rest of us got slices of overdone venison on under-seasoned mash and crunchy vegetables.

Once the tables were cleared, Georgy Chernoy stood up to speak at a lectern in the corner of the room. The Bund's rather childish sense of humour and habitual bids for attention (the soup was a classic example) had this effect: that its spokespersons were earnest to a fault, dry as bones and solemn as owls.

'We take this truth to be self-evident,' Chernoy began, 'that death is a mistake.'

It was ground he had covered many times, in the press and on the radio, and it was not a subject with which I felt comfortable. To take my mind off his words, I looked about the room. The girl with the jewelled ear wove past our table on her way to the toilets. This was my first chance to see her properly and her spareness surprised me. Her slim black skirt shifted tight over her thighs as she moved. High heels explained her mesmerising walk but meant that she was even shorter than I had imagined. She had a hungry look: a female Cassius, Stella would have said. Hungry and determined. I thought of foxes. I thought of crows. I watched her leave the room: her hair was shaved short at the back, a chaotic dyed-black shag everywhere else; it must have cost a fortune.

Shiny things sparkled under her hair as she pulled open the door. I assumed her to be one of the angrier 'creatives' brought to decorate a gathering whose average age must have topped sixty.

When she was gone, I studied the room, out of sorts without really understanding why.

It was easy to tell the Bundists from the rest of us. They tended to be either very short or very tall. They did not share any particular facial characteristic. They put the lie to the notion that beauty lies in conformity. The strangest-looking of them, be they elves or ogres, displayed a health, happiness and animation that contrasted painfully with our sallow, sagging, relatively immobile faces. I wondered what they did, that they thought it worth being here, and how involved they were in government. I wondered how many backroom conversations our civil servants might conduct with them this evening, over sherry, perhaps, or spirits, or at any rate over wine markedly better than any served during our meal, in private rooms away from the dining hall. But these were idle thoughts and for all I knew the entire evening might be adding up to no more than a series of empty, well-meant platitudes.

'To Alexander Gavrilovitch Gurwitsch, then,' Chernoy declaimed, raising a big glass of purplish stuff. (I expect it was Vimto, though neither I nor anyone I had ever asked knew what accident of history had caused the Bund to fall so madly in love with that stuff.) 'Brother of a concert pianist, he mastered Beethoven; pupil of Kupffer and Boehm, he conceptualised the developing shark brain; and with Vladimir Vernadsky, in that little hut in Kazan, why, it is not too big a claim to make that he dreamt up the Bomb! This modern Aristotle, for whom "the whole" was never a static entity, but rather an invariant dynamic law pertaining to the entire process of development! And as Gurwitsch moved step-by-step in that direction, trying never to lose contact with real biological data, may we uncouple his *Kraftfeld* from the body itself, never losing our wonder or our rigour, so we might realise the potential plasticity of all living matter, and weave for ourselves new natures, for the men and women who are to come in his name, on this and other worlds!'

By which time most of his listeners, exhausted, had set down their glasses and had to snatch them up again for the toast. We drank, not too sure of what we were drinking to, and some of us numbly suspecting that whatever it was, it was but another small, friendly, well-meant step towards our own dissolution. The Bundists around us, strictly teetotal, drained their Vimtos and grinned their bright-white grins. A second dignitary – tired, stoop-shouldered, obviously not a Bundist – stood to speak.

I took advantage of the lull to slip out of the room.

The nearest bathroom was a public toilet. Its steel trough and elbow-operated taps were incongruous fittings among the elderly brickwork and pitch-black wood.

I dried my hands on a paper towel, left the bathroom, and then, when I came to the gift shop, I continued walking until the corridor turned and deposited me outside on a gravel path. I crossed over to a stone balustrade and studied the garden below – or as much of it as could be seen in light shining from the windows of the castle.

The garden was arranged to a formal plan: a sheet of

paper folded, cut about with nail scissors and spread out flat again. The planting was sparse and precise. I smelled roses.

I heard her footsteps on the gravel path before I saw her, approaching from out of the darkness. Her shoes were dangling from one hand and she was walking slowly, barefoot, over the stones. The weakness of the light, and the slowness of her walk, suggested some marine space, and it startled me when she looked up, right at me, and stopped: a first contact between separate worlds. I raised my hand in uncertain greeting. She turned to the left, along a narrow path between low bushes of lavender. As she brushed by them, their scent rose into the air. Just at the edge of vision, where the darkness prepared to swallow her again, she glanced back at me.

Small dog-like stone lions guarded a flight of steps that ran flush to the wall. I followed them down into the garden. Once out of the glare of the castle, my eyes adjusted quickly. The night was not so very dark after all. There was a full moon. The air along the lavender-lined path was heavy and astringent. It was a smell that, much later, I would recall every time I used Fel's soap: lavender and thyme, with something metallic in the mix.

She was waiting for me. 'You're supposed to be listening to my dad.'

I took this in. Chernoy was her father? Then she was a Bundist. 'I thought you were a painter or something.'

'Why can I not be?'

I thought about this. 'Not with those nails.'

She lifted her hand and looked at them: impossible to tell in this light whether her nails were black or red. 'Perhaps I brush up well.'

I walked on, hoping she would follow. The path widened and she came to walk beside me. I slowed down, conscious of her bare feet on the stones. 'Unless you don't use paint,' I said. 'Being what you are.'

'What would I use? Being what I am.'

'Light. Plasma. Solidified air.'

'You're funny. What else?'

'Dad's rays, maybe. I reckon you spend your days sculpting living forms for new natures, on this and other worlds.'

'Did he really say that?'

'Yup.'

In the garden's centre there was an oval bed of carefully topiaried evergreen shrubs. She said, 'This is a garden for people who don't like nature, isn't it?'

'I think that's the point.' With a sweeping gesture, I took in the town below the castle, the railway, the foggy effulgence that was London. 'Be glad there are such things as gardeners. Out there it's chaos, haven't you heard? The wasteland.'

'And there was I thinking you were a romantic.'

'Really?'

'I meant in the intellectual sense.' She turned to the castle. Her face, lit by distant windows, was as grey and fragile as paper. 'So. You're not a nature lover.'

I thought about the West Riding, my narrow upbringing there, how my father's love had straitjacketed me, and how glad I was to get out. And at the same time, how much I missed weekends fishing with him in the fast-flowing brooks above the town, and how bitterly I regretted my brother James's disappearance into the toils of military security. We used to go walking about the moors until . . .

I might have touched a dental cavity with my tongue, the shock was so sudden, the pain so sharp. I covered my confusion as best I could. Hands in pockets, surly shrug: 'Nature has its moments.'

'Dad'll sort it out.'

'I'm sure he will.'

'There will be order. Fel.' She extended her hand. Her nails on the back of my hand were cool and sharp, like the edges of teaspoons.

'Stuart.'

She smiled. There was something on her front tooth. It glittered. 'And I don't paint.'

'I don't paint, either. We have that in common.'

'Let's leave it at that.'

'We'll prolong the mystery.'

'Only you buttonholed La Cosgrave and sat with her all evening, so I assume you're one of her harem.'

'I'm her nephew.'

She looked at me. 'Really?'

'This makes you and me practically related. From how she tells it.'

'God, don't, she's worse than he is.'

She appeared easy with the idea that her father was sleeping with an actress. I wondered what had happened to her mother. 'How do you get on with Stella?'

'Not very well at first. Now she's roped me into this television project of hers.'

'*DARE*? She told me about that.'

'Every week I arrive at a small film studio in Shepperton, West London, in a gold car with batwing doors.'

'Star treatment, then.'

'That's the title sequence, silly. Personal assistants with big hair saunter past me in hotpants.'

'Several flash you a leer.'

'Careful.'

'Trust me to know my aunt. What's the film studio about?'

'It's a cover: behind the glitz and tinsel of Shepperton lie the central headquarters of a surreptitious supra-governmental organisation dedicated to the defence of the planet.'

'The Desk of Abominable Rectal Examination.'

'Or something. Don't interrupt.'

Beyond the formal garden was a grove of trees, and a narrow path between ferns and steps down to a pool, and a waterfall splashing, and an artificial cave behind the waterfall, and in the darkness I kissed her, and her hands moved across my back, and she opened her mouth to me, and she tasted of berries and all the concentrated juices of the summer. (Only later did I remember: Vimto.) The thing on her tooth was meant to be there. It was a jewel, set in the enamel, reflecting light that, given where we were, hidden from the castle and its windows, could only have come from the Moon.

5

Since any Bundist, staring at a screen (and when did they ever do anything else?) could follow any number of live video feeds transmitted by machines already anchored on the Moon, already digging, mixing and building, it was and remains a puzzle why any of them found Stella's television show worth their investment. *DARE*: the glacially paced saga of men and women on a fictional moonbase plagued by a perpetual clothing shortage.

And this, *Punch* tittered, came as no surprise since the rockets necessary to supply the moonbase were themselves fictional.

DARE's world was one powered by gigantic chemical rockets of the sort that had, one after another throughout my childhood (eager ear pressed to the radio), come to spectacular grief in the deserts of Woomera. No doubt the art of sending payloads into orbit by rocket would be mastered eventually. But in the Bund – that peculiar ethnic combine in frozen, far-distant Birobidzhan, Lenin's Siberian homeland for the Jews – a new technology had been born.

The Bund used balloons to lift small payloads into the stratosphere, then gently accelerated them into orbit using the same proprietary mechanism that allowed the Bund's aircraft to land vertically on any square of level ground.

The payloads their technology could handle were light indeed – just a few pounds, far lighter than any living human being. Steadily, however, their technology had amassed in orbit, constructing itself out of parts, so that Bundist machines were even now scuttling over the surface of the Moon.

Woomera hoped to leapfrog the Bund's lunar ambitions with their planet-hopping HMS *Victory*. And if, God willing, the *Victory* flew, then the present would diverge even more sharply from Stella's imagined future of aeroplane-sized space shuttles and orbital docking platforms.

At least Stella had the sense not to put a date to this redundant future of hers. She gave me a draft of her pilot script to read over the summer holidays. When I handed it back to her with proofreader's scribbles, I teased her about her concept. She countered, 'Who says there can't be more than one future?' This with the touching melancholy of a girl who has asked for a puppy *and* a kitten.

Though I knew my aunt and her reputation well enough to distrust her performed naivety, I did think at first that *DARE* was most likely a mere vanity project. I couldn't imagine the show ever getting made. I couldn't imagine who would want to watch it. But if it gave Stella, in the autumn of her career, the sense that she was breaking new ground, learning a new skill, exploring a new medium, or however you want to put it, then where was the harm?

Georgy Chernoy, I had assumed, was bankrolling his lover's project, though his name never appeared on the project's paperwork, not even as one of the show's more-than-a-dozen executive producers. I do know he arranged the permits necessary for Stella to film south of the Thames, in the purlieus of Medicine City. One bright August morning, when I should have been working through my second-year reading list, I went, armed with a camera, to help Stella to scout locations for her series.

It was my first visit to Medicine City, and for all the press that had greeted the project, both gushing and hostile, I was quite unprepared for what I found there. It felt as though the tram trundling us from London Bridge Station to Peckham Rye were slipping us through theatre flats into an entirely different reality. A weak enough commentary, since this was more or less exactly the impression the City's designers had been aiming at.

I had been living and studying in London for slightly less than a year; in that time Medicine City had spread at visible speed across the compulsorily purchased streets of its south-east quarter, turning schools into clinics, cinemas into surgeries, whole avenues into 'memory lanes', re-creating Londons past and gone – and this with technology the Bartlett staff themselves could hardly fathom, let alone teach to us.

Who were the unknown architects of that extraordinary and controversial transformation of the south-east, from the Thames at Deptford, through Peckham, to the very mouth of Forest Hill and the valley William Blake had dubbed his 'Vale of Vision'? How many of them were there? Where did they live and work? Had Medicine City's construction relied upon ordinary, unaccommodated talents, thousands of them would have been needed to realise the project. But it was no secret that the entire look and feel of Medicine City – 'An Oasis of Reminiscence and Regrowth' – had been envisioned by machine, down to the smallest details: the tasteful lighting embedded at the edge of every pramway; the walnut detailing of Medicine City's step-free streetcars.

My sense of rushing disorientation began the moment our tram, starting from outside London Bridge Station, turned the sharp and squealing corner onto Tooley Street and a view of the first and most well-reported of Medicine City's architectural novelties. Around the cool white walls and dappled niches of a second Saint Paul's Cathedral – smaller than Wren's original and opened out, a kind of exploded maquette – strolled the medicalised infants generated by the Chernoy Process.

Some infants wandered unaccompanied, but most held the hands of nursie. For those not yet able to walk, an elevated pramway swooped around the structure.

The point of the cathedral was simple: it existed to jog, in these ersatz infant minds, memories of the actual cathedral, which lay hardly a mile away on the opposite bank of the Thames. Much of Medicine City was directed to this purpose: it was a theme park dedicated to the awakening of memory. And if it seemed gimcrack, absurd, even insane – well, no one involved in the project, not even Georgy Chernoy himself, was likely to disagree with you there. It wasn't as though they had planned it this way.

No one had guessed, at the start of the project, how

difficult it would be for Chernoy's Processed infants to remember their past. And once the problem was recognised, no one had any idea just how baroque the solutions to this problem would become.

Memory, after all, was the most labile of mental gifts, the one most susceptible to suggestion – no? It would be enough, surely, to show these forgetful infants certain pictures; or play them certain pieces of music; or feed them, *in extremis*, mouthfuls of madeleine dipped in tea – no?

No, no, and no. The medicalised infants generated by the Chernoy Process turned out to be maddeningly resistant to reminiscence. Nothing short of full immersion in the past seemed capable of waking them to it.

So then the problem had become: how to immerse an infant in a vanished world? Various lacklustre systems of 'virtual reality' were developed: ugly concatenations of pressure suit, visor, gloves. Nothing worked. It proved cheaper, in the end, to re-create entire environments, at least in little. To resort, that is, to the artisanship of theatre makers, fairground engineers and theme-park designers.

Saint Paul's was not only Medicine City's most famous 'attraction'; it was also, from Chernoy's point of view, its most successful prompt to memory. It turns out that all of us hold Saint Paul's in mind in much the same way. Most everyone, whatever their background and personal circumstances, remembers *the same cathedral*.

London's less celebrated landmarks, however, were more of a struggle, requiring redundancy and repetition to be effective. Our route led through endlessly reiterated miniature versions of the same places. I lost count of the number of Oxford Streets we rattled by: tatty barrow and hawker Oxford Streets, shuttered and hostile Oxford Streets, Oxford Streets lit here by flames (a memory of the Great War), there (a happier, more recent memory) with Christmas fairy lights; all small, none built above waist height, a vast, cluttered multiversal Oxford Street containing all imaginable prompts to memory.

Vernacular memories were the hardest to bring to mind through this bizarre architecture. And this was an abiding worry for Medicine City: vernacular memories are, after all, what define a personality. Yes, everyone remembers visiting Saint Paul's Cathedral, but few personalities are profoundly shaped by the experience. What shapes a person is the colour of the bedroom curtains; the pattern of the linoleum in the kitchen; the sound of muffled arguments in the hall. What shapes a person is the daily grind.

Bedrooms, bathrooms, office cubicles: these did not require endless versioning so much as an extensive, dull, generic running-through of elements. There was only one office building in Medicine City, but it stretched all the way from New Cross Gate, up and over Telegraph Hill to the leafy crescents of Brockley. It had been built outsize to most effectively prompt, in the infantile minds of Chernoy's patients, memories of the times they had spent in such places. The cramped conditions. The irritation, the boredom, the drudgery. Here furniture substituted for buildings: desks five, six yards high, and office chairs as tall as street lights. Anglepoise lamps loomed over the street like great white eyes, while calendars as big as billboards scrawled over in marker-black ('provisional deadline', 'sales strategy', 'accelerator hub') provided curtain walls, dividing the district up into discrete memory-packets: post room, sales, marketing, human resources, even a trading floor. This last was the most abstract area of all, a series of giant blocky, geometrically simple maquettes sporting the bright striped blazers (rendered in wire-reinforced tarpaulin) of the most venerable London firms. A bell tolled as we rattled by; more likely, the recording of a bell.

Hauled through a cutting at Telegraph Hill, at last Stella and I found ourselves amid a sanely proportioned architecture: a practical, habitable architecture built for use. We boarded an elevated travellator at Brockley which promised to take us to One Tree Hill and the southern edge of Peckham, but which for the longest time led us a circuitous dance through the thickly arboured avenues of Ladywell.

'All the gentlemen from the City set their mistresses up around here,' said Stella, pointing out handsome red-brick villas through gaps in the rhododendron. I glimpsed gabled frontages and doors and upper windowpanes heavy with stained glass.

These houses had since swapped their knick-knacks, closets and cocktail cabinets, their Everyman Libraries and Schirmer's Classics, for padded pneumatic chairs and lockable cabinets, for wall calendars and anatomical charts, for drills and mirrors, and had opened their doors to dentists, chiropodists, opticians, reflexologists and all the other ancillary crafts and services that hung off Medicine City's great enterprise. We saw infants in perambulators and buggies. We saw newborn infants bundled up in the arms of young nurses. We saw infants staggering out of driveways clutching their freshly drilled jaws, and peering out of the windows of private cars, owl-like in new spectacles. We strode as the elevated walkway pulled us along, the air fresh on our faces. We passed a girl on crutches, and sidled around twins in a pushchair, and were nearly bowled over as three boys barged past us, playing tag. On the travellator running beside us in the opposite direction, I saw one medicalised boy trying to fly a paper kite, though these walkways moved at nothing like the necessary speed.

Stella turned to me and grinned. She had her youthful colour back, as if the air itself must be tonic. 'What do you think?'

I had no thoughts, just a few futile and incoherent premonitions. I felt as though I had been reduced to the size of a mouse and left to fend for myself inside the toybox of a spoiled and distracted child.

Now came Honor Oak, and the hill from which Boadicea, Queen of the Britons, is said to have led her last and fatal charge against the legions of Gaius Paulinus. A cable car carried us over that, and down through modest residential streets which by pure coincidence had already been named, a good century before Medicine City was ever conceived, for the Crimean War and for the work of Florence Nightingale. We walked the length of Scutari Road and came at last to the Rye.

A breeze had picked up and across the fields children were flying kites. Dogs ran about among them, barking. Families picnicked on squares of blanket. A railed-in section of the park afforded a little shade. The flower beds were planted with red-leaved ground cover, grasses, ornamental thistles and other sculptural plants. There was a bowling green, a café selling Italian ice creams, a playground.

'We've come a long way,' Stella said to me as we set down our coffees at a table outside the café, opposite the lake. Children ran back and forth, squealing. I couldn't tell if they were real children this time or more of Chernoy's medicalised infants. I nodded agreement, too tired to ask what Stella meant. She might have been referring to our journey today, or even to our involvement in the ostensibly glamorous business of television production. Perhaps she meant the life-journeys we had each taken, out of the West Riding and into the Smoke, into careers no one back home would have foreseen for us, and which among some locals were no doubt, and at this very moment, raising sneers of reverse-snobbery.

Theatre. Architecture school. Should the HMS *Victory* ever leave the ground, Jim would be following the most remarkable trajectory of us all. It was his adventure, if anyone's, that would earn our family its footnote in the history books. Were we particularly gifted, particularly blessed? The way we had scattered felt more like an accident than anything else. How had a family with roots in iron and coal and labour haemorrhaged so suddenly, in the space of less than a generation, and scattered its energies on so many grand-sounding but empty projects? Plays that people no longer came to see. Bridges and buildings that machines could make better. A giant spacecraft that had yet to fly.

Fel arrived at the café laden down with laundry bags. I went to get her a drink and when I came back the table, my chair and a great deal of the decking round about were strewn with swatches and squares of material.

Fel was helping Stella design the costumes for *DARE*.

She cleared my chair, dumping her fabric samples unceremoniously back into the bag. The piece she and Stella were agonising over had an open, interlocking weave; it looked as if it had been made by a spider. 'I can make this out of wire,' Fel explained. 'I can distort it to fit any shape, like armour. It doesn't have to be fabric at all. It could be a sort of exoskeleton.'

'Well.' Stella stretched the fabric over the table. 'It's you that has to wear it.'

'If we choose the colours carefully you won't be able to tell the difference between the fabric version and the rigid one. We could pretend they were the same suit. A responsive fabric. A kind of safety garment.'

Stella liked that. 'What else?'

Fel had been running off samples at a nearby medical fabrication lab. With a computerised loom she had created materials that looked half-mechanical, as though there were tubes running just under the weave: compression suits, Stella explained glancingly to me, for use in the vacuum of space. What interested her most, though, were the flimsy, shiny stuffs that would ultimately appear on the show as fashion wear. 'Can you make these up?'

'I've had a go,' said Fel, doubtfully, pulling out a tabard and a microskirt made of white vinyl, each piece stamped with a bright red *DARE* decal. 'I thought this might work for the crew of the submarine.'

Stella was far too busy with the fabrics to notice the glances Fel and I were exchanging. We had been seeing each other for more than three months, and I still had no clear idea who Fel was, beyond that she came from the Bund and seemed to own her own time. I did not know what she did, and had yet to realise that among the Bund the question 'What do you do?' made little sense. I knew what her mouth tasted like. I knew the jewel in her tooth was a birthday present she had given herself. I knew she lived away from the Bund, pursuing an independent life in a place of her own, a studio flat near London Bridge Station with a bed that pulled out from the wall and an upright piano and a bathroom stacked with funky, off-piste perfumes, all moss and wet rope and cat piss and cigarette ash. I knew she didn't so much sleep in a bed as in a nest of pillows and duvets and clothes and bathrobes and anything else that lay to hand, and that her blood ran so hot that she barely covered herself at night, but lay snoring on top of the heap she had made, like a young dragon. I knew she had a teddy bear called Boethius and that when she was alone, cuddling Boethius brought her consolation. I knew that she had read Boethius's *Consolations*, and it was rare that I met anyone who had read what I had not. It was an effort for me not to talk about books with Fel, but I tried to hold back because I knew that the more we talked, the easier we would be with each other, and the easier we became with each other, the more we ran the risk that we would defuse whatever was driving our mouths together whenever we were alone.

I didn't want Stella to know about us. I didn't want it in her head that she had somehow brought us together. That my aunt was sleeping with Fel's father was more of a family connection than Fel and I knew what to do with, and we already had a tacit understanding to treat Stella simply as a wealthy, eccentric lady of a certain age; someone for whom we did amusing favours. This was the game we were playing with each other, the fiction we were trying to maintain.

I glanced up and saw Stella looking at me. Stella knew. Any fool would have guessed that I was smitten. Fel was naturally discreet; 'wily' might be a better word. But me? I may as well have worn a sign around my neck. I coloured up.

Stella was far too intelligent to say anything, though.

Fel packed up her samples and her notebook. She was staying on at the café – her father was due to meet her there for tea.

'Give him my love,' Stella said. 'Tell him if I'm not home before him, I won't be far behind.'

I wondered what Fel really thought of her father's blousy new girlfriend. I wondered if her father had taken many partners. It was strange, thinking of him about to turn up here. He was still lodged in my mind as a celebrity. The man who had defeated death.

'Now, Stuart, shall we go and make some use of that camera of yours?'

Stella and I said goodbye to Fel and walked north to the restored lido – one of the few structures remaining from the old Peckham. From here we worked our way back to London Bridge by taxi, on foot, and by taxi again: a three-hour zigzag in pursuit of locations, vistas, angles, and in all that time my eye hardly left the viewfinder of my camera. Stella was a tyrant when she wanted to be, and tireless, and – I had to admit it – inspiring. We did good work that day.

In the course of it, we discovered that the whole of Peckham had been transformed, all the way north to its hazy junction (razed by Zeppelin bombardments in the Great War) with Bermondsey, where the old Peek Freans and Hartley's Jam factories had given way to pharmas, hacker labs and synbio start-ups.

And while the warm air gathering in the bowl of New Cross had hardly changed from the fug Stella said she remembered from her boarding house days – still laden with Chindian and Cypriot kebabs, mutton in sticky rice, eels, pies and liquor – the streets west of there and around the Queen's Road had, we discovered, acquired a quite different olfactory signature, stringent and sickly citrus, reflecting the food habits of Medicine City. Wheatgrass and spirulina. Goji crackers. Smoothied spinach. Crispy kale with chia seeds. Stewed kelp.

Three months had not been time enough for our sex-delirium to dissipate and reveal just what Fel and I had let ourselves in for.

I was not, she told me, her first unaccommodated boyfriend. I was, however, the very first not to look into her eyes and say something catastrophically ill-judged like, 'Are you even real?'

Fel, true to her corvid appearance, proved a first-class mimic. Once, over her first ever (and, for her, highly transgressive) half of pub cider, she performed these lines of reductive male incomprehension to the company with a precision that had my male friends wincing in self-recognition and the girls throwing up a little into their mouths.

I can't for the life of me remember the name of the pub

but it was a block away from the High Street in Tooting in south London, and I would often be there with my friends, catching a routine or a band. Two of my housemates had a stand-up act. They dressed as pirates. We went to see them every month, whenever the comedy circuit brought them back near the house. Their routine was never the same twice, and it never improved.

When Fel and I met, I was sharing that house in Tooting with seven others. None of us had any money or knew how to cook an egg. There were so many of us, and so much traffic on the stairs, that the ground-floor ceiling plaster was coming down. The door to the downstairs bathroom had no lock, but the bottom edge had swollen so you could jam it shut for privacy. Two smallish strides carried you from the door of my room to the bed, assuming the floor was clear, which it never was. You could open the window and climb out onto the roof of the kitchen extension. Fel and I perched out there some nights drinking cheap white wine from Balham Tesco, chilled almost to freezing to make it palatable. We drank it out of mugs because all the glasses in the flat had been broken. Sometimes the others would join us on the roof, bringing beer.

The Tooting crowd liked Fel, but they weren't sure what to make of her. A stray fox. A feral cat. They knew, and sometimes said aloud, that I had bitten off more than I could chew. Stan Lesniak once went so far as to draw me aside and give me a stern talking-to. 'You know she's slumming it with you, don't you?'

I wasn't angry. I knew Stan was jealous, and drunk, and unhappy. I was even prepared to accept that he was right. I knew I was overly submissive around Fel. But how else was I to behave? She was a Bundist, and I was not. Her mind ran on high-octane fuel. Next to her, I was a wood-burning thing.

Though she excelled me in the speed of her thought, in her wit, in her knowledge, that is not to say that her mind had no shape. It was particular, as specialised in its way as any piece of technology. It had edges. Even limits. She hated abstraction. I learned quickly not to offer her my hidden depths. She absolutely would not engage with my important agonies about life. She wanted things from me. People. Facts. Objects. She was a collector. This was her purpose in life, and all the purpose she needed.

She liked me to explain things to her exactly. She wanted details. When I sat at my drawing table, studying the Cripplegate plans, or simply working on something that to her must have appeared quite ordinary – a staircase, perhaps, or a curtain wall – she would pull up a chair and kneel on it, elbows on the table, watching with a seriousness that was utterly, charmingly childlike.

I told my housemates that Fel designed costumes for television, because it was true, and because whatever else she did remained a mystery to me. Or not a mystery, exactly, but difficult to explain. What did she do all day?

Fel had money. I didn't. I remember saying early on that this situation was bound to grow old very quickly: that I would not be able to keep up with her. I did, in the end, manage to convince her that taking me out to dinners I could not possibly afford, though good for my stomach, was bad for my spirit. But still she treated me to concerts, to song cycles at Wigmore Hall, to opera at the English National and the

Royal. She knew every piece. She knew every performer. Every soloist. She listened to music. Really listened, sometimes with the score in her lap. There didn't seem to be any part of the cultural life of the city that she didn't know like the back of her hand, and I couldn't work out how she had acquired so much knowledge or how she sustained such a lively engagement with everything. She put me in mind of an ambitious foreigner, acquiring the trappings of a culture not her own. Which was, of course, exactly what she was. And like an ambitious foreigner, the culture she had acquired by diligent study was easy to parody. It was undeniably off-beam, and often yawningly over-serious. At the same time, it was richer than anything a native like me would ever gather out of the air.

She took me to lectures at the Whitechapel and the Barbican and the Tate. She wasn't a student. She wasn't an artist. She wasn't a musician. She wasn't working on a novel. She didn't fit any art-school pigeonhole. Still she knew more about art, music, books and architecture than anyone I'd ever met, Stanislaw Lesniak included, and this is why, in time, Stan came to hate her so. She sucked everything in but she was more than a buff, more than an anorak in a pretty wrapper (this was her description of herself, one night among friends).

All she did was live, and so she lived, intensely and well. Her mind was like a steel trap. She forgot nothing. I had no idea what she saw in me. What I saw in her was someone who was used to considerably more than I could ever give her, and whose talents – even if, in the end, they simply boiled down to smart acquisition – ought to have earned her a sight more than a supporting role in Stella's *DARE*.

'What do you reckon?'

Thigh-high boots and brassiere. Open-weave tabard. Platform heels. A long dress made of translucent plastic, split to the thigh. Playsuit. Plastic camisole.

'You've got to be kidding,' I said.

'This is just for the submarine. You should see my Moon gear.'

'Please.'

Purple fright wig. Silvered eyeshades. Microskirt and thong. 'Stella kept me behind an extra hour today for screen tests. I think she might have been hitting on me.'

'Please take that image out of my head.'

'Oh.' Fel folded her arms. 'You're no fun.'

Stella wanted Fel to play the captain of DARE's global fleet of stealth hunter-killer submarines. In *DARE*'s ever-expanding show bible, this was defined as an executive position involving active service, frequent dry-land contact with the upper echelons of the DARE bureau, and regular face-to-face contact with defence crews on the Moon. That way Fel could wear virtually everything Stella designed.

When *DARE* won match-funding and received the green light from the broadcaster, life became easier. I told people Fel was an actress.

My female flatmates were subdued around Fel, the boys puzzled, though sympathetic. Some – Stan Lesniak in particular – were quietly concerned that I might be bad for her. They fed her herbal teas and shot me looks as though sceptical of my motives. As well they might have been: she got drunk very easily and more than once Stan leaned out of his cupboard of a room to find me manhandling Fel up the stairs. At night we tore into each other the way a starved cat tears at a bird.

Fel gave herself a hard time, always. She never took her brilliance for granted. She was conscientious. She never took her body for granted, either, moving with an oiled slickness that suggested the expert operation of a complex mechanical system. When she reached orgasm, she laughed, and while her happiness was evident, at the same time her climaxes were not a release for her, nor any hackneyed falling back into self. She was energetic afterwards, elated, as though together we had enabled her body to accomplish a new thing.

It was a part of Fel's heritage that she was insatiably curious about all kinds of processed food and unfamiliar tastes. Dog treats. Mealworms. Cans of winter melon tea and pressed fish roe. Though she agonised over it, interrogated it, poked it and pilloried it often, she ate virtually everything. Bacon. Black pudding. Growing up on the Bund's peculiar, delicate and by and large processed diet, she was fascinated by the rawness and bloodiness of my own meals. Once I cooked her some steak, and she grinned and chewed and slobbered and enthused right up to the point where she was violently sick just a couple of feet short of our toilet.

She thought in ways that were studied and contrarian. She treated other people's opinions the way a fox treats an unsecured bin. She gave herself no quarter; she said, 'The way I've been taught, I tear everything down to white light.' Until she said that, it had never occurred to me that, young as she was, she might actually have finished her education, and been given mastery over all the tools she would ever need.

Towards Christmas in my second year, Fel decided it was ridiculous, me having to commute from Tooting to the Cripplegate site every day. 'There's too much going on. You've too much to worry about. It's going to drive you crazy,' she said. 'Leave it with me.'

The next evening she turned up at the Tooting house dangling a set of keys in my face. She said, 'Daddy says we should move in together.'

'Well.' I thought about it. At least, I made a good show of thinking about it. 'Daddy knows best, I suppose.'

'Is this Georgy's?' I asked, moving as if in a dream from one large, airy, day-bright room of the Barbican flat to the next.

'One of them,' Fel replied. 'It's not a place I know.'

'Why is he doing this for us?'

She came and stood by me and we gazed out through the patio door at the water and the strong, brutal lines of the buildings. Sunlight against brick and cement render. 'He's going to have to accept what I want,' she said. 'And I want you.'

Kissing me, putting her arms around me, sliding her tongue into my mouth, she stopped me from formulating the obvious question: whether her father had asked her for anything in return.

My Tooting housemates helped us pack and made us promise to come back and visit, but we never did. I was sorry to lose that easy, effortlessly decent community in Tooting. Looking back, I can see that I was at my happiest there, and at my best.

But love will have its day. I imagined I was surfing with Fel through new territories. ('Surfing.' This is what she called the business of acquiring information.) Books. Music. She played me Wagner, Mozart, Schumann. We read poetry aloud to each other in bed. Cavafy. Keats. Eventually it would come to me that I was not 'surfing' anything; that I was simply wallowing along in her wake. In the meantime I was drunk on her difference. The weird flexibility of her limbs. Her scrawny strength.

'We frontload our health,' she told me once, in bed. I sucked on her tit as she spoke for the Bund. 'Many of us go blind before we die.'

Fel had time for Stella's TV show. I didn't. The spring term of my second year ended with important exams. In the end, in a desperate bid to balance favours for Stella with my course requirements, I persuaded my tutors to grant me a placement at her studio, so that I could design the interiors she needed and have that count towards my qualification. Submarine. Moonbase. Moon interceptor. Tank-like 'mobiles'. The subterranean offices of DARE's Shepperton HQ. I sold it to the Bartlett as an opportunity to design for the new fabrication machines spilling out of Medicine City. I showed them Fel's open-weave exoskeleton-cum-jumpsuit, in both its fabric and wire versions, and I explained I wanted to accomplish equivalent innovations in the built environment. I used expressions like 'built environment'. They gave me six weeks and expected me to write them a 30,000-word dissertation about the experience.

Because Georgy Chernoy's personal worth was astronomical, it was easy to forget that Stella was a commercial success in her own right. She owned a house in Islington and a holiday cottage in Shropshire, to which she used to repair whenever she had a script to work on. When she heard about my dissertation deadline, Stella gave me the key and told me to top up the oil tank, keep the dehumidifier running in the master bedroom, and otherwise do with the place as I liked.

As if holing herself away in an old crofter's cottage at the edge of a village just shy of four hundred souls was not isolation enough, Stella had had a hut built at the top of her garden. The garden ran all the way up the hill behind the house. Though the property deeds presumably marked a border, in truth it was possible to walk all the way up through the garden, past two handkerchief-sized lawns, past gooseberry and blackcurrant bushes, and a terrace barely big enough for a set of rusting garden furniture, up more steps to the hut, and beyond, into trees, and out again to a view all the way to Wales, and there imagine that the entire Clun Valley was one's own.

I took an extended Easter break there. On my first night, I woke up at about 4 a.m. to an unfamiliar chill and could not get back to sleep. I went downstairs, made coffee in one of Stella's several coffee makers, fetched the key from beside the back door and carried my drawing equipment up to the hut along bark trails and flagstone paths treacherous with moss and lichen and dew. The hut was small, watertight, and the bottled gas heater warmed it up in minutes. There was a chair and a tilting table large enough for me to draw on. It became a routine. I started work before dawn, finished around eleven and spent the rest of the day either walking in the surrounding countryside or tending the garden.

It took me about a week to shake off the persistent feeling that I was working on *DARE* out of weakness – an inability to say no to my aunt when she needed a cheap favour. By the end of the second week I was obsessed. I spent evenings on the phone to Stella and to Fel, arguing for more budget, better materials, more ambitious sets. I drew ceaselessly, inspired by the scripts I had read the night before. These arrived almost daily. The series, originally planned at six episodes, was now budgeted to run for twenty. Our available funds were increased, but I still had to design sets that were more convincing, more sturdy and more easily mended for less money per unit of screen time.

Strong colours and extensive lighting notes replaced expensive materials. The moonbase grew airier, lighter and less cluttered, the submarine even more of a human sardine can. Only a skeleton staff remained to operate DARE's subterranean HQ.

Though she brought in friends to help with the dialogue, Stella wrote the additional storylines herself. Under the pressure of extra work, the scripts, though crude, were acquiring a distinctive flavour – an urgency and coherence the original episodes had lacked. Whether by accident or design, Stella's notion – that the world has room for more than one future – began to be realised. The show's inconsistencies, its departures from reality, no longer bothered me. I began to inhabit the world of the show. In my mind, it ceased to be a drama about underdressed people in space. It ceased to be a show that deliberately, wilfully ignored the Bund, the chickies, or the half-dozen other human variants that rub more or less uncomfortably against each other upon this crowded and irradiated Earth. *DARE* became for me another world entirely: imperilled, certainly, but in many ways happier than our own. It was a world without civil war, without nationalism, without tribes. It was a world that had never been exposed to Gurwitsch's ray, a world in which the ray had not yet been discovered or, better yet, did not exist. It was a world whose dominant species was still one and entire: a single, healthy, well-bred human family.

A scream startled me out of my reverie. It came from the bottom of the garden. I leapt up, looked out, but it was still an hour before dawn and all I could see was my own face, reflected in the glass of the door. I ran outside. 'Hullo?'

There was no reply. I hurried as fast as I dared down the garden. I'd taken my shoes off outside the hut and the dew soaked through my socks as I ran.

I found Fel catching her breath by the back door.

'Fel? What are you doing here? Are you all right?'

She pointed at the path. 'What is it?'

We were in pitch darkness. I stepped forward to trigger the outside light and there, in the centre of the path, frozen stiff as a garden ornament, was the toad that lived in the rockery wall. I bent down and made to take hold of it. It jumped between my feet. I chivvied it away.

I took Fel in my arms and kissed her. 'What are you doing here?'

'I thought I'd surprise you.'

'Darling. Come see the hut.'

She pulled back against my hand. 'Not up there.'

'Come on.'

'I'm scared,' she said, pouting, only half in jest.

I laughed, put my arm around her and led her into the cottage. 'I'll make you a coffee. How come you're so early?'

We spent the next four days together. I would wake at four and work in the hut until daybreak. We would breakfast in the garden around nine, and then I would go back and work into the early afternoon, when we would visit some town or other, some castle or stately home, that Fel had spotted in the guide she had bought. I tried to take her walking with me but the countryside bothered her. Things kept moving about in her peripheral vision: sheep, cows, crows, tree branches bending in the wind. She was always tripping over roots, stones, her own laces. She was not equipped for the natural world and lacked the lore necessary to survive it. If a cow's in your way, wave at it and keep walking. Stand still for a wasp, and check the rim of an open can before raising it to your lips. 'It stung me! It *stung*!' I kissed away her tears but Fel was not to be comforted. 'Let's go back. Urgh! There's another one!'

'That's a bee.'

'I don't like the outside. The outside is mean.'

The paper guide she had bought in Ludlow was exhaustive, but Fel missed the Bund's information glut. The day we went to Stokesay Castle, she asked me: 'How do we know if it's going to be busy?'

'It's Saturday. It's a castle. It's going to be busy.'

'But what if it's too busy?'

'Then we'll queue or we'll go somewhere else. Come on, Fel.'

She carried her absurd do-everything, know-everything phone around wherever we went, though a lack of signal rendered it virtually useless. The phone had a camera in it so her carrying it around made some sense. She worried about losing it, though. 'Nothing's backing up,' she explained.

'It's your phone. It's in your hand. Why would you lose it?'

'I just don't want to lose our pictures.'

'You're not going to lose them.'

'Don't be angry.'

'I'm not angry.'

When we got home, she made me sit with her and look through her camera roll, for all the world as though the day recorded there had not already happened.

'Nice. Good one. Yes.' I had no idea what I was supposed to say.

When it was time to return to London, Fel dialled a number on the house phone, listened, dialled some extra numbers and put down the receiver: 'All done.'

In the evening, a car drew up outside the door. It was large, white, brand new and unlike anything I had seen before. There was no driver. We put the luggage in the boot and climbed in. The interior smelled of leather polish and new plastic. This is how Fel had managed to arrive so early, the morning she came to the cottage: she had booked one of these vehicles for herself and slept the whole way. She snuggled against me as our vehicle wound steadily through narrow country lanes to the M54. I clutched at her, petrified. The motorway was worse. I was convinced we were going to crash. How can a car have no driver? I cricked my neck craning to see out of windows dialled dark against the street-lamp glare. When we got back to the Barbican, I was so tired I had to go straight to bed. The mattress felt as if it was moving in waves under me.

6

'No one need be too surprised by the pace at which we build,' Georgy Chernoy had said, over dinner in Windsor Castle. 'The rules by which we operate are no different from the rules that have pertained to progress, fecundity and expansion on this planet since life began. They are no different, if I might for a second speak as a Bundist –' (a strange thing to say, since to my knowledge he never did anything else) '– no different from those which led our unaccommodated forebears to their own achievements.'

Even Stella, who had sat shiny-eyed through his whole performance – wrapped up in his vision, or at any rate spellbound by his delivery – admitted to me later that Georgy Chernoy's *noblesse oblige* at this point had made half the room suck its teeth.

Oblivious, Chernoy had continued: 'I say "rules", but there is only one rule, and everything follows from it. Not a rule, even, but a simple mathematical truth. I mean the exponential function. If the Bund has deviated from the general course of human progress, it is through their knack of comprehending, embracing and exploiting the consequences of the exponential function.

'And how strange that humankind, the tool-builder, the city-maker, the census-taker, should be always tripping over such simple mathematics!'

Here Stella's report broke off in typical style: 'Oh, I've no head for numbers!'

I had just got back from Shropshire and Stella was treating me to one of those expensive hotel teas she so enjoyed. It was May, the first anniversary of my meeting Fel, which meant it was also a year to the day since the dinner at Windsor Castle. This was how we got talking about Georgy Chernoy and how I came to hear, slightly garbled and second hand, a speech Fel and I had missed. 'Something about how things double every few years. You must know all this from your college work.'

I poured milk from a silver jug into Stella's cup. 'I just spent a whole month in Shropshire drawing curves. That doesn't mean I understand them.'

'Curves! Yes! He talked a lot about curves. About how the Bund thinks in curves. It all sounded rather pretentious, if you ask me.'

Had Georgy Chernoy sought a living example of general mathematical myopia, he could not have found a better subject than Stella. I remember thinking darkly: perhaps this is exactly what he has done – picked her as a sort of glamorous mascot of human limitations. A human pet he can watch as she paces stereotypically back and forth, back and forth, against the plate glass of her own incomprehension.

Chernoy's point – and it was a valid one, however galling – was that some vital truths about the world, though well known and widely broadcast, absolutely refuse to stick in the unaccommodated mind. They are well understood, and yet they invariably fail to inform action.

Multiply the natural logarithm of two by a hundred and you get seventy, or as near to seventy as makes no odds. Divide that number by growth expressed as, say, so many per cent per year, and you get the number of years it takes for a steadily growing thing to double in size. A tree growing at five per cent a year will double in size every fourteen years.

From that, everything follows. Since the first protozoa assembled themselves, species have been expanding to fill the niches available to them; have reached carrying capacity; exceeded it; and died. 'The greatest human achievement was its magical ability to cheat the limits of carrying capacity by altering its environment. The Bund's more recent achievement is to accept, and act upon the knowledge, that this human magic also has its limits.'

I think this is what, above all, puzzles non-Bundists and fuels our occasional hatreds: our sense that the Bund is hypocritically preaching restraint on the one hand while throwing off all shackles to expansion with the other. For heaven's sake, it has begun to mine the Moon! The Bund, to the contrary, would have it that its own dizzying, so-fast-as-to-be-unfollowable growth is possible because it understands the limits to growth better than anyone else. 'If bugs in a jar reproduce once every minute, and by midnight the jar is full, at what time is the jar half-full?'

This Stella had remembered. Familiar enough as I was

with the riddle, it still took me an incredulous moment, a split-second of scepticism, before I confirmed the answer in all its enormity: 'At one minute to midnight the jar is still only half-full.'

'You see?' Stella clapped her hands, delighted.

One minute to midnight, and the future looks bright, the possibilities endless, or almost endless. A whole half-jar remains unexploited!

A minute later, everything starves. Everything dies. Everything ends. This was the Bund's point of pride: that it understood the exponential function in its bones; was trained up to it; was born to it. It thought in curves and, in so doing, knew how to evade environmental limits long before impacting with them.

'Do have another little cake.'

'I'm done.'

'Not at these prices, you're not,' Stella snapped. 'At these prices we're licking the bloody plates.'

I picked one with a strawberry on top as the healthiest-looking option. Underneath the fruit was a *crème pâtissière* so thick I needed an extra cup of tea to wash it down.

Stella took the opportunity to check her phone. Georgy had got it for her to help her organise the shooting schedule for *DARE*. The first live-action filming was just a fortnight away, and a second-unit crew made up of final-year film students was already at work making stock footage of the models I had built for the show: submarine, mobiles, interceptors, satellites, assorted Earth- and Moon-based launch platforms; also some simple pyrotechnic work.

She pecked hazily at the screen, saw me looking, sighed

and dropped the phone on the table. 'I'm never going to get the hang of this thing.'

'I'm sure you will,' I said, but only out of form's sake. I knew how impossible it was. Just the night before, Fel had cuddled up beside me in bed and tried showing me how she planned our evenings on the tablet she was always hauling around with her. Images sprang from the screen in 3D and she started knitting patterns together as though plucking a harp. All I could do was laugh.

'What? It only takes practice,' she said. Perhaps she was trying to be kind. We both knew it wasn't true.

Stella had tried moving her scripts onto glass; the logic of text manipulation had held reasonably fast in the transition between media and she spoke enthusiastically about the speed at which she was able to turn cast scripts into shooting schedules. Suddenly the (Bundist) lighting cameraman and the cinematographer were accessing her work even while she was tapping away at it, her whole screen blizzarding in green and purple. She'd had to abandon the work to them. She was enough of a professional to know that film-making is a collaborative business and that her film crew knew a lot more about the mechanics of a shooting schedule than she did. You could see that it hurt, though: how work she had assumed would take a week came back to her, without her input, late in the evening of the same day.

Episode seventeen upped the ante by launching a story arc to carry the first series to its cliffhanger conclusion. (Stella had it in mind that a second series of *DARE*, if green-lit, would eschew standalone episodes altogether. She would run the show, developing its narrative 'spine', while professional writers drawn from theatre would collaborate on individual episodes.)

In episode seventeen, the aliens launch a concerted attack on the moonbase – DARE's first line of defence. At first, the attack appears tactical, but by episode nineteen it is clear that the UFOs are arriving for the long haul. Despite swingeing losses, they begin to construct a nigh-on impregnable bridgehead on the Moon's far side, using material time-shifted one second into the future. Cut off from their lines of communication, the crew of DARE's moonbase lack vital intelligence on the nature of the aliens' 'chronoconcrete'. Unaware that their attacks are simply strengthening the enemy's hand by providing them with a vital extra source of 'chronic energy', they succumb, one by one, to mysterious, invisible ground-assaults.

With extra episodes to devise, Stella was using me as her sounding board. Our teas were more frequent, which pleased my sweet tooth, but they were closer to script meetings than family catch-ups. As Stella's ideas for *DARE* developed, it grew clear, at least to me, that I was not the best reader she could have chosen. It was all too obvious where her latest ideas were coming from. She seemed to me to be working out her feelings about looking after my mother – none too subtly, neither.

By episode twenty, DARE's secret Shepperton HQ has developed an effective portable countermeasure involving resonant crystals, and the aliens are flushed from their bridgehead.

Submarine-launched interceptors land successfully within the perimeter of the now abandoned alien station, and ground crews set out to explore the structure. In the final reel of the final episode, they find the moonbase's 'dead' crew.

They are not dead, but they are not really alive, either. Helpless, strapped to gurneys, dripping blood and worse, many have had their organs harvested and their vital functions are being maintained by sophisticated machines.

'In the second series, brilliant surgeons will pack these life-support systems into the victims' still-living bodies, and these cybernetically enhanced personnel will form a new, elite line of defence for the DARE organisation,' Stella explained. 'They're not just stronger, not just faster; their ordeal has bestowed on them a deep insight into the minds of the invaders.' She could see I wanted to interrupt and, to stop me, she turned her attention to the teapot, adding hot water, stirring, pouring, talking all the while: 'But with this knowledge comes a certain sympathy for the aliens – these last desperate representatives of a dying world. As the second series builds to a crisis, you won't be entirely sure whose side these familiar characters are actually on.'

'I think,' I began (I knew I had to tread carefully), 'I think we're getting a bit ahead of ourselves. You want the first series to end with a shot of the show's most engaging characters eviscerated on surgical beds?'

'It doesn't have to be graphic.'

'It doesn't?'

I didn't want to be angry with her, but it was all I could do not to shake her. Betty was only just out of her latest bout of 'life-saving' surgery. I assumed this was where Stella had got the idea. By now my mother had hardly any internal organs left.

*

It is a measure of the love Betty and Stella felt for each other that, almost until the last, it survived the radically different choices they had made in life. As a young woman, Stella had chosen a life in which she could decide things for herself. Betty, marrying young, and marrying Bob, chose to have her life dictated by a husband. She never thought to resent her sister's success, and I suspect this is partly because she did not recognise it as success. In my memory, Mum, while fond of Stella, always spoke rather disparagingly about what she was 'getting up to'. The real fullness of life, in Betty's opinion, was to be obtained through home and family. And given that these, in our case, consisted of a tin bath in the parlour and Bob rolling in drunk every Friday and Saturday night, you could only admire her faith.

I had just started my second year at the Bartlett, and was watching my first houses rise in Cripplegate, when Betty moved to Islington to stay with Stella. I didn't visit often, and they did not encourage me. Chemotherapy left Betty weak, prone to viral infections of one sort or another. There was no prohibition on my visiting, but an odd reticence kept me away. If I phoned Stella at home in Islington, it was always to talk to my mother or, if she was resting, to ask after her. But when Stella and I met in person, it was never at the house, and the subject of Betty never arose.

Had I known my mum was going to spend the rest of her life in London, I would never have let such an unnatural state of affairs persist. But I always assumed that Betty would return to the West Riding after her treatment.

I wonder, at what point did Betty's affection for Bob entirely die? He never, to my knowledge, behaved badly towards her, not even in his blackest moods, not even in his deepest drunk. She never had to hide behind lace curtains of a Monday morning, as I recall some bruised and battered neighbours doing.

Betty never went home. She spent her last years in a room not her own, in a city she didn't know, being ministered to by a sister she loved dearly but with whom she had nothing in common. I realise now, and far too late, that she was disorientated. That she did not know what she was doing. That she did not know what she was agreeing to.

How long did Betty hide the symptoms of her cancer? She must have been aware of her illness even before I left for college. I remember when I was still at home, and distracted by the business of moving to London, she was constantly visiting the toilet. But this sort of thing seems significant only in retrospect. Once or twice I found pink piss in the toilet bowl. But even this is no smoking gun. With bladder cancer the bleeding stops and starts. It can disappear for weeks. Even months.

Whichever way you cut it, Betty's silence killed her. Once in Islington, the pain in her lower back became so bad that Stella had to manhandle Betty to the surgery. It was the first time in her professional career that Stella had ever missed a matinee. Much later, she told me how startled she was at how light her sister had become: 'Like a bundle of sticks.'

Had this medical emergency unfolded in the West Riding, I don't doubt the doctor would have sent Betty away with painkillers and some nonsense about sleeping on a harder mattress. In London it was a different story. Stella's GP gave Betty an immediate referral.

The cystoscopy revealed suspicious lesions, too far gone to be removed surgically. Betty returned to Stella's with a sore arm from a BCG injection and a letter for the GP to continue the course, but it was only ever a holding measure. Within the month she was back in hospital, an inpatient this time, awaiting an operation to remove her bladder.

It was the autumn of my second year, while I was having to commute daily from Tooting to Cripplegate. I suspect now that Mum's operation was the main reason Fel and I moved in together when we did. Fel was worried about me.

'There's too much going on. You've too much to worry about. It's going to drive you crazy.'

At the time, I was bowled over at the thought that Fel liked me enough to live with me. It never occurred to me, until later, how much she wanted to care for me.

I went to see Betty before the surgery. Her bed was a pile of forms, handbooks, diagrams. She was trying to understand what life would look like after the operation. She was confused, humiliated.

Further operations followed to create a new bladder for her, using a loop of intestine. She grew even thinner from that procedure, as was only to be expected. Released from hospital, she stayed with Stella, learning to self-catheterise, learning to live with incontinence.

She never went home. She never went back to my dad. She reminded me of those women of the Middle Ages who, disappointed in their political manoeuvrings, retire to a religious establishment. And though it feels strange to me to be casting Aunt Stella, of all people, as a nurse, her performance was, as always, immaculate.

Why Stella did what she did then is still a mystery to me. And I can't quite get it out of my head that she waited till I had spent a month in Shrophire, designing her precious TV show, before she dropped her bombshell on me.

'It's not the end of death,' she tried to explain.

It had seemed strange to me at the time, that she had wanted to meet me so soon after our last teatime, when we had shared jokes about that strange meal in Windsor castle. It turned out that both occasions were of a piece: Stella was preparing me for what she had done.

Our sandwiches lay neglected on the silver tray and the tea grew cold in its pot. Had she really thought to lure me into an easy understanding? Was she so complacent? The hotel's faux-Louis XV chair frame dug hard across the backs of my legs as I crouched forward, wanting to run, wanting to fight, wanting this not to be happening. Stella, for her part, must have guessed what my response would be: her shoulders were hunched, her whole manner defensive. 'What it does,' she explained, 'is it obviates one's personal extinction. Obviates. Is that a word?'

I had no idea what to say to her. What could you say to this? Georgy Chernoy's patented Process was unprecedented. It was revolutionary. It was, frankly, bizarre. 'For God's sake, Stella. What were you thinking?'

'She will not leave us. That's what I'm trying to say. That

what your mother is – and you have to think of her as a performance, Stuart, that's the point, we're not things, we're performances, you see? We rehearse ourselves. Well, that rehearsal will continue.'

'Does Dad know?'

Stella would not look at me.

'You know he can stop this. Don't you? He's her husband. He has that right.'

She forced herself to meet my gaze. 'We cannot let her die, Stuart. Can we? Think of the possibilities!'

When I got back to the Barbican, I was too upset to go up to the flat. I headed to the Foresters instead and used the payphone by the gents to call Bob's pub, the Arms. I asked the barman to give my dad a shout and after a few minutes Bob called me from the usual payphone. 'What is it?' he said, assuming the worst. He had been preparing for this call for a while.

'It's Stella.'

That foxed him. 'Stella?'

The pips sounded. 'I'll call you,' I said.

I rang him back – we had called each other like this often enough that I knew the number – and I explained what Stella had done. I told him what she had planned for Betty. I couldn't tell if the silence that followed indicated anger or confusion or grief or what. 'Has Stella talked to you about this?' I asked.

'No,' he replied. 'She's not spoken to me.' This in a tone that would have told me, had I been paying attention, that it was quite pointless putting any responsibility for action onto him. Bob's fear of confrontation was pathological. 'I think this is Mum's choice, don't you?' he said.

'No,' I said. 'No, I don't think this is Mum's choice. I think Stella's railroading her.'

'Why would she do that?'

'I don't want a conversation about Stella. I want to talk to you about Mum. Will you come and see her, at least? Speak to her?'

Robert hummed and bumbled.

'You can take a couple of days. The factory will give you a couple of days.'

'But where will I stay?'

'You can stay with Fel and me,' I said, out of my mind with frustration.

Which left me having to explain to Fel why my father was visiting: because Stella had persuaded my mother to sign up for the Chernoy Process. The emotional complications of all this would surely drown us, so I decided to make a last-ditch effort and visit Medicine City myself, to see if I could dissuade Betty from undergoing the Process.

'Why am I meeting Mum outside? I can't see how that's going to be comfortable for her.'

Fel, sprawling across our bed in the Barbican, gestured at her tablet. She twisted and fiddled with the air above the screen: ghosts rose from the glass and spun. But even Fel was bested by Medicine City's overmediated user portal. 'I'm not sure "inside" and "outside" mean very much in Medicine City any more.'

I bit my tongue. The baroque complications the Bund larded over everything had long since ceased to captivate me. 'I just need to know where I'm going.'

In reply, Fel dug about under our pillows and pulled out the glass wafer that was her new phone. 'Take this.'

'You know I don't have a clue how to operate that.'

She tapped it. A miniature colour-coded urban landscape appeared. 'Ladywell. Follow the blue dot.' She waved the phone at me to take. 'It won't do anything else, I've locked it to the app.'

I had no idea what she meant by that. I did know she was trying to be helpful. I knew, too, that without her help I would never have been able to make an appointment in the first place. This, after all, was how the Bund was locking the rest of us out of its accelerated territory: by the sheer weight of its offering. Options, menus, mirrors, proxies – what did these words even mean? What concepts lay behind them? No door was ever barred in the Bund, but no door was ever the right door, either. The Bund was a party at which, unless you knew everyone already, you were never able to strike up a conversation.

'Thanks,' I said, pocketing the phone.

She got up and kissed me. I ran my hands over her head. It felt as though I were stroking a cat. Filming had begun on *DARE* and Fel was sporting a haircut appropriate to submarine commanders: close-cropped, and shaved over the ears. She kissed me again. 'I hope it goes all right.'

'"All right"?'

I didn't mean to be awkward with her. She was only trying to be kind.

She let me go. She was out of patience with me, and trying not to show it. 'I don't know what you want. Not really.'

I took a breath. I had no desire to take my confusion out

on her. The least I owed her was an effort to be honest.

'Your father's treatments.'

'Yes.' She let go of me and climbed back under the sheet.

'What do you think?'

'What do I think?' She paused a second, letting me register the inadequacy of my own question. 'I *think* they work.'

'Yes.'

'In fact, I know they do.'

I sat beside her on the bed.

'Maybe,' she said, 'you're asking me the wrong question.'

I took a breath. 'I can't ask you how you feel about it,' I said. 'It wouldn't be fair of me. I don't know what I feel about it myself.'

'I am the wrong person to ask,' Fel agreed. 'I'm too close to it. I grew up with Daddy's work. It seems normal to me. Inevitable, in a way it doesn't to anyone else. Not yet. Not even in the Bund. I don't think it does you and me any favours that your mother's been invited to go through with this. I know that's selfish of me.'

I took her hand. 'I feel the same. I know I shouldn't but ... There's something else.'

'Yes?'

'My father's coming to town to see her. He's going to need somewhere to stay.'

It took Fel a moment to realise what I was getting at. 'I'll book him a room,' she said.

'He wouldn't feel comfortable with that.'

She lay back on the bed, staring at the ceiling. 'Right.'

'It won't be for long.'

I lay beside her on the bed. Her hand found mine. 'I'm

sorry,' she said. 'It's fine. I didn't mean to be a bitch.'

'It's not that.'

She turned to look at me.

I said: 'If Bob asked you about the treatments, what would you tell him?'

Fel thought about it. 'I'd tell him the truth. That Daddy's a genius. That the Process he's invented is the future. That death has lost its sting. Beyond that, what other people believe is irrelevant. Don't you think?'

That Georgy Chernoy's triumph over death would usher in a new world was evident. But I could not imagine Bob wanting to take up residence in that world. It would surely repulse him. All his life, Bob had lived for the weekend. A long rest by a sunny brook and fish enough to catch. What was Death to him but an everlasting weekend, an eternal release from the labour of living? I could not imagine anyone less likely to consider the Chernoy Process a victory. Seen through Bob's eyes, in fact, it could only be thought a betrayal.

'Go.' Fel kicked me under the sheet. 'You'll be late.'

To get there quickly I caught the Tube but it was already four by the time I arrived at London Bridge. This station being a Bundist development, I was not surprised to find the layout changed since my last visit and extra exits added for streets I'd never heard of. The gloss and finish of the place did surprise me, though they offered but the barest hint of the bizarre transformations I would encounter above ground.

The conceit of the designers was that London Bridge owed its existence to bones. And I had read enough at college to know that this was, in a strict historical sense, perfectly true: Southwark has risen from the marshes of the ancient Thames on the bones of its settlers and their animals, accreting layer by layer like a coral. The same is true of many long-settled places.

Because the Tube line had been dug deep here, the remade station had been fashioned as a slice through history. The walls were lacquered earth, and in the earth were the leavings of past ages of London. Potshards and wooden clogs. A trove of coins. Chicken bones in the ashes of a fire. As I ascended the escalators to street level, so I moved through time, through timbered frames and broken arches, pools of shattered stained glass, swatches of stained brocade. Then ironworks. Pipes and pumps. The homogenous tilth in which the station's faux-relics had been 'buried' (set in lacquer, polished, cunningly lit) vanished entirely, squeezed out by a tangle of ducts, drains and brickwork vessels – the innards of a world coming to mechanical life.

The story these corridors were telling was not subtle. It was coarse, triumphalist and irresistibly exhilarating. As I neared concourse level, iron ceded to plastics and glass and ceramic, and the whole fabric of the building seemed in motion, responding as an anemone might to my passing. The entire subterranean structure was a narrative of human progress, writ according to the Bund's rigorously materialist creation myth, in which the poor, bare forked folk of the Earth had assembled, out of dirt and heat, generation by generation and oh-so-painfully, a living thing out of dead stuff – a city that first had breathed, then gushed, then felt and cried, and now, at last and with the coming of the Bund, had begun to speak.

I had a moment's panic while I fished for my ticket, then

remembered that Fel's phone itself would let me through. I held it up to the plastic barrier, which slid open, letting me onto Tooley Street and a project that, since my last visit, had taken a strange and baffling new direction.

The tram stop was where I expected it to be, and the tram, though wheelless, propelled on a cushion of magnetised air, was in all other respects as I remembered it. The street, however, had quite vanished, broken into pieces and rearranged as if within a giant's kaleidoscope.

There was no longer any second Saint Paul's, but fractured pieces of that structure hung about the street as though projected on the air. Look again, and you would see that these shattered baulks were solid enough, artfully suspended by wires thin as silk from distant sky-grey gantries. Some of the rubble was shrunken to the size of a bin or a bench, while other fragments had been blown out of proportion, so that the statue of Queen Anne, for example, which, like its original, had stood at the foot of the cathedral steps, now spanned the entire thoroughfare, with a tunnel for traffic drilled through her skirts. The whole effort here seemed directed against the comprehending eye, destabilising and dethroning it, making every angle as legitimate as every other, as though the whole view were a canvas by Picasso, that avant-garde Parisian artist whose career had been cut so cruelly short by the wartime gassing of that city.

Out from under Queen Anne's skirts, the vistas rolling by grew stranger still. There were no recognisable streets any more, but only the most fractured arrangements of materials through which we swooped in perfect silence on a raised concrete track, like privileged tourists of the future scouting some terrible and ancient wreck.

As I had understood it on my last visit, these playful zones – colossal filing cabinets like blind high-rises and chairs the size of bridges – had served a psychological function. Such outsize fragments of the real were meant, I had thought, to help the labile and disorientated infants of the Process keep the world in mind. They were props, in other words, for people whose grip on reality would otherwise have been fatally loosened by the Process.

It was clear, however, that this year some new strategy was being tried. Outside, there were no objects, but only the parts of objects; no reality, but only the ingredients of one. My brow furrowed and my head ached as we rolled by acre after acre of incomprehensible stuff: the levers from adjustable office chairs, carpet squares, coat hangers, phone sockets, bicycle handlebars, cotton wool, the lids of take-out coffee cups, fluorescent tubes, paint, staples, sandwich packaging, a pile of faceless wooden men, red and blue, unstrung from table-football games, all of it gargantuan, monumental, none of it readable. It was as though the everyday world had been torn apart and discarded, leaving only the components, as meaningless and minatory as the letters of a sentence were you to jumble them and cram them, spaceless, upon a board.

What breakthrough had Chernoy's researchers made to necessitate this shattering transformation of their playground? Were they trying to actually ape and echo the psychic disintegration of their patients? To what end? What would be the point of that unless it was to prepare their clientele for an altogether different sort of reality? The weightless, hypermediated, so-complex-as-to-be-chaotic reality of the Bund?

When Betty's Process was complete, she would wake into a new world, that was clear – and not a world I could ever be part of.

Beyond the cutting, the tram slowed and settled, purring, onto its concrete bed. In my hand, Fel's phone blinked 'Brockley', and I disembarked.

Parties of Processed infants were walking under the lime trees of Ladywell, catching the last of the daylight. The air was fresh, and I was certain that it was only my imagination that filled the streets with the faint ghost of an echo of a dentist's drill, the fleeting suggestion of mouthwash, the yeasty smell of fresh Band-Aids.

On my first visit, with Stella, it was obvious at a glance how this area had been given over to various ancillary medical services. Aside from anything else, there were signs all over the road, severe speed restrictions, crossings at every junction, lights in the kerbs and ramps up to every door. All that I had seen last August, just eight months earlier, had been removed. Had the Chernoy Process somehow done away with the need for dentists, GPs, sports therapists and all its other hangers-on? Or was Medicine City simply learning the art of disguise? I passed along an avenue of cherry trees. It was easy to imagine that the area was restored to what it had been before the Great War: a leafy and fashionable suburb of the City.

The infants of the Process moved awkwardly along the pavement in bands of between half a dozen and a dozen. They moved too sedately for children, though now and again

I saw, pelting in another direction, groups of runners. They bashed along the pavement together, equally silent, equally serious, as though fleeing for their lives.

Too slow. Too fast. I tried to imagine what Chernoy's Processed infants were going through as they struggled to come to terms with their strange new bodies. Half-remembered. Half-familiar. Too small. Too strong by half.

Everyone was civil, letting me by on the narrow pavement, but the way people here travelled in groups unnerved me. I wondered what their common purpose was. Half a dozen overtook me at a run. Instinctively, I brought Fel's phone close to my chest, protecting it. Were all these infants following an exercise regime, I wondered, or something more atavistic? The boast of the Chernoy Process was that the mind lived on in a new body – but what if the body had its own agenda? The body of a child, flexing, expanding into the space afforded it, testing every limit: such a body would have its own ideas. What must it be like, to take a ride in that body? To be tied to it? Committed to it?

I came to a street that must once have been a main traffic artery; now it appeared to have been given over entirely to promenaders and runners. I climbed wrought-iron stairs to a rolling walkway raised above the road. I travelled east.

I tapped Fel's phone. I was meeting my mother in an indeterminate zone, a white space on the phone's projected map, near buildings, near a park. Now I understood Fel's confusion. It was impossible from the map to tell whether I was meeting Betty outdoors or inside. There were no other details beyond a time of meeting.

Someone barrelled into me from behind and I fell,

dropping the phone. I saw a bright trainer, a stylised skull stitched to the heel, and a hand snatching up the phone. I got to my feet. The young man leapt from the handrail of my walkway into the trough of the one moving parallel to mine, in the opposite direction. The combined speed of the walkways caused him to spin and tumble when he landed. He was already far behind me when he got to his feet. He was unhurt. He stood, arms folded, staring me down as he vanished in the fading light.

My heart hammered in my chest. Panic fizzed through me. But it was over and done and there was nothing I could do about it: I had been mugged. I don't know whether it was the absurdity of the incident or what, but I felt strangely insulated from the assault. I was shaken, and stayed shaken a long while. At the same time, I found the incident impossible to take seriously. Here, in a place technologised to the point of incomprehension, someone wanted to steal a phone? Was this area haunted by unaccommodated criminals? Or was my assailant one of Chernoy's patients, testing the limits of their regained youth? Exuberant. Out of control ...

I should have run after him. I should have leapt from walkway to walkway and pursued him. But I had never been athletic, and I lacked the reflexes that make quick action possible.

So it occurred to me far too late that without the phone I wouldn't be able to find my mother. And even as I thought this, the road, which had risen to cross water, met with a walkway, and the boards under my feet meshed and slowed.

I took metal stairs down to the waterside. There was a small river here: a well-domesticated suburban tributary of the Thames. Along its banks were trees in full leaf, and leading away from the river, a peculiar, maze-like public park made of narrow gravel paths between hillocks no more than a few feet high. These must have been artificial. Between the hillocks, raised on wooden posts wrapped around with coloured scarves, were tents, marquees and gazebos of every size and shape. The tents were brightly coloured, lit by lamps that gave off a warm, organic glow. These lamps were hung from the tent posts, or placed upon the ground behind screens of ornate punctured tin. In each shelter lay a couch. Some tents held two couches, I suppose for partners who – not to be parted by death – had chosen to undergo the Chernoy Process together. And on each couch sprawled a living human form.

Some were naked. Others lay smothered in a thicket of metal branches which, growing up around their couch, threshed about, dipping in and out of that prone and defenceless flesh as if spooning it up.

My eyes fought to adjust, my mind to comprehend what I was seeing. The back-and-forth of metal blades as fine and sharp as grasses in the wind should have made those tents tableaux of violent atrocity. But as I walked, glimpsing each figure – here a man, there a woman, here two women, there a family gathered around a relative gone so to fat and out of true that it was not possible to guess the person's sex – it came to me how happy everyone was here. How unconcerned. Around me rose a great contented murmur of calm and private conversation, which my ear, in passing, muddled to a giant, restful hive-hum.

The reclining figures, naked on their couches, watched

my progress without embarrassment or self-consciousness of any kind. Those whose bodies were hidden under thickets of threshing blades were hardly less passive. Their half-closed eyelids and small smiles suggested that they were drawing from the experience, and in full view of everyone, some small, innocent pleasure.

Here and there a figure, unattended at present, lay virtually hidden behind that sharp, weaving stuff. But I saw no blood, the blades dipped but did not appear to penetrate, and I began to wonder if that dangerous metal foliage was, after all, anything more than a sort of massaging mechanism.

I saw children – real children, not Chernoy's Processed infants – by several of the couches, holding the hands of prone men and women who must, I supposed by their age, be their grandparents. Some were staring up in wonder at the faces of these ancient beings. Others, bored at last, were playing tag around the tents while their parents – who after all were only grown-up children themselves – kept vigil around the beds of their parents.

So many sensations and ideas pressed upon me all at once. It was only as I walked, snatching furtive glimpses, that I was able at last to parse what I was seeing. I was in a great tented gathering of the dying, where the naked dead-to-be held hands with the yet-living. The prone, plump, pinkish bodies on their couches never moved. Each tent was a tableau, warmly lit and calm. A series of nativities. The metaphor was an apt one, I saw now, for once the initial shock was past, I was able to register what was surely the point of the whole Process: every naked figure on its couch, young or old, man or woman, had a belly swollen with new life. Everyone lying here, regardless of their age or sex, was pregnant, and in dying they would, I supposed, give birth to themselves.

Standing lost in all that fertile dying, I knew then that I could not do what I had come to do. How could I presume to dissuade my mother from this new chance? What right had I to tell her she should die in the old world, she who had taken the decision to live in the new? Why had it even occurred to me to do this? Because I was afraid for her? Or because I was afraid *of* her, and what she would become?

The great warm human buzzing around me became a scent in the air, neither spring nor autumn, neither new life nor rot, but something else, something unprecedented, new to the Earth, which could not ever be the same again. I breathed it in and found myself, quite unaccountably, in tears.

I wondered how I would ever find my mother; and if I missed her, if I would see her before she was a child again.

Bob paid his only visit to Fel and me. He arrived late one Friday evening in June, right in the middle of my end-of-year exams, wandered goggle-eyed around our new apartment, and in the morning insisted that he go on his own to Ladywell to talk to Betty. And when he panicked, lost beyond all saving somewhere out in Woolwich (as had been inevitable), he rang, not me, but Stella, from a kindly stranger's phone ('I have a gentleman here says he's lost, he says you're his sister-in-law.')

Stella put as brave a complexion on the afternoon as she could. But it was clear enough, once she had rescued Bob and led him to that place where Betty was at rest, dying and being reborn at once, that Bob would prove inadequate to the occasion. I imagine him there, on the threshold of that tented fairy space, frightened and affronted. What on earth would he have found to say to his wife, in such surroundings, and after so long an estrangement?

Well, it turns out he did not enter. He never got that far. He stood on the travellator platform, talking to his wife on Stella's picturephone. They cannot have been more than a couple of hundred yards apart.

It took me most of the summer to shake off my anger towards Stella. Eventually she managed to persuade me to break bread with her. Or at very least, fork cake, in the lobby of her usual hotel. She had decided to meet the controversy head-on, and insisted on playing me the recording of Bob's conversation with Betty.

'Stella,' I protested, 'it's private. What were you thinking, recording this?'

'Oh, don't be silly,' she said, as oblivious as her boyfriend to old notions of personal privacy. 'The phone records everything.'

I persuaded her to show me only snatches of Betty's side of the conversation with her husband. Betty's face, withered more by suffering than age, loomed large in the frame of Stella's phone.

'The thing about cancer,' Betty said, 'is that it hurts. So you learn to fold the pain up inside you. You crumple it up, so that, even as it gets stronger, it's all the time getting tighter, denser, smaller, like a stone. And then you throw the stone away. You see? You throw it into the sea. And though the waves will return it, again and again, you throw it back into the water, again and again. And so it goes, back and forth, back and forth, thrown and returned, thrown and returned, day after day, and you hope that at last the waves will erode the stone. You hope, one day, there will be no stone. Though there always is.

'But Stuart, this is the point. When you take pain like that, every day, and squeeze it tight, squeeze it into a stone, and throw that stone away, eventually you realise: you can do that with anything. Any part of yourself. And that's why this has been easy for me. Do you see? I've been doing this for years. Stuart. Feel my belly.'

'That's enough,' I said.

Stella leaned forward, over the table, the phone firmly in her grasp. 'Watch.'

Betty had turned the camera upon her body. Waving steel grasses tipped across her supine form, hiding her gravid belly. Out of focus, writhing and spiralling, they stirred her flesh as though it were a soup.

I sat there, helpless.

'Touch my belly. Feel how hard it is. Like a stone. Are you going to catch it, Stu? Are you going to catch this stone? Are you going to look after me?'

The picture went out.

I got to my feet. 'You had no business showing me that.'

'What are you talking about?'

'That's between Mum and Dad. You had no business recording it.'

'*Stuart.*'

I buttoned my coat.

'Did you not hear? She was talking to you. That was all meant for you.'

I shook my head. 'She was talking to Dad. She's confused.'

'Please, Stuart.'

I threw a twenty pound note on the table, a calculated slight since Stella always paid – pointless, too, since the hotel no longer accepted paper money – and I left.

Bob's own interpretation of Betty's state of mind had been refreshingly straightforward. 'She wasn't interested in anything I had to say. Mind you, she never was.'

Following his aborted trip to Ladywell, Stella saw him back to our flat. He spent the evening with me and Fel, saying very little, and the next day he returned to Hebden by the noon train. His visit, which I had expected to be both awkward and intrusive, proved in the end too short for us. Fel felt she must have done or said something wrong. 'I don't think he liked me very much,' she said as we pulled sheets and bed covers from the couch where he had slept, and I said nothing, because in all honesty she was probably right. It must surely have occurred to Bob that the Bund, which had won dominion over so much already, had now won dominion over his wife. And if that was the case, then who was Fel but the agent through which the Bund would win dominion over his son?

I lived in two worlds, and until that point I had always imagined I would be able to hold them apart: my unaccommodated life, and that part of my life that nudged up against the Bund. I had managed until now. I had remembered not to rub my father's nose in my higher education. I had always toned things down when he was around. I wanted him to be proud of me, but I knew not to make too much noise about all of the important things I had learned, nor opine too vigorously about political matters of which Bob, living where he did, and doing what he did, could not possibly know anything.

But the stretch between life in the West Riding and life in London was as nothing to the chasm the Chernoy Process was opening up between the unaccommodated and the Bund, and for the first time, I felt myself tear. I loved Fel, and I loved my father, but as time went on and the world continued to change, playing out with a cold logic the speciations triggered by Gurwitsch's ray, I could see that I might be forced to choose between them.

7

We none of us visited Betty very often during her pregnancy. And this was no tragedy, since day by day there was less of her to visit. By the autumn, when we were carrying umbrellas to Ladywell and splashing along gravel paths from tent to tent, it was impossible, when we got to her gazebo, for us to glimpse the oh-so-precious core one likes to imagine lies at the root of a human self. Betty's body alone remained. That and a wrapper of words and associations unbound by anything you could call consciousness.

Betty's tent was sagging by then, its crimson canvas faded in streaks to a fleshy pink. Mildew grew in the corners and its seams bled in the rain. There was mud trodden into the rugs around the couch, and things living under the weave, and the tin lamps scattered round about, which had lit Betty's confinement from beneath like a Victorian nativity scene, had tarnished and dented, and many had ceased to function. By then, Betty was spared the sight of this dilapidation. The stand of blade-like grasses had receded back into the earth, but now her head was smothered by hordes of silver bees. It was a sight familiar enough by then to make my last visit, at the end of November, easier than perhaps it ought to have been. Not very charged with emotion at all, in fact – it was as though I had already lost her. When I squeezed her hand for the last time, her fingers found mine and yet I knew, deep in my heart, that this was merely an autonomic response, and that she was consumed. I stared at her swollen belly. Its late fecundity was still disturbing to me: a youngish belly parasitising on an old woman. An unnecessarily bitter way of looking at the Chernoy Process, but given Betty's medical history, how could I think of it differently?

Oblivious to my grim metaphor-making, Betty hurtled towards her triumphant rebirth. At Stella's request, the clinic sent us regular video reports. Through them we sensed her belly swelling day by day, and heard the bees swarming in and out of her mouth and nose in pursuit of strange honey, reading her mind even as they burned away her brain.

The clinic controlled every nuance of this process, including the moment of death. For Betty's demise, they picked Christmas Day: the very day the family were meant to cheer Jim off to Woomera.

Stella's house in Islington stood on the corner of Inglebert Street and Myddelton Square. It had an impressive front door, but the easiest way in was by the garden. I pressed the bell and after a long shivery moment the side door – set in a high, lilac-topped brick wall – unlatched itself without buzzing. I let Fel through first. Though much of the planting had died back, the garden still felt overgrown. I gathered Fel to me and kissed her in the shadow of the long-neglected apple tree. Laughing softly, she pushed me away and I nearly toppled over a planter moulded in the shape of a classically proportioned human head. I took her hand and led her, more by feel than by sight, along a narrow brick path to the top of a spiral of slippery iron stairs.

Light from the basement dining room lit our way. The kitchen door was ajar. From it spilled a current of warm air, heavy with asafoetida and cumin. Stella, who had never cooked for Fel before and who claimed never to have done more than spiralise a few vegetables for Georgy ('We always eat out') was attempting a feast compatible with the Bund's strictures on diet. There was no trace of Christmas in her cooking, no decorations in the windows, no sign of cake anywhere. I put a brave face on things but it had somehow slipped my mind that Christmas was not universal. I was as disappointed as a child, though grimly determined not to let it show.

'Come in, come in,' Stella harried. 'Don't let the warmth out. No, don't shut the door, leave a gap, we won't be able to breathe.'

'How are you doing, Stella?'

'Have you come straight from Cripplegate?'

'Pretty much,' Fel said.

'Drinks. Would you like a drink?'

'I'm fine.'

'I've got juices, Rose's Lime, Vimto.'

Fel laughed.

Stella's smile was uncertain. 'You all drink Vimto, don't you? At least, Georgy does.' She shot a look at me.

'It's fine, Stella. They do all drink Vimto. It's practically a religion.'

'Do you have a beer?'

Stella blinked at Fel. 'Of course.'

'Fel drinks alcohol.'

'Oh.'

'And Vimto,' said Fel. 'But a beer would be lovely.'

'Stuart, can you go and get Fel a beer from the fridge next door?'

I slipped off my shoes and stowed them under the bench just inside the back door. I crossed the dining room to the heavy, lime-green fridge-freezer. The room was nothing like I remembered. Stella had it fitted out with subfloor heating under marble, and a set of wilfully eccentric pieces from Portobello Road Market had taken the place of the old cupboards. This evening, in preparation for the gathering, the room was all lit up with tea-lights and candles. It looked like Stella was trying too hard. I returned to the tiny galley kitchen with Fel's bottle of Pils. 'Is there an opener?'

Fel, recognising the brand, took the bottle, screwed off the cap and stuck her tongue out at me.

'Now, Felicine, do go and sit down. Stuart, give me a hand.' Stella thrust a handful of coriander at me. Some of it dropped on the floor. 'Here,' she said, pulling a chopping board down and over the sink: the fit was precarious but there was no other surface to use. She had already taken the dining table out of action with place settings and glasses for Vimto and wine. 'Can you manage there?' She fished about in an open drawer and fetched out a mezzaluna. 'As fine as you can.'

'A knife would be better. I need one hand to steady the board.'

She found me a knife too small for the job; I sawed away at the stuff in my fist, pressing down to keep the board in place.

'Oh dear,' said Stella, gazing at the mess her cooking had made of the kitchen. 'I don't know what I'm doing.'

'It all smells fantastic.'

'Everything smells fantastic when it starts to burn.'

'There. Is that fine enough? Good. Now, what else is there to do?' Having got through that labour with my fingers still intact, I was game for anything.

Because the Bund only ever ate meat of its own devising – vegetal meat, efficient, sterile and relatively homogenous – Stella had elected to stick to vegetarian food. She was not a bad cook, but she was out of practice and the recipes she had chosen – I read them over her shoulder out of books with titles like *The Incredible Spice Wunderkammer* and *Adventures on the Cardamom Route* – had far too many stages to them.

'Just grind all that into a paste and fry it,' I told her, pointing to a particularly knotted passage in *Under the Tamarind Tree*. 'Make life simpler for yourself.'

'But it'll burn!'

'It won't burn, it'll be full of liquid from the onion. Just toss it about in some oil until the water evaporates.'

She looked up at me with wide eyes. 'You think so?'

'Go and talk to Fel,' I said. 'She's on her own in there. I can fix this.'

She kissed me on the cheek.

It was easy enough to handle. Stella had forgotten the rice. It was still soaking in far too much cold water. I drained half of it off, added cardamom and butter and salt, and was just sealing the pan with a sheet of foil when the back door opened and Bob and Jim came in.

'I found him,' Jim bellowed, putting his arms around me. 'I found Dad, bet you can't guess where.'

'How'd you get in?'

'Some pillock left the garden door open.'

I wanted Jim to be still and let me look at him: I had seen him twice in the past two years, both vanishingly brief encounters on his way through London, and none of us had received so much as a letter from him since he'd been selected for the army's Space Force. He had just finished a month in purdah at a submarine base in the Firth of Forth, doing whatever passed for basic training in that bizarre and brand-new organisation. Tomorrow was Christmas Day and he was off by air for Woomera and the rocket construction effort there. After that, there was no telling when we would see him again. If all went well, the next time we saw him he would be on television: first Yorkshireman in space.

If Jim's ebullience hadn't already given him away, his breath certainly would have. 'Good drink?' I asked him.

'Should have come with us, bro.'

I wrestled Jim off, one hand still steadying the rice pan. 'Christ, you'll have me tipping this over.'

Jim laughed and ruffled my hair.

'How're you doing, Stu?' Bob's face was flushed, maybe from the sudden heat of the kitchen, more likely from however many hours he had spent drinking with Jim.

'Go through. Take your shoes off. There's beers in the fridge.'

Stella appeared at the living-room door and hugged the new arrivals. Once the rice pan was sealed, I set it on a low heat, checked my watch and followed the others into the dining room.

Stella's new dining table was very small: a find from her scavenging expeditions in search of props for *DARE*. She told us it hailed from the mortuary of a defunct hospital. The zinc wrapping was tarnished here and there, and you could not help but try to guess which had been the table's head end and which the other.

Fel sat at the end of the table, Jim near her and Stella next to him. 'Food in fifteen minutes,' I announced, taking a seat opposite Jim. Dad sat beside me. This left the chair at the head of the table vacant for Georgy.

'I don't know where he can have got to,' said Stella, finding things to fret about. 'He said he'd be here to help.'

Fel must have asked Jim something about his work because the next thing I knew he was moving all the glasses about the table in an effort to explain the hydrodynamics of small nuclear devices.

Bob was aghast. 'Should you be telling us any of this, lad?'

Jim laughed. 'It's no secret, Dad. The ship's half-built. You half-built it!'

Bob smiled a guarded little smile. 'Only shift work, son.'

'Anyway,' said Jim, 'I dare say if you lot had wanted, you'd have blasted off years ago and this Earth'd be riddled with holes like a Swiss cheese.'

I looked from Jim to Fel, unsure what was going on.

Jim saw me and shrugged. 'The Bund, I mean.'

Fel smiled him a cold smile. 'Blowing things up is not our style.'

Jim laughed and raised his beer. 'Trusting us to do the heavy lifting, eh?'

'*We* don't trust *you* to do anything,' Fel said, holding my brother's gaze.

No one knew how to react – no one, that is, but Jim, who met my eye and whistled his appreciation. 'Got a live one here.'

'Bob?' Stella placed her fingertips on the table: a subtle call-to-order. 'How was Betty?'

Bob met Stella's smile with a rare smile of his own but he said nothing.

Jim filled the silence so quickly, there might not have been any silence at all. 'I thought she looked jolly fine. Stuart?'

'I saw her last month,' I said. 'She seemed – well, she seemed healthy, didn't she, Fel?

'God, she must have been glad you were there, Felicine!' Jim exclaimed, thumping the table. He pronounced her name to rhyme with 'twine'. 'The daughter she never had.'

What that was supposed to mean, I had no idea, but Fel took it in good part: 'How much have you drunk?' she asked him, laughing.

'We sank a couple, didn't we, Dad? Christmas cheer and all that. You two should have come along.'

It occurred to me then why Jim was coming at everything from such an odd angle, exhilarated and aggressive. He was nervous. And realising this, I realised why. He was covering for Bob. Bob had once again failed to visit Betty. It must have been obvious to Fel as well: she felt for my hand under the table and gave it a squeeze.

'When I come back,' Jim said, 'I expect Mum'll be ... well, I hope—' He hesitated, finding himself suddenly on dangerous ground, and something else occurred to me: how strange all this must seem to him! He had spent most of the last year, prior to basic training with the Space Force, on a peacekeeping tour of Sri Lanka. Of all of us, he had the least understanding of what Betty was going through, and the least notion why anyone could have thought it was a good idea.

'Well, of course,' Stella exclaimed. She laughed. 'Everything'll be different in a year.'

As though her assurances were a cue, Georgy Chernoy entered the living room.

'George! Where have you been?' (Only Stella ever anglicised Georgy Chernoy's name. I suppose it was a sort of endearment. I wondered what he thought of it.)

Georgy strode up to Stella's chair and kissed the top of her head. 'I'm so sorry,' he said. 'I could not get away.' He took in the table, his daughter, me. 'You must be Robert,' he said to my father. 'And James.'

Jim stood up, none too steadily, to shake his hand.

'Congratulations.' Georgy pumped his hand. 'When do you fly out?'

'But I only just got here,' Jim shot back, and over laughter, 'Tomorrow morning.'

'And the big launch?'

Jim grinned. 'I'd be the last to know that.'

'Jim's been telling us how their ship's drive works,' Fel said.

'Oh yes?'

'Did you know that the bomb-delivery mechanism is based on a Vimto dispensing machine?'

'Yes. I did.' This flatly, and without humour. I wondered why Georgy was trying to shut his daughter down. To Jim: 'Well, I wish you luck with it.'

Try as he might – and I was not convinced that he was trying especially hard – Georgy Chernoy could not let go the *noblesse oblige* of his people, for whom such pyrotechnic adventures were, according to their conceit, quite superfluous.

'There's something splendidly muscular about this effort, isn't there? Yes?' He fished around the table for signs of assent and, ignoring their absence: 'Here we are – in the Bund, I mean – setting off firecrackers from high-altitude balloons, spreading sails to catch the sunlight, spitting ions out the back of flameless rockets, sending up fist-sized microsatellites on pencil-thin laser beams. And here you are, shipping ruddy great pipes halfway around the Earth and threatening to nuke an entire desert so as to get a frigate into orbit.'

'The point of space,' said Jim, 'is being there. Don't you agree? No, you don't,' he continued, not letting Georgy respond. 'You'd rather send up machines. Each to his own, but I want to see the Earth spread below me with my own eyes.'

Georgy cocked his head: a predator sizing up prey. 'What a pity you only have one pair.'

Stella shot me a look. She didn't like the combative turn the conversation was taking. But what was I supposed to do? Get the two sides of this dinner to meekly agree on their mutual incomprehension? I said: 'I suppose, having given birth to the dead in Catford, it's a relatively small step to give birth to them on the Moon.'

Georgy's smile tightened.

'That is the idea, isn't it?'

'It's certainly a possibility,' he conceded.

'Already you're populating other planets!'

He did not look at me. 'Quite why everyone is so fascinated by the population curves of the Jewish race, I'll never know. It has always been like this. As if we're a sort of human isotope. Don't let them reach critical mass!'

His angry defensiveness astounded me. Why now, here, among friends, was Georgy referring to his community by the old, unhappy name? The whole point of the Bund had been to repudiate its tribal past. Of all the bizarre figures forged in the inferno of the Great War, the Bundist – thoroughly modern, rigidly materialist, crushing the rabbi under his proletarian heel – had surely been the most compelling, the most exhilarating.

'If it was critical mass we were afraid of,' I said, 'I think we'd look at London and declare that battle lost for good and all.'

By Georgy's expression, I could see that he still thought I was attacking him. Fel had let go of my hand. Perhaps she thought so, too. I did not care. My blood was up. I knew what he thought I was. All I could do was answer fire with fire. 'When you've finished snatching racial failure from the jaws of political victory,' I said, 'you might just possibly see that I was paying you a compliment. Whatever the Space Force accomplishes – men in space, men on the Moon, men on Mars – it's obvious to me that you will still be first to settle these places. That is, I assume, what your machines are for? To build for your arrival?'

'First to settle?' This from Bob, for whom none of my oh-so-important opinions had made any sense at all. 'Well, I don't know about that. I think Jim and his mates might surprise you there, Mr Chernoy.'

Chernoy did not miss a beat. 'How very proud you must be of your son,' he said, reaching across the table.

Bob, blinking, rose as if hypnotised to shake Georgy's hand.

I glanced at my watch. 'Stella?'

Stella and I served the food while Jim, in the lull occasioned by my absence – what on earth had I been thinking? – held forth about his training. Bob, at least a little tight and with a second bottle of beer on the go, listened intently. Georgy had relaxed at last, though as usual his open, warm smile gave absolutely nothing away. I couldn't catch Fel's eye to see what she thought of my altercation with her father. It hadn't been my finest hour, but of one thing I was sure: he had started it.

'I don't know how we're going to fill the days of our voyage, exactly,' Jim admitted. 'There won't be much to master about the ship itself: it's the size of a frigate, as you say, and a damn-sight easier to sail.'

'And where will you go?' Georgy asked. 'All being well.'

More rearrangements of the glassware: 'So you see, even Jupiter is not outside our range.'

Georgy looked impressed. 'And do you have special suits prepared for Mars?'

Jim blinked, blindsided by a question so specific and

so very much off the point. 'I'd be the last to know about details like that,' he said again.

'Only I've heard it said that it's going to be easier to run on the Martian surface than it is to walk,' Georgy said. 'So I suppose the designers are going to have to think about that.'

You could see Jim taking confidence from the question. You could see him thinking: *Here we are, two men together, thrashing out the technical detail.* 'True enough,' he said. 'Your power-to-weight ratio is different in lower gravity – more like a child's. The smaller you are, the stronger you are relative to your size. And that's why little kids are always running about from place to place. It's *easier* for them to run than walk.'

I remembered the strange combination of awkward slowness and pell-mell speed exhibited by Chernoy's Processed infants: old souls in bodies adapted to a more accommodating physics.

Before I could put any of that into words, however, Georgy once again launched himself into wild territory. 'A lot of little kids running about on the Red Planet!' he cried.

Everybody looked at him.

He blinked at us. 'Well, isn't that what it'll be like? It's charming. The thought of James here skipping about Schiaparelli like a toddler.'

Silence.

'Oh, *come on*, why go all the way to Mars if you're not going to have a bit of fun?'

It occurred to me that it was we who were being thin-skinned now. Grown men playing tag in the red dirt? The vision *was* charming! Especially so in the eyes of a man who had fused the infantile and the aged into one constantly renewing – and therefore immortal – form.

'Fel,' said Georgy, serious suddenly. 'What is that you're drinking?'

Fel reflexively wrapped her hand around her bottle. 'It's beer,' she told him. I had never really taken any notice of her interest in alcohol, which anyway never exceeded the odd half of cider down the pub. Hearing the tremor in her voice now made me realise that breaking with the Bund's teetotal tradition was a big deal.

'Really?'

'Really.'

'Well.' Even Georgy's control slipped occasionally: he shot a glance at me. A corrupter of women as well as an anti-Semite.

'Has everyone got enough?' Stella asked. 'Oh, God. The beans.' She ran back to the kitchen.

'They're on the side,' I called, and when she didn't respond, went into the kitchen after her. Stella was peeling the foil off the pan. 'Oh, look, they're burned!'

'They're not burned.'

'The garlic's all brown.'

'Not very brown. It's supposed to be toasted, it's fine.'

'You can't do that with garlic.'

'Yes you can. With this, you can. Stella, look at me. What do you think I cook for Fel? I cook this kind of food all the time. It's perfect.'

Stella mouthed a thank you and carried the dish out to the dining room. I fetched a spoon.

The beans were perfectly fine. Trust Bob, though, to be meticulously cutting off each tip and edging it with his knife to the side of his plate. Had Stella noticed? No: her gaze was glued to Georgy Chernoy who, having got everyone's attention with his potentially belittling remark about playtime on Mars, was holding forth on his favourite subject: the reconciliation of what, in a more formal setting, he would probably have dubbed 'the human family'.

'It's absurd!' he exclaimed, and Jim chimed in, banging the zinc with his beer bottle. (Stella winced.)

'We're not afraid of you!' Jim asserted, slurring slightly.

'Well, of course you aren't!' Georgy laughingly agreed. 'Where could the conflict possibly lie? The moment you're in space is surely the moment you realise how absurd all this scaremongering is. Do you know, I read an op-ed in one of your papers the other day that raised the spectre of us dropping Moon-rocks on London? That's the word they used: "dropping"! As if the Moon were above the Earth! It's positively medieval. Ptolemaic, even.'

'Anyway,' said Jim, overcome with fellow feeling, 'you live here. You people are half of this city. You'd have a few words to say if anyone dropped rocks on you!'

Chernoy beamed at him. 'No one's dropping anything. No one's throwing anything.'

Bob, joining in, raised his bottle. 'And to hell with the red-tops!'

'The tabloids. The papers,' Stella explained, seeing Georgy's confusion.

At that, Georgy raised his own bottle. The bottle surprised me, the label even more: now he, too, was drinking Pils. 'Well, yes, to hell with *them*,' he exclaimed, and drank.

Fel was working hard to ignore her father and so had

managed to strike up a conversation with mine. Bob had that poleaxed look I had noticed men got when they talked to Fel for the first time – as though he was being truly understood for the first time. 'Pumps, in the main,' he was telling her. 'The pipework for pumps. They made me a checker.'

'It's a big deal,' I told her, chipping in.

Bob shot me an angry glance. 'It's shift work, as always.'

'On spaceships.'

'The *parts* for spaceships.' Poor Bob: he was trapped. Whatever he said about it, his work carried the smack of glamour.

Georgy drew the back of his hand across his lips, stood up and crossed to the fridge. He wanted people to notice him. Above all, he wanted Fel to notice him. He pulled out two bottles of Pils from the door, unscrewed them both as he returned to the table and handed one to Bob. Fel was still managing to ignore him, but Stella wasn't. I sensed that this was new: that she had not seen Georgy drink till now.

'An engineer is an engineer,' Georgy announced, and raised his bottle to Bob to chink.

Bob stared at him.

'Whatever the engine,' Georgy added, and took a deep draught of his fresh beer.

Bob frowned. It was all very well him putting his own work down, but what was Georgy about? I could practically see the clockwork turning in him: should he be offended or not? How I hated that about him: that old pendulum inside him forever swinging between pride and fear.

'God, Daddy,' said Fel, 'don't tell us you're an engineer now.'

Georgy sucked at his bottle. 'Well, what would you call it?'

'Medicine isn't an engineering problem.'

'Everything is an engineering problem.'

'Really.'

'You'll discover this in time.'

'Here we go.'

The pair of them, father and daughter, each nursing their bottles of forbidden alcohol, had been building up to a row ever since Georgy came through the door.

'What?' Georgy smiled a combative smile. 'You think all that art and music you're so fond of aren't engineering problems? Talk to any painter! Any composer!'

'You don't know any composers.'

'What, you think you're the first to step outside the Bund? Stuart, tell her: is there anything you studied at that school of yours that *wasn't* an engineering problem?'

'Well.' I was painfully aware what his likely opinion of me was. 'Yes.'

'*Yes?*' Georgy laughed, incredulous. 'In that case, remind me to bring a hard hat and good insurance next time I visit any structure of yours.'

It was such a clumsy attack, I couldn't help myself: 'An open mind will do.'

Georgy was delighted, or made a good show of seeming so. 'Oh, bravo!' He raised his bottle in a toast. While he drank, he kept his eyes on Fel. He was showing her how little her trivial dietary rebellion mattered. It would take more than a bottle or two of beer to count as secession. Measure for measure, Daddy could match his brat of a girl. Only it was apparent that he could not match her: his eyes had already acquired a dangerous glassiness.

I expected Stella to head the conversation into calmer waters, but she sat there in absolute silence. In the end, it was Jim who poured oil on troubled waters by offering a little homespun philosophy of his own.

'Now hang on, Doctor Chernoy. I mean to say, there wouldn't be much point in good engineering, would there, in making something well, or doing anything well, if others didn't stand back once in a while and say it was well done? Would there? And isn't that what art is?'

Georgy clapped, rather slowly. 'There you are! "Lonely on a peak in Darien"!' He winked grotesquely, at me or at Fel or maybe at both of us, it was hard to tell. 'Poetry.'

'Silent.' Fel's voice was taut with anger. '"Silent, upon a peak in Darien." Though what Keats has to do with anything beats me.' She reached for the pitcher of Vimto Stella had prepared. It was still full, the ice almost melted.

'I'll have a sup of that,' Jim announced, ever the diplomat, and thrust out his water glass. Fel poured for him. 'And –' he drank it off '– and I'll be off home. No, no, I'd better,' he insisted, gathering himself. Sobriety, or a decent impression of it, had become like a jacket he shrugged on at will. 'Reveille's at five a.m.' He got out of his seat and in one swift, elegant move that made Stella squeal, he gathered her into his arms and brought her out of her chair in a hug tight enough to wind her. 'Auntie!'

'Give over! Oaf!'

'Thank you so much for tonight.' He planted kisses on both her cheeks. 'Such a terrific send-off.'

'Great fool,' Stella cried, flushing with pleasure.

It was clear enough, whatever we said, that Jim was determined to leave, so one by one we got out of our chairs and hugged him.

'Till tomorrow.' Stella sighed, kissing him. 'Get some good sleep.'

Jim hugged me, kissed Fel on the cheek and came around the table and into Bob's arms. Neither man smiled as they held each other, and the party fell silent a moment, solemn suddenly at this parting of father and son.

'Here,' Jim said, pressing something into Bob's hand. The moment went by so fleetingly, I didn't take it in. It was only much later, when I returned to Yorkshire, that Bob showed me what he had been given: a wristwatch from the rocketry school in Peenemünde, the logo from the film *Frau im Mond* surfing starlight on its engraved underside.

Georgy had the sense to hold himself back in this moment of leave-taking; or perhaps, rising from his seat, he had suddenly felt the effects of the evening's alcohol. Jim and Georgy shook hands, more formally than before, their smiling eyes locking. For all Georgy's earlier nonsense about reconciliation, the evening had, if anything, drawn the lines between our races even more clearly. Georgy said: 'We'll see you when you get there.'

He meant the Moon. Jim's grin at the challenge was without mirth. 'Your machines will. Have them prepare our supper for us.'

'Don't be late,' said Georgy, still holding his hand.

Bob and I saw Jim to the door. When we came back in, we found Fel and Georgy staring daggers at each other across the table while Stella gathered up the empty plates.

Georgy wheeled around in his seat. 'Robert!'

Fel, a desperate expression on her face, looked from her father to me and back again.

'Robert, tell Fel what it is you actually do.'

Stella passed me bearing plates into the kitchen. For all her doubt and her little-girl-lost routine, the meal had been a success. We had demolished every dish; there was barely anything but sauce in the serving bowls. Only Bob's plate remained full. He took his seat and began picking at his dinner again, his face drawn. 'Well—' he began.

Chernoy interrupted him. 'Robert measures the widths of holes, Fel. Day in, day out. Imagine that.'

I felt Stella come back into the room beside me, felt more than heard the breath she drew.

'Dad,' I said quickly, before she could say anything, 'stop messing about. Come and help me clear up.'

Georgy shot me a look that might have been admiring. I ignored him; I just needed to get Bob out of the room. Let the Chernoys fight among themselves if they wanted to.

In the kitchen, Bob emptied his plate into the bin and handed it to me. He'd eaten hardly anything.

'Too spicy?'

He shrugged.

'Come and help me wash up.'

I washed, Bob dried. *What did you do all day?* I wondered. Traipsed around the city. Supped tea in cafeterias. Rolled up at the pub at last. What? You told Jim but you won't tell me. 'You should have gone to see Mum,' I said.

Bob glanced at me, and quickly away. 'I did.'

'Right.'

'You calling me a liar, lad?'

'Yep.'

Stella came bustling in. 'What are you two still doing in here? Come out! Leave that. There's dessert.' The party was coming to pieces in her hands. I felt sorry for her, but really, what else could she have possibly expected? Had she imagined that all the bits of unresolved family business she had hurled together willy-nilly this evening would unlock each other, as neatly as a stage comedy? But of course she had. This, after all, was the world she lived in: the scripted world of the stage, where complications only got tangled up in Act Two in order to unwind in Act Three.

Only there wasn't going to be any Act Three. Not tonight: not with Georgy drunk and raiding the fridge for another beer, and Stella, suddenly losing her cool, pulling hard on his arm to stop him. The fridge door flew open and a carton of milk toppled out of the door and landed at my feet. I snatched it up but it had burst and it leaked all over my hands and down the front of my trousers as I juggled it into the kitchen.

By the time I came back, Georgy was shifting, none too elegantly, into a penitent gear. It was already arranged that Bob would stay over, so Georgy was going to have to mend fences somehow. He said to Bob: 'I honest-to-goodness didn't mean anything bad by it.'

Bob was the taller of the two men, but his baffled, hypnotised expression revealed that Georgy, even as an unaccustomed drunk, knew how to handle men like Bob: simple working men for whom even their own sense of self-worth acted as a brake on their self-assertion.

Fel ordered an autonomous cab for us. We rode most of the way home in silence, until at last she said: 'Your mother dies tomorrow.'

I looked out through the window. It was a dry, clear night. Christmas Eve. I was surprised the streets were so empty. 'Yes.'

'No one said anything about it.'

'No. Well, Jim and Bob went to see Mum earlier today. In the end, there is nothing to say, is there?'

'Isn't there?'

'For crying out loud, what do you want me to say?'

'I'm sorry.'

'That I'm losing her again? You need me to spell this out?'

'It's all right.'

'That I've never particularly liked her?'

'That's not true.'

'Love and like are different things. Deal with it. God knows I've had to.'

She put her arm around me. I tried to calm down. I did. Only I didn't want to be put on the spot. I couldn't bear the way Bob had sloped off again, and I couldn't convince myself that I was any better. And the way the evening had ended: that still rankled. 'Your father's an arsehole,' I said.

'Yes.' She offered nothing else. She didn't laugh. She didn't turn it into a joke. She didn't want to be angry with me. She waited for me to calm down.

I took her hand. 'I'm sorry.'

She squeezed my fingers. 'What will you do tomorrow?'

'Do?'

'Are you going to Croydon to see Jim off?'

'Of course.'

She took my hand and massaged it, as though trying to read something there. 'And your mum?'

'I've been to see her,' I said. 'There's nothing left.'

'There's the birth.'

'I'm not interested in that.'

We were approaching Moorgate when she said, 'I'll go there tomorrow. I'll go to Ladywell. Someone should be there.'

I shrugged. 'If that's what you want to do. I guess you understand it better than I do.'

We got to the flat and undressed and huddled together under the duvet. I'd had enough. I couldn't bear the thought of talking any more. But as usually happens whenever I try to force sleep upon myself, it didn't last. In the middle of the night I woke up, brain ticking and buzzing as though it were already morning, only I was convinced there was a stranger in the room.

I stretched out for Fel but found only bedlinen. I sat up abruptly, sure that by doing so I would shake off what could only be a dream. A glitch of the sleeping mind.

But the presence persisted. It was real enough, though invisible, and felt tied to Fel's absence. I stared numbly at the empty half of our bed. Fel was not in the bedroom. I blinked, orientating myself.

The door was ajar. Light fanned in from the living room. I got up. The laminate flooring was cold and sticky against my feet. The French window was open, letting in distant traffic sounds, the city never quite sleeping. Fel was on the balcony. She glanced at me and smiled and the diamond set in her tooth and all the stones in her ear glittered in the moonlight.

She turned back and looked up at the sky. I followed her gaze. A half-moon was rising above the blocks of the estate. Where the Moon's dark half should have blocked out the stars, there were lights. Just a few, very faint. Four or five of them. Six. Maybe seven. My eyes, adjusting, caught the hint of more, though I had to look to one side of the Moon to detect them. They were faint enough that they disappeared when looked at directly.

They hung in no particular pattern, and shone with the same modest brightness as the surrounding stars so that it appeared, after a few seconds, as though they were indeed stars, and the dark half of the Moon was entirely missing. A few seconds later, the illusion righted itself, and reason took hold again, and I was looking at the unlit half of the Moon. And there were lights. Lights on the Moon.

The Moon was inhabited. I'd read the papers. I knew the inhabitants were only machines. Diggers, cranes and drills. But still. Fires were burning. I had not seen this before. Not with the naked eye. I must have said something. It was quite a sight.

Here, however, memory breaks down. It fails me, and I can't be sure which of us next spoke.

'Fires are burning.'

Nonsense.

I took Fel by the hand. 'Come to bed.'

8

Champions of the Process called Georgy Chernoy's medicalised infants the 'reborn'. Critics dubbed them the 'undead'. To me they were just strange children. Their bodies, though growing at an accelerated rate, never quite managed to catch up with their impatient, adultish minds. I was never able to take them entirely seriously, not even when one of them was my own mother. Fel persuaded me to visit my new mum around the time she was three months old, and had started to use sign language. Fel was infatuated. Whenever the weather allowed she had been wheeling Betty around the memory parks of Medicine City, and the therapy was having the desired effect. 'Betty knows who she is now,' Fel assured me. 'She's been asking after you.' As though this would encourage me. But Fel's enthusiasm was winning, and my own curiosity was growing. What finally tipped the scales was Betty leaving the nursery. Stella took her back to her house in Islington to look after her, now that she no longer needed specialist care.

'It's just a matter of patience,' Fel explained to me. 'Your mum's memories are all there. It's just a question of encouraging her to work through her old life. She needs to call everything to mind. You should go and see her. You should talk to her. You should make the connection.'

I didn't know about that. But I had lost too much of my mother already – to cancer, and to Stella – to ignore altogether this strange new chapter in her life. Though I was sceptical about who or what I would find rattling the gaily painted bars of Stella's newly installed staircase, I felt I had better stake an early interest.

I arrived to find Betty in Stella's basement dining room, strapped in a high chair, splashing sickly, sweet-smelling rusk porridge all over the zinc dining table. Now Betty was out of Ladywell's care, Stella had to rely on local shops for her supplies. Betty's stiff plastic bib had a locomotive on it. Her sippy cup was embossed with cartoon giraffes.

'Here she is,' Stella said, tone cheery, eyes wide as she faced me and nervous as hell. I wondered if her mood was triggered by my arrival. It was just as likely that Betty herself was keeping her on a constant knife's edge.

Her feeding, for a start, was painful to watch. An ordinary baby, knowing no better and anyway lacking coordination, will throw porridge around as a kind of wild experiment. The infant before me, however, already knew perfectly well what a spoon was, what a table was, what up and down were and what porridge was for. She just lacked the coordination to handle them. There was no joy in her movements at all – just incapacity. She looked to me to be exactly what she was: a shrunken adult struggling with a motor dysfunction. She glared up at me, her chin thrust belligerently forward and dripping with milky, greyish stuff. She dropped her wide-grip plastic spoon. It fell half into her bowl and toppled out onto the table. She weaved her stubby little arms in front of her face.

Stella translated: 'She wants to know what took you so long.'

Fel was in the kitchen, wringing out a rag. She returned to wipe up the worst of the spills and detach Betty's bib. Betty sat still throughout the clean-up. No actual baby would ever have done that. I tried hard not to show my discomfort, but I found it very difficult to watch. I felt I was confronted with something pretending to be a baby. Which, I suppose, was not far from the truth. The imposture was more than unsettling. It was disgusting. My whole body sang with tension. It occurred to me that it would be the most natural thing in the world for me to stove this thing's head in with a pan. The shock was so intense, I mumbled an excuse, rushed into the kitchen and leaned over the sink. There was a glass on the drainer and I fumbled it under the tap and filled it. The drink helped. *Thank God that's over*, I thought. My heart steadied. I came back in to find Fel wiping Betty's face with a damp tissue, and it was all I could do not to rush in and save her, pulling her out of range of that dangerous, gummy mouth and those tiny, stubby, grasping hands.

They weaved about.

Stella, translating again, said: 'She wants to know about your work.'

So I sat there sipping milky coffee, trying to control the trembling of my hands, trying to explain to my newborn mother how the kinds of technology that (among other things) made her possible were eating my career before my eyes. 'They print buildings now, Mum. Draw and print. The machines do everything.'

Whatever sign-system Betty was using, it had to be tiring, and she was constantly trying to form words in the back of her throat, her immature tongue weaving around inside her gaping mouth like something trapped. I tried to ask her about herself, about what she was going through and how she felt. She waved these questions away impatiently. Replying to them with arm gestures would have been both difficult and exhausting – even assuming that Stella was up to translating them.

Fel steered away from us as we talked; over Betty's head I could see her busying herself in the kitchen, sorting out piles of baby clothes. Georgy Chernoy was not at home. I wondered what he made of these novel domestic arrangements: about being confronted, at the end of every busy day, with a living, breathing, defecating example of his creation.

In the taxi back to the Barbican, Fel said, 'What do you think about kids?'

'She's not a kid,' I replied. 'I don't know what she is. Well, I do. I get it. She's something new. Still, I don't know how you do it. They grow up fast, don't they? Faster than normal. That's what I've read. I can't imagine Dad coping with this. Not until she's older, anyway. Not until she can speak, at very least. How long will we have to wait? A couple of months? She's developing so fast.'

I looked across at Fel. She was looking out of the window, away from me. Her arms were folded.

'What's the matter?'

She took a sudden interest in something outside, though there was nothing to see.

Eventually, she said: 'You didn't answer my question.'

In the game of Set there are no turns. The dealer shuffles a special deck and lays twelve cards face up in a rectangle. Players identify and remove sets of three cards from anywhere in the array. Each card contains one, two or three symbols, which are lozenges, squiggles or diamonds, and these are either red, green or purple, and solid, open or striped. There are 81 cards in the box, and there is a 1:33 chance of there being no set present in an array of twelve cards.

'Set!' Stan Lesniak exclaimed.

'No.' Fel pointed to two of his cards. 'These two are diamonds. That one is a lozenge.'

He still didn't understand.

'You can't have two characteristics the same,' Fel explained, 'unless all three are the same.'

Stan blew a raspberry. 'This is boring,' he complained. 'Have you at least got some better wine?'

Stan, star of my academic year, editor of *Responses*, was following my brother to Woomera, albeit in the employ of the Commonwealth Office. For years the army had been detonating atom bombs in tarmac-lined hemispherical basins dug all over the desert. It was the quickest way they knew of producing the valuable, short-lived nuclear fuel called tritium. Now local campaigners were blaming the production cycle for an increase in stillbirths, birth defects and childhood leukaemias. Stan had been hired to establish whether these claims had any scientific credibility.

'You would have thought, when they heard the loud bangs, people would simply have had the sense to move away,' he complained. He sipped at what I'd just poured him and winced.

'Stan's a sensitive soul,' I said for Fel's benefit, trying to keep the evening light.

But Stan was caught in an embarrassing position and, being Stan, wanted to take his embarrassment out on us. Somehow he had heard about Betty – I don't know how – and he must have assumed Fel and I were looking after her. He was irritated to find that Betty was not with us when he visited; worse, that neither Fel nor I wanted to share parenting stories with him. He insisted on staying in the flat though, even though we had a restaurant table booked, and then he acted all put out that our home life was boring. Well, whose isn't? 'What do you do all day here, anyway?'

It was a good question, though not one I had any intention of discussing with him.

What did we do all day here?

Listlessly, and without much conviction, I revised for my finals, which were now only a month away. I had been a conscientious student. I knew I would pass. I knew, with equal conviction, that I would not excel. For all my brave words in Art's defence around Stella's dining table, I was not very creative. I had learned how to use rulers and protractors. I had learned how to project a three-dimensional structure onto a piece of graph paper. I had learned how to turn sketches into lists of materials and plans of work. I had, over three years, acquired competence in the very skills that were even now being automated by the Bund.

Whenever the futility lay too heavily upon me, I got out my designs for the second series of *DARE*. The sad fact was, Stella, my first client, was likely to be my only client for some while, and if I wanted to stay in London, then the only way forward for me was to do the kind of work she had offered to find for me: concept artwork in television and film. *DARE*'s balsa-wood moonbase and extruded polyethylene submarine were amusing enough, and I had undeniably enjoyed designing and assembling them. Series two was already well into development, and I was having a lot of difficulty trying to dream up suitably otherworldly shapes for the aliens' lunar beachhead, an important recurring locale. Stella had so far deemed everything I had sketched 'too tellurian'.

'Too what?'

'Too Earthlike, dear.' She poured out more tea. 'Too *grounded*, somehow. I don't know. I mean, what do we really know about these aliens?' She gazed off into the Barbican Centre café's bright orange middle distance.

Now that my work for *DARE* involved maquette-making as well as sketching, Stella was renting space for me in the Barbican itself, in workshops that were meant to serve the theatre in the art centre's basement.

Being handed the keys to these well-appointed workshops sped my work along. It meant I could walk to work in minutes. It also meant Stella had an excuse to call in at our flat with Betty. Fel, hearing the bell, rushed to the door. It was a novelty for her, to have friends surprise her in the day. Such casual arrangements must, I suppose, have been absent from her own carefully invigilated childhood. And she adored Betty. She scoured charity shops for cast-off toys and games. They were the only second-hand items Fel ever let through our door, and she filled the flat with them. Wooden train sets. Dollies. Toy xylophones. There was always something new at our flat for Betty to play with.

It was strange watching Betty and Fel playing together on the living-room rug, and impossible to say who was humouring whom. Fel talked a good game, always couching her charity-store purchases of toys and games in terms of Betty's locomotor development, her hand–eye coordination and so on. When they got together, Fel played with Betty the way I imagine she would have played with any toddler. My mother's uncanniness did not seem to disturb her at all. It made me wonder if Fel had ever played with young children before. Could she simply not see that there was a difference here? A weirdness?

Betty did not so much play with Fel as play along. The Process had her growing so fast you could practically hear her creak, and her mental development was more advanced every time I saw her. By the time my finals were over she had begun speaking: a curious, very unchildlike honking from the back of her throat, all hard 'g's and aspirants, as though she were suffering from a bad cold. But she never spoke to Fel except through the sign language that had served her in her first month. It was as if she didn't want to break the illusion of babyhood. As if, around Fel, she wanted to stay a child.

Betty liked having Fel make a fuss of her. Day after day

of Stella correctly and assiduously treating her like an adult undoubtedly made Fel's attentions, by contrast, into a sort of holiday.

More than that, though: I think Betty genuinely liked Fel. Among the many exasperated glances Betty shot her when she thought Fel wasn't looking, there were other, much softer, much more melancholy expressions. Once, I came in from a morning at the workshop and found Fel and Betty sitting on the floor, some sort of bead game spread out between them, with their foreheads pressed together. Neither spoke or let my appearance disturb them.

Then Fel was up on her feet asking me how the lunar beachhead was coming along, and Betty, in a striped jumper with buttons at the neck and red rompers and one shoe, was looking up at Fel with an expression, on that unformed toddler's face of hers, of what I can only call love.

As that summer ended, so the distinction between the two parts of London – the East and West, the Bundist and the unaccommodated – grew ever more visible.

The Bund's soft annexation of South East London was an injury to the whole so huge and so sudden – the quick hacking-off of a limb – that the unaccommodated city, still dizzy, incredulous and drunk on the endorphin high of injected capital, was only now waking to the pain of its mutilation.

At the end of a working day, I would stretch out by walking east, into the Bund. With a new phone to help me ('Here,' Fel said, handing it to me, 'it's simple. There's only one button,' – as if that wasn't half the problem), I decided I would conquer my dislike of exercise and wove a route – never the same twice – to the river, and watched commuters piling home, ever more exhausted, ever more pale and wraithlike, onto ferry boats at Canary Wharf and Millwall Outer Dock. I would ride back with them as far as the Tower. It struck me that my fellow commuters – guest workers, visiting the Bund by day from the unaccommodated half of the city – were beginning to resemble ever more closely the dead-eyed drones drawn by the more hostile newspaper cartoonists. Half-men. Robots. Indentured labour. Working conditions in the Bund remained excellent; in fact, if anything they were improving, with more allowances made for unaccommodated 'guests'. But something had changed. Watching them stumble off the jetty at the Tower and Charing Cross, you would be forgiven for thinking they had just been hauled, blinking, from the airless depths of a mine. It was hard not to read buyer's remorse into the blank looks they gave the Thames's southern banks. Not that there was anything for them to see there. Those zones of the city were by now entirely transmuted, all fairy glitter and constructivist gesture. Structures – you could not call them buildings; for a start, they had no doors – rose and fell there in real-time. There was no solid building anywhere. The very substance of the place had been turned from architecture into something very like metabolism.

In the newspapers, columnists all of a sudden found themselves reminded of the South London of their youth. School nature walks on One Tree Hill. A favourite aunt in Peckham. A visit to the Horniman Museum. The taste of jam fresh from the factory in Deptford. The smell of leather clinging to the maze of little streets in Rotherhithe. Where, the opinion-writers asked rhetorically, had all this past got to? Was it possible that it was gone for ever, transmuted into a dramatic yet finite flow of capital investment? Had the city's appetite for new construction become so overpowering that it had induced us all to gobble up our past?

It became the fashion, even among those snobs who had never set foot south of the river, to claim some connection with those lost lands. Gift shops sold old postcards of the area, antique advertisements from businesses long dead, road maps that no longer squared, in any particular, with the area they once covered. Between cushions printed with photographic renderings of wide, empty, untarmacked high roads in Brockley and Sydenham sat scale models of the Crystal Palace, the TV transmitter, the full-size plaster dinosaurs grazing in the nearby park. A flyer arriving in our postbox invited us to subscribe to a heritage project: the accurate, brick-by-brick reconstruction, in a derelict corner of Hackney, of Brockley's demolished Rivoli Ballroom.

Such cheap nostalgia would most likely have faded and been forgotten, were we not constantly reminded of our territorial loss by changes within the Bund itself. Compared to the baffling erasures to the south, the changes wrought in the city's old financial centre were, on paper, relatively modest. And something had needed doing. Over the few short years of its habitation, the Bund had grubbed up London's old, war-damaged financial district and amalgamated the pieces into towers like the building-block constructions of a hyperactive child: here a brick-clad wall; there a glass curtain; over there a virtually windowless obelisk. The district's ancient street plan had not been obliterated so much as upended. Vertical thoroughfares wove through its towering and peculiar constructions, along suspended glass tunnels, over footbridges and platforms, up escalators and moving walkways, so that navigation – already notoriously difficult for the unaccommodated visitor – had begun to tax even the people of the Bund. Some general solution was needed: a way to tie together all these pavements and public spaces.

The solution was light. Lots of light. Moonlight in particular: that cool, blue suffusion. So the Bund built artificial moons: huge fizzing lights mounted on scaffolds that reached so high they topped its tallest buildings. The Bund's whole bizarre mass lay like an accident beneath these six unblinking eyes. Residents basked in this rational light, navigating with ease, at last, the night-time maze of their city, and celebrating, through a contented silence, their conquest of the night.

The rest of us hated these six ghastly eyes gushing electric ice, freezing the Bund in a silence that – compared to the bustle in our unaccommodated half of the city – could only suggest the silence that hangs between the detonation of a bomb and the screams of its first victim.

The Bund erected ingenious baffles so that light from the Bund would not spoil the night-time of our half of the city. Still, come nightfall, the Bund's high towers shone in their reflected light: a bug-zapping effulgence that, according to those old enough to remember the War, brought to mind the terrible first seconds of an atomic explosion. It felt to us as if the Bund was bathing nightly in some terrible, malign radiation. Though, after all, they were only glorified street lights, and only there to help people find their way in the dark.

The uncanny and pitiless glare shed by the Bund's urban 'moons' was a source of exasperated humour for a while – the stuff of acid editorials and pithy stand-up routines. The truth is, though, it unnerved us – and by 'us' I mean the unaccommodated majority to the west. Compared to the unbending horror of those rays, the West End's own piecemeal illuminations – the mass effect of a thousand thousand street lamps and headlights and shop signs and God knows what – felt positively homespun.

And so it came to us that, unlike those strange, friendly folk to the east, we loved the night, and darkness was our friend. Night-time made up part of who we were. Without the night, why would it ever occur to us to gather together? Were there no night, why would lovers ever turn to each other in the dark? We didn't want to conquer night. We wanted to make light of our own – ordinary, human-scale light – and gather around it, creating little bubbles of humanity in the dark. What were our street lamps and headlights but lanterns? What were our lamps but candles? The night was for stories, for song, for sleep. Summer was hardly over and the gift shops were filled with candles, oil burners, old-fashioned spirit lamps and huge, dim lightbulbs with ornate filaments, not lights so much as ideas of lights; gestures towards illumination. We did not want the day to last for ever, and we wondered at those who did: the ever-industrious Bund, who appeared not to need the night any more. The sleepless Bund who, we reckoned, must have lost the use of some quintessentially human part of themselves.

And thinking this, we began to rage, as surely as a chimpanzee in a zoo, confronting some simple, animatronic version of themselves, will panic and scream and tear the toy to pieces.

Who were the Bund, who did not need the night? Who were they, to buy up half our home and wipe its memory off the face of the Earth?

Capping the matter nicely came the Bund's long-promised workings on the Moon itself. Once these became visible, I think we all very slightly lost our minds. Who were the Bund, that they were remodelling our Moon? The red-tops, casting around for some means to express their existential outrage, grew literal. And the pictures splashed across their front pages were real enough. Whatever your politics, it was undeniable: the Man who once resided in our Moon had been entirely erased.

On the Day of Atonement – which was also the day I learned I had earned an upper second from the Bartlett – someone splashed graffiti over Stella's garden wall. The next day, Fel and I stood across the street, watching two men in blue council overalls scrub away at the mess: a boy with a shaved head and a much older man who paused every few minutes to wind a fringe of thinning hair around his scalp, only so the breeze could unwind it again.

'We'd better go in.'

Fel took my hand and led me across the street.

'I didn't expect anything that bad.' I was quite shaken.

Fel said nothing, and I wondered if I was being naive.

Stella and Georgy were in the dining room with little Betty. Sprawled across a rug in the corner, she was painstakingly constructing a tower of brightly coloured wooden blocks. She had outgrown the game already, and she moved the blocks about dextrously in her chubby little hands more in the spirit of exercise than play. I wondered if she knew what had been happening, and if so, whether she had recouped enough of her old self to understand its significance. Her air of exaggerated seriousness aside, she looked to me like any child occupying itself while the grown-ups argue.

Stella was saying to Georgy, 'If the BBC wants to interview you, you surely have an obligation to go.' Stella had a producer's belief in the moral as well as the material benefits of publicity.

Their familiarity with and love of the microphone had been one of the few bits of common ground Stella and Georgy shared. Today had wreaked a change: 'I am sick and tired of explaining things,' Georgy snapped – then, raising his hand, he revised his opinion. 'No. I'm sick and tired of explaining *new* things. I'm sick and tired of being the voice of the fucking future. And the fact is, no one around here is interested in the future. They're interested in old things. Aren't they? The same old things. For two thousand years the same old things.'

So much for a drink of something and 'congratulations on your degree'.

'George, please—'

'Go and read what's on the fucking wall, woman!'

'I've read what's on the wall.'

'And?'

'It says "Yid".' Stella retorted. 'It says "Yid scum". I can read. I do know what you're getting at. I'm not stupid.'

'Actually,' Fel said, 'it says "Kill yid scum". If there are points here for accuracy.'

Georgy, who up to this point had hardly marked our arrival, flew at his daughter: 'You think this is a *joke*? This *amuses* you?'

'I think,' Fel replied, deadpan, 'that you could do with calming down.'

Stella leapt in: 'It's the BBC. It's a chance to explain—'

'Do you think the oafs who daubed our wall listen to the fucking *PM Programme*?'

'I just think it's good for people to know what's going on.'

'I think,' I said, 'we all know what's going on. Don't we? Isn't it obvious?'

Georgy watched me carefully.

I met his eye: 'You're smarter than us, less sentimental than us, more ambitious – whatever words you want to use. We used to write off our differences as cultural. As upbringing. Everyone's different, we said. Just as everyone's the same. What a wonderful, rich, diverse world we live in, and on and on. But you are different. Fel's different.'

'Thanks,' said Fel.

'Fel, listen. The difference between the Bund and the rest of us is getting bigger by the day. Once we began using the ray, some speciations were obvious from the start. Who thinks chickies are human? Who ever thought they were human? Was there ever a time? A few weeks after the irradiation of the Somme, maybe, but by their second generation? No chance. With you and us it's different. The divergences haven't been so great between us, or haven't shown up so fast. So we cling to the idea that we're supposed to be the same somehow, "underneath". That's why you're getting called those names. The names are offensive, sure, but that's not all they are. They're also – you made the point yourself – they're also *old*. They're a way – clumsy, disgraceful, yes – but a way of clinging on to the idea of there being one humanity.'

'Is your point,' Georgy asked, acidly, 'that these hooligans are trying to be affectionate?'

I felt a tug at my hand.

I looked down to find Betty looking up at me. 'I want to go pee,' she said.

I was confused. 'Can't you—?'

She tugged at her groin. 'These bloody poppers are impossible.'

'Oh,' I said. I led her out of the room.

She ignored the bathroom and led me to the front door. 'I can't open this,' she said.

'You want to go outside?'

'I want to get *you* outside.'

'What have I done?'

'Given vent to your advanced education. Open the bloody door.'

I turned the lock and followed her out. On the top step, she took my hand and turned me around. 'Look.'

A six-pointed star had been daubed over the door in red paint. Since the door was painted red anyway, this didn't look nearly as bad as it might have done.

'They weren't the brightest,' said Betty. 'I think they wanted it to look like blood.' Her voice was thready and raw. Even the

Process couldn't tune immature vocal cords to adult use.

I had to ask: 'What do you think brought this on?'

'You mean, "What did we do wrong?"'

'You know that's not what I mean.'

Betty shrugged: another oddly adult gesture. 'Maybe someone spotted me. Maybe someone realised what I am and didn't much like what they saw.'

I said nothing. What Betty was suggesting was certainly possible. Were feelings running so high against the world's still pitifully few undead?

'How's James?'

Only Betty ever called Jim by his full name. It was one more proof that my mother really was residing in that crisp, fresh, infantile frame, and the realisation, as usual, dropped the temperature of my blood by a couple of degrees. I recalled how I'd felt when first confronted with her: the recidivist urge I'd had to get rid of this monstrous thing. This impostor. This 'child'. If her son had felt that way, how could anyone be surprised if strangers, liquored up and fed fright stories by the cheap papers, felt the same way? Naive or not, I couldn't shake the feeling that the anti-Semitism that agitated Georgy so was no more than a desperate and inept scrabbling for vocabulary, and that these hatreds were a new beast masquerading in old clothes.

'We don't hear from Jim much,' I said.

Betty skipped down the steps, stopped at the gate, and skipped up them again. If this was her way of allaying the suspicions of passers-by – just a little girl playing on some steps, nothing to see here – then it was ill-judged. Physically she looked only about two years old.

'No letters?'

'Sometimes. I'm pretty sure they're being dictated.'

Betty paused on the steps. 'I wonder if James knows he's picked a side.'

'A side.'

'In the war.'

'Oh. The *war*. That.' I said, with sledgehammer irony.

'Oh, Stuart.' Betty sighed and flopped onto the top step, exhausted by her game. 'Do try and take your head out of your arse.'

I laughed, as who would not, barracked by a child? But Betty's attention had been caught by three youths who had come to linger at the corner opposite the house. One leaned against park railings, watching us. The other two seemed to be paying us no mind. One was fighting to light his cigarette in the breeze. The other, with his back to us, had a baseball cap pulled low over his face.

I leaned towards Betty: 'Is that them, do you think?'

Betty stood up, arms folded. 'Let's go in.'

We found Stella alone in the kitchen.

'Where's Fel?'

'Upstairs with Georgy. No, don't go up.' Stella rattled the dishwasher shut. 'He's in one of his moods.'

'Can I give you a hand?'

'It's all done. God!' Stella picked a dish towel up off the floor and threw it onto the counter. 'I am so sick of clearing up.'

Given their resources, it had not occurred to me that Stella might be feeling the weight of a domestic burden. But little Betty's arrival must have ushered in a dramatic change of pace for her. And from the times I had met him, I was confident Georgy was not a man to look after himself. He had that preppy, over-mothered quality. Not one to keep the laundry in check, was my guess. Not adept in the stacking of dishwashers.

Fel came into the room. She had been crying. She held my eye long enough that I knew not to ask any questions. Betty went over and took her hand, and though Fel smiled and gave her hand a returning squeeze, nothing came of it: no talk, no game.

'Is it time we were going?' I asked.

Fel nodded.

'Stella, call us any time. Is Mum going to be all right?'

'We'll be fine.'

'Any time.'

'Yes. Thanks.'

Fel and I bent down and took turns to kiss the top of Betty's head. We left through the front door. Evening was drawing in. The boys lingering near the house had wandered off; there was no one on the street.

I said, 'Let's walk along the canal a bit. We can get a bus from the Roman Road.'

Fel followed where I led, without enthusiasm. We met the canal at the southern end of the tunnel, where it emerges from its underground passage of Islington. We picked our way down leaf-slimed steps to the towpath. It was a bright night. Most of them were, since the Bund had begun to light the Moon. We glimpsed it through damp, bare branches: a new moon, illumined by the lamps newly lit on its surface. Like this, it hardly seemed a solid thing at all: more a scaffold of lit strings stretched across a small, circular void.

'Mum thinks there's going to be a war.'

'Is that what she says?'

'She reckons the *Victory*'s a warship. I don't know where she gets this shit.'

'My dad. Upstairs he was telling me much the same thing.'

'Really?' I was disconcerted. I had assumed Betty had been listening to the local phone-in shows. Maybe they both had. 'Georgy buys into this idea?'

'Daddy just had death threats daubed over his garden wall.'

I had no reply to that. 'What did he say to you?'

Fel did not reply.

The roads running parallel to the canal descended slowly till the only thing separating the towpath from the road and its council housing, the bricks curdling under bright orange sodium lamps, was a low chain-link fence. Houses like these, I thought, were likely to be my only mark upon the world, and then not for long. The economies of the Bund were ungainsayable, and the whole city would be a Bund construction in time. Rage towards this future, though ugly and to be deplored, was not an unnatural response. 'We should get out of here,' I said.

'What's the matter?'

'I mean we should get out of London altogether.'

'Are you so frightened?'

'It's not a question of being frightened,' I said, 'it's a question of being expected to take sides in a conflict that as far as I can see is entirely fatuous.'

We walked in silence. Beyond the estate were retail parks, more housing and, as we neared the Roman Road, the iron fences and towering plane trees of Victoria Park.

Fel said, 'My mother rejected the Bund. Did I ever tell you this?'

'You've never told me anything about your mother.'

'She was Moldovan. Her family were boatmen before the War. Farmers before that. Peasants. Not thinkers. The last people you would ever expect to make a stand over an idea. When she left the Bund, she tried to take me with her to Palestine. I was too little to remember. I'm told that when we reached the Mandate, the authorities tore me off her and put me on the first boat home. I do think I remember Daddy waiting at the dock as we sailed into Tilbury. My mother died a year later during a typhus outbreak in Jerusalem. I have no idea why she suddenly decided to cling to the old faith, and it's hopeless asking Daddy, all he ever does is quote from his own speeches. The debt we owe future generations. The promise of technology. Maybe my mother embraced Jehovah as the only voice strong enough in her head to contend with Daddy's.'

The moral to all this did not need spelling out: the sides choose you.

'We could go to Shropshire,' I said. 'Stella doesn't use her house there. It needs someone to look after it.'

'What would be the point of that?'

'We could do what your mum tried to do. We could try to lead a normal life. You keep saying that's what you want. Would you like a normal life with me?'

The look she shot me revealed how much she hoped for, and how uncertain she was that I would commit.

'Nothing's off the table,' I said, careless and (strange how the feeling had crept up on me) desperate. 'Absolutely nothing.'

If that had been true, I would have been prepared to utter the word 'baby' out loud. But some calculating part of me still clung on.

'Let's have a normal life,' I said.

The smell was overpowering. A yeasty, cheesy, sour stench.

Fel stared into the dark of the hall. 'What is that?'

I felt for the light.

Stella's Shropshire cottage was infested with chickies. We could hear them scuttling about behind the furniture. Upstairs they thumped and bumped their way into hiding. They were as big as children but had the timid instincts of mice.

The carpets downstairs were smothered in scraps of paper. Every book in the place had been torn to pieces and chewed up for nest materials. The flock had been pulled out of the living-room sofa through rents in its covers. There was a foul-smelling stain in the corner of the living-room ceiling, so it was easy to guess where in the house the chickies went to relieve themselves.

Fel gazed about her at the ruin: 'How is this even possible?'

'The neighbours must be away.'

'Jesus.' She fished out her glass slab of a phone. Naturally there was no signal. 'Where's the land phone again?'

'Over there. Who are you going to call?'

'The firemen, of course.'

The fire brigade would bring exterminators. 'It's not that bad,' I said.

Fel dialled. I came over and, gently, took the receiver out

of her hand. 'It's not that bad. Let me deal with it.'

'You're kidding.'

'Let me assess the damage. If we call the fire service, Stella's insurance premiums will go up.'

'Are you serious?'

'We can go to Ludlow and find a hotel. Give me tonight to assess the damage and if necessary we can call the fire brigade in the morning.'

Fel spotted the stain on the ceiling. 'Oh, God.'

'Let's find you a nice hotel.'

By the time I got back to the house, it was after eleven. The rooms were silent. Perhaps the chickies had already evacuated. I doubted it. I went into the kitchen. The radio on the windowsill was tuned to a music channel. I scanned for a talk show and turned the volume as high as it would go. Human voices were a more reliable deterrent. Use music and you were as likely to get chickies dancing as running away.

The player in the living room had no radio but I found a cassette of *Third Kingdom*, a popular if rather overwrought radio drama that imagined the state of continental Europe had Germany's most notorious post-war chancellor not choked on that grape.

I went upstairs, letting the din on the ground floor do its work. Upstairs was far worse. There was a nest in the main bedroom, extending from the end of the bed and covering the window. It was made in the main of plastic waste which they must have dragged from fields above the cottage: fertiliser and feed bags, tarpaulin, bubble wrap. It was held together by stuff that had been chewed up and urinated upon to form a smelly cement. God knows what else had gone into it. Fabric. Paper. Bits of carpet. I fetched a broom out of the upstairs closet. I poked it into the nest. There was no sound. I wiggled the broom handle and heard the delicate interior crumble. The nest appeared to be empty.

I went through the hall, clapping and shouting. Nothing I did felt particularly effective, but I had to try something. Ever since the episode on the moors, I had found the idea of doing violence towards the chickies unconscionable. This sounds like a reasonable attitude, but I am afraid it wasn't. Saving chickies where I could was not a moral imperative with me, or anything in which I could take pride. It was more on the order of a superstition. A childish taboo. Tomorrow, Fel would insist I saw sense and called the fire brigade, and then it would be too late for them.

The study door was shut and obstructed from the inside. I pushed it open enough to edge through into the room. A blanket had been pulled from the daybed under the window and used to block the door. The smell in here was extraordinary. Warm milk and fresh-baked bread. Though far too powerful to be pleasant, it shared nothing with the sour, blocked-drain smell downstairs.

Most everything had been pulled off the shelves and out of the cupboards and spread over the floor: clothing, paper, also the balsa sheets and knives and clothes pegs and tubes of glue I had been using to fashion set designs for *DARE*. I scuffed through the mess to reach the work table. Bizarre to find my notebook there. The phone and lamp had been pulled off and dangled by their wires over the table edge. But the book sat squared to the edge of the table as though set there for me to read. I picked up the chair and put it back on its feet. I sat and opened the notebook.

It was as I had left it. What else had I expected? I flicked through the pages, one at a time, past my last, abandoned doodle – a sketch of the aliens' lunar beachhead – and through to the end of the book. The pages were blank. As they surely had to be. And yet I was disappointed, as though denied some revelation. I stood up and, from force of habit, rolled the chair in under the table.

The chair legs hit something soft: something which shifted in response to the impact. I pulled the chair out and knelt down. Under the table I found an old coat of navy-blue felt. There had once been hi-vis patches sewn on its back and elbows, and there were still tattered lines of the bright stuff fastened to the felt; the rest had been torn or eaten away. The coat slumped and shifted. I reached under the desk and pulled it out by the collar. Little hands closed over mine. I jerked back. From over the top of the coat a face appeared. The chickie was very young: practically newborn. It was still blind. Dark jellies moved behind its yet-to-open, tissue-blue eyelids. It opened its mouth in a yawn. I stared down its pale, pearly throat. It raised its head, extending its neck, begging for food. I stood up and felt in my trouser pockets for something to give it. My fingers closed around a ball of something. I pulled it out. How long the corn dolly had been languishing in my pocket, I could not remember. Anyway, it had come entirely to pieces: now it was just a handful of grass tangled up with short lengths of red ribbon. The infant chickie reached out for the thing. I dropped the mess in its hands. 'I'm sorry,' I said. At least, I remember saying something absurd.

Outside the room, somewhere in the house itself, perhaps, the chickie's parent would be scavenging for food. I didn't want to get caught between them so I left the room, closing the door behind me.

The scent of the room seemed to follow me into the hallway. I felt overloaded and unclean and, in spite of myself, aroused. I looked into the bathroom. The toilet was blocked and in the corner between the toilet bowl and the window was a pile of scat. I went back downstairs and through to the kitchen. I found the key to the back door and let myself out. The porch light snapped on automatically: absurd that this light should still be working when the house as a whole was so evidently broken. Like windscreen wipers clicking back and forth on a wrecked car. I climbed damp, leaf-strewn stone steps to the first lawn. Beyond it lay blackberry and gooseberry bushes; grown out of trim, they suggested the beginnings of a fairy tale: a thicket of thorns.

Above them, up wooden stairs that were succumbing to rot, there was a shed and a greenhouse and between the two, coiled there among weeds, a hose attached to a standpipe. I looked around. I don't know who I expected to be there, spying on me. The smell from the study had followed me even here. It didn't make sense. I sniffed my fingers. The odour had come from the dolly. It was spreading up my wrist, my arm. I undressed. I had an erection. I turned the hose full on and doused myself. I forced my head under the biting cold water. My penis throbbed. I turned the jet on it. It bobbed under the downpour like a salmon trying to leap a fish ladder. The baked-bread smell rose through my head and milk spilled in a strong stream from my erection. The water carried it away into the earth.

I wrenched the tap shut, gathered my clothes to my chest and ran on tiptoes, shivering, up a bark-lined path, up more stairs, past a table and iron chairs, to Stella's writing hut. The key was where I had left it, by the door under a large stone ammonite. The hut was as I had left it. I closed the door behind me, dug about in the desk drawer for matches and got the gas heater working. There was a blanket folded up on the rocking chair at the back of the room. I shook it out, scrambled into the chair and wrapped the blanket around me. I fell asleep almost immediately.

The heater woke me hours later, puttering away on fumes from the empty bottle. The room was so hot, I had to peel the blanket off my sweating skin. The hut had a glass door and I stood in the cool air seeping around its edges, watching a smeared winter sun top the edge of the hills.

Later that day, in a tea house in Clun, near the old castle, I tried to explain to Fel the decision I had come to as the sun had risen to dissolve the mist filling the valley. 'London's bad enough with your dad paying our rent, but this place is no different; we'd still be taking handouts from Stella. What we'd have here isn't an ordinary life at all.'

'What do you want to do?'

I thought about it. I thought about Fel in my bed in the shared house in Tooting. How impossibly cramped it was. How uncomfortable. How lacking in privacy. I thought about her bed, how it fell squealing out of its niche in her little studio flat in London Bridge. How house-proud she was. How clean everything was, how antiseptic. The curve of her back as she played the piano. I thought how strange and sad it was, that no stream may be stepped in twice.

'I want an ordinary life with you. I do. Only this isn't it.'

'I understand,' she said.

'The house is a wreck.'

'We can't live here.'

'No.'

'No.'

I didn't know what else to say.

'We'd better call Stella,' she said.

Fel returned to London the next day. I stayed on for several weeks to organise the refurbishment of Stella's house. I got a private contractor in to do the extermination. By then the chickies were long gone. 'You should have called us the moment you noticed them.' The white-suited exterminator tutted, shaking his head at the dim-wittedness of his clientele. 'It doesn't do to disturb them. Once they've formed an attachment to a place, they'll only keep coming back.'

I hired a firm of industrial cleaners to drive out from Telford. They arrived in a van with a rose painted in incongruous soft-lit detail on its side.

As soon as they saw the upstairs bathroom, they tried to renegotiate the price. 'Who on earth did you have in here? Students?'

I asked Stella for any photographs she had of the cottage, and to leave me to re-create the place as best I could.

'You don't have to go to all that bother.'

'I want to,' I said. 'It's become a kind of project.'

It was obvious I was trying to avoid coming back home.

Stella didn't say anything, and neither did Fel. Somehow the pair of them had intuited that I needed my space.

'Don't forget to watch tonight,' Stella reminded me.

The first season of *DARE* had begun airing on a pay-per-view channel. When I told Stella her television was broken (it wasn't), she arranged the delivery of a set twice as large and a box to suck the relevant channel off a distant satellite. I was out of excuses, so I sat down to watch.

Stella's style was all gloss and chrome and nylon and the shock of the new – or as close as her minuscule budget could get her. Every shot went on far too long as she squeezed every drop she could from my oh-so-brilliantly detailed *mise en scène*.

Episode three was called 'Time and Tide'. It involved a plan to drain and transport the Earth's oceans to the aliens' homeworld using a temporal pump. Time, moving faster inside the pump, meant that water was leaving the Earth at a fantastic rate through a pipe of economical dimensions. This neat conceit not only made the device hard to find, giving the episode its narrative thread, it also kept the climactic shoot-out and destruction of the device within Stella's modest budget.

Or that, anyway, had been the logic behind the script I had proofread for her. In execution, though, things slip about in odd directions. Stella must have been offered a deal on cheap location shooting, because the episode, which was supposed to have been a claustrophobic affair set almost entirely within the chipboard confines of DARE's stealth submarine, had been opened out to include a romantic interlude in somebody's back garden and moody establishing shots of the beach at

Dungeness (standing in here for an exposed seabed). Towards the end of the episode, even the submarine came apart into a series of surprising real-world cutaways, including one extended sequence in which Fel, playing the submarine commander, crawls inside the ship's weapons system to effect a vital repair. In the script, Fel's risky adventure was conducted off-camera, via regular, increasingly desperate reports over the ship's Tannoy system. Stella had somehow found the resources to visualise the whole thing. No wonder she had wanted me to watch the episode.

It surprised me that she had chosen to shoot in such cramped locations: there seemed very little here that Stella could not have got me to re-create in plasterboard and hot-knifed packing foam. Concrete walls and pipework; a floor with a drain. Signage whose significance escaped me but which, being in an easily legible and serifed font, no doubt belonged to the location itself rather than to Stella's set-dressing.

At one point, Fel entered a cell-like, windowless space and took her mark behind a drain set in the floor. Her costume was a silver one-piece, sturdier than the foil-thin suits that were the usual daywear of her crew. She wore no wig: her head was close-cropped, shaved over the ears. (I remember that cut; the feel of it under my hand.) From the drain in the floor, water welled. It rose in a column, fluted and swirled by the pattern of the grating, and spread over the floor. It hit the back wall of the cell and broke, foaming: salt water. The flow strengthened and the cell began to fill. Soon the flow welling from the grate was no more than a dome of disturbance on the surface of the rising water. Inch by inch, the water rose around Fel's body.

It was over her chest now, and in a weird breaking of the fourth wall, Fel looked directly into the camera lens. Not into the distance, as the shot seemed to demand. Right at me. The water got to her neck. The camera was mounted to match her eyeline. The water was nearly at the level of the lens. Wavelets plashed against a glass screen protecting the lens. Was the camera in a glass box, or were they shooting through a window?

The water rose over Fel's face and the camera at the same moment, losing what was surely the most dramatic moment of the shot, the moment Fel's face, her nose and mouth, became submerged. The image was a mess of distortions, foam, shadows, gloom. Not until the water level had risen above the lens did the scene stabilise.

Fel remained in shot, holding on to the pipework. The film lamps, adequate enough to illumine the dry cell, struggled to penetrate the seawater, so that Fel's impassive expression, her apparent relaxation, her utter indifference to the water, may have simply been an artefact of poor lighting. Was she even in the water? Perhaps there was a glass wall between her and the water, just as there was a glass wall between the water and the camera. But how could that be? Surely the water had pooled around her feet? Surely I had just seen that – seen the water rise, not just in front of her, but *around* her? Yes. I had seen that. The impossibility of it – that she should be submerged and show nothing, and minutes later still show nothing (why on earth were they holding the shot?), impressed me. I wondered how it was done.

I was still wondering at Stella's special effect, still impressed by its realism, as I pawed the bathroom door open and retched all my pent-up horror violently into the toilet bowl.

I wiped my mouth with toilet paper. I swilled and spat. I went back into the living room and phoned Stella. I wanted to know how she had pulled the trick off. I wanted some reassurance. I didn't get any reply. I phoned Fel. She picked up straight away.

'Hi,' I said.

'Hi. What's wrong?'

I laughed weakly. 'It's that obvious?'

'What's the matter?'

'I've just been watching *DARE*.'

'It's not that bad.'

'I've just been watching you—'

'What?'

'Drown. I've just been watching you drown.'

When I finally got her to understand what I was talking about, she laughed at me. 'I held my breath, Stu. What the hell did you think?'

I couldn't tell her. With the vividness of nightmare, the airlock sequence had realised my suspicion that Fel was advancing beyond the human. That she was changing from the woman I knew into something else. That she was leaving me.

'I was just going to phone you,' she said.

'Yes?'

'There's some bad news.'

My heart skipped a beat. 'Mum.'

'What? No, Betty's fine, don't worry. Only Daddy and

Stella. Well, they've decided to split up.'

'Good God. Why?'

There was a pause.

'Things aren't getting any easier here,' Fel said.

There were Christmas lights strung across the main streets of Islington. For some, the party had already got itself started:a balloon was stuck in a tree near Stella's house, and spent firework casings lay trodden underfoot by the park gate.

With Georgy gone I had assumed Stella might dress her house for Christmas this time. There was no garland on Stella's door and no tree in her window, though it was hard to be sure because her windows were barred on the inside by white steel concertina railings. The bell was gone from beside the garden door so I went around to the front. Stella let me in. Though it was after noon, she was still in her dressing gown. 'I didn't get much sleep last night,' she explained. 'Some boys were throwing firecrackers at my window.'

Betty was in the dining room in the basement, playing *Operation*. Her dexterity was almost adult. She nodded me hello but otherwise ignored me. The Process had put us at a remove hardly greater than that established already by her long absence. Would we have grown any closer had it not been for her cancers? I doubted it.

Reminded, I asked Stella: 'Have you got any greens? I'm out.'

Stella fetched a freezer bag from the kitchen, full of unopened tubes: 'Here. I don't take them any more.'

'Why on earth not?'

'I've been rayed.' And when I didn't understand: 'Georgy rayed me. At the Gurwitsch. I'm resistant now, or so he says. It's a new treatment he's been developing.'

'That's—' I fumbled a green into my mouth, crunched it, swallowed it down. 'That's amazing.'

Stella shrugged, as if developing an inoculation against radiation poisoning were just another of her ex-boyfriend's eccentricities. Which, perhaps, from her perspective, was just what it was.

Remembering to drop the affectionate anglicisation of his name must have taken effort. It was something she wanted me to notice.

I duly noticed it: 'What's happening between you and George?'

Sighing, Betty hopped down from her chair and left the room. She had been here throughout, a witness to their break-up. I could not begin to imagine how awkward that had been.

Stella sat down at the dining table and lifted Betty's *Operation* game, buzzing angrily, onto the floor. She drew a tissue from her pocket and absently worked at one of the old, indelible stains in the zinc. 'I suppose you were right, after all,' she said. 'I suppose the differences between us and the Bund are becoming unbridgeable.'

'But he took you to the Gurwitsch. He's been treating you. Why didn't he just—'

'What?'

'You know. Why didn't he make you—'

'"One of them"?' She shook her head. 'He offered. He suggested it many times. But why would I want that?'

I had nothing I could say to her. For a long while now I had wanted nothing else. Of course I wanted to be 'one of them'. A Bundist. Bright – genuinely bright, not just over-educated. Odd. Different. A match for Fel, since as I was, I was – what? A companion? A pet?

I think Stella sensed my turmoil; anyway, she squashed it flat. 'The Bund hands out the treatments it wants to hand out, to people it wants to hand them out to. It's a cult. It's always been a cult.'

'It's certainly a business,' I conceded.

'It's a cult. I honestly think I prefer those nutters causing trouble in Palestine. At least they don't pretend to be doing everyone else favours. How is the house?'

'The house?'

'My house.'

She meant the house in Shropshire. 'Oh. Good. It's good. I hope. I mean, I hope you like it.'

'I'll probably just put it on the market.' Stella sighed. She saw my disappointment: 'Well, I did tell you not to go to all that effort, didn't I?'

'Yes. You did. You might still have warned me.'

'I didn't know I'd need the money then.'

'Is everything all right?'

'Everything is fine. The network wants a third season of *DARE*, so I need to free up some capital to tide me over next year.'

'That's good,' I said, uncertainly.

'Don't tell Fel. The ink's not dry and I still have to think about casting.'

I couldn't imagine Fel losing sleep over whether or not

she would get yet another chance to strut around one of my cardboard sets in a purple fright wig.

'Does Georgy know?'

Stella woke up to what she was doing with the tissue, the pointlessness of her scrubbing, balled the tissue up in her fist and tucked it into the pocket of her dressing gown. She frowned at the stain in the zinc. 'I'm going to have to get rid of this table. These marks don't bear thinking about.'

I looked at it. It was a dreadful thing. 'Where did it come from? Could you take it back?'

'From the Gurwitsch,' Stella said. 'They don't want it, they threw it out. I found it in a skip.'

It was some ungodly hour of the morning on Boxing Day. Fel was sitting up in bed with her bedside light on. She was unclothed, a sheet over her knees and a book balanced open in the shallow nook of her thighs. I had just woken out of a deep sleep. I sat up, drinking in her spare and pale body, and she held up the book to shield herself. Playing along, I bent forward and read the faded spine. She laughed at my surprise: Virgil's *Aeneid*. And, closing the book, she said: 'The old stories are the best.'

I kissed her. She touched my face. 'Go back to sleep,' she said.

I don't know how much later it was but when I woke again, I found the bed empty. The sheets were cold. The room was in darkness. I turned on the light. I felt certain that there was someone in the room with me. Someone behind me. Someone hiding out in the corner of my eye.

I got out of bed and went to the window. The Moon was rising behind the flats of the Barbican. It was a very different Moon from the one I had seen with Fel just a couple of weeks earlier. It was a new Moon, bright with artificial light. The light was spread unevenly over the Moon's surface, gathering in streams, knots and pools which, to the informed observer, might well have echoed the geographic features of the Moon itself. At a glance, however, the far stronger impression was one of regularity: off-kilter lines of longitude and latitude gridded the Moon's sphere.

I thought of bacteria and bell jars. I thought of clocks and curves. I thought of the exponential function. The HMS *Victory* would have to hurry if it was to land the first living people on the Moon. Even then, their efforts would only be token. The evidence was shining there above our heads: whole Bundist cities were rising from the regolith, empty and bright and inviting. Some people found it strange that the Bund, for all their activity on the Moon, had built no rockets worth the name, no spaceships, no Space Force. But it was not the way of the Bund to waste time on a journey. To them, the destination was everything. I had been to Ladywell. I could guess well enough the means by which the Bund would one day settle the Moon – if indeed it had not already begun. I wondered which of those lights up there were hospitals.

I heard Fel in the living room, turning over playing cards. I slipped on a dressing gown and went to join her. She was sitting on the floor, laying down cards, gathering them up. She was playing Set.

If no set can be found in the twelve-card array laid out at

the start of a game of Set, three more cards are added. The odds against there being no set now increases from 33:1 to 2500:1. 1080 distinct sets can be assembled from the deck. Though there is no such thing as a 'good' card, or a 'good' pair of cards (each of the 81 cards participates in exactly 40 sets, and each pair of cards participates in exactly one set), some players have hypothesised that the ratio of no-sets goes up as sets are removed from the array.

Fel paid no attention to me. She was focusing on the cards. She played too fast for my eye to follow. In the space of two minutes she had ordered the whole deck, leaving three discards. She gathered them up, shuffled and began again.

I said, 'Why did you ever play me at this?'

She saw me and put down the cards.

'You always won. But you made it look hard.'

She shook her head.

'Yes you did.' I came and sat opposite her. 'You made it look as though it was a game worth us playing.'

She gazed at the cards. 'I liked playing this with you.'

'Why?'

'It was fun. Playing you.'

'Humouring me.'

She shook her head. 'If that's what you think.'

'What else am I to think?'

It was a stupid question. A mean question. She was right not to answer it. There were tears in the corners of her eyes.

I said, 'What else did we do together that was like this? By which I mean: totally fucking pointless?'

'Not pointless.'

I wish I hadn't raised my voice. I wish I'd had at least that much sense. 'Well, what would you call it?'

She stared at me, the way you search a wall for a door that isn't there. 'Love,' she said.

That shut me up.

She said: 'That's what we do together. That's the point of it. That's why it's worth doing.'

It wasn't that I disbelieved her. It wasn't that I didn't understand. But we had started to talk of ourselves in the past tense and it was too late trying to change. 'I know you've been slumming it with me.'

'Oh, for crying out loud.'

'Well, you have!'

'According your friend Stan bloody Lesniak I have.'

I hadn't expected that. 'What?'

'Your friend Lesniak. He's shared his important thoughts about our relationship in his fucking student rag. I thought you'd seen.'

'I don't read *Responses* – I didn't even know it was still running.'

'He's had a fine old go at us. In fiction, but it's pretty bloody obvious who he's talking about.'

That took the wind out of my sails. It made my blood run cold to think that Stan had so easily identified the breaking point in our relationship; worse, that he was actually finding something entertaining in it all. Was our being together so obviously unworkable? Was Stan the only one of our friends to be raising his eyebrows at the thought of us? I doubted it.

'I didn't know,' I said. 'Anyway, what's it got to do with him?' I wanted all of a sudden to paper over the cracks, to heal what was broken, to withdraw every complaint.

She gathered the cards up from the floor, split the deck in two and put it back in its box.

'What does it matter?' I said. 'His readership can't number more than a couple of dozen.'

'All our friends read him. All your friends, that is.'

'What's that supposed to mean?'

'When was the last time we went out with friends?'

'We can do that.'

'Not now we can't.'

I gave her a minute to calm down. 'What does he say? Exactly?'

'Read it yourself. Only I threw it away.'

I tried not to smile. 'Good,' I said. Then: 'Do you want to come back to bed?'

She shook her head.

I took her hand and led her to the sofa. We sat together, intimate but not touching. We had not sat like that before. It felt very grown up.

We both knew what this was. Knowing it, we managed to be kind to each other.

She said: 'I know people, they get a lot out of having a kid. They get a different kind of relationship out of it. Satisfaction. A lot of fun. Being stuck in their little monster's perpetual present – it makes them young again, in a way. Do you know what I mean?'

'I know what you mean.'

'But you don't feel it.'

'No.'

'You like the life we have. The music, the books. You can

work. We go out together in the evenings. It's good for you. It's what you want.'

'Yes.'

It was the worst possible moment I could have chosen to be honest. Sometimes the words have to come before the feelings. You may not mean them, but that doesn't make them untrue. They are a kind of promise to yourself. A challenge to yourself. And I failed that challenge. Even at the time, sitting there beside her as her tears came, and me there feeling so very sad, so very noble that I had managed to be honest, I knew that I had failed. 'In time—'

'What time?' She got up off the sofa. She pointed out of the window. She screamed at me: *There is no fucking time!*'

I looked where she was pointing, but there was nothing to see. Only the Moon.

She said: 'I'd better go.'

Returning in the new year to the West Riding, to the valley, the furnaces and all those narrow streets, I decided to move back in with my dad for a while. Though Betty had left him years before, Bob was feeling especially lonely now that she had passed away. And despite Stella's best efforts, her unwelcome letters and even less welcome day visits, he refused to let her reconcile him to the idea that there was another Betty waiting to see him, and talk to him, and reminisce with him over past happiness. Death was death to Bob: a boon companion he refused to abandon.

I told myself that I would not stay long. That moving in with my dad would be an opportunity for me to regroup, while giving Fel some much-needed space before she and I took up – in a more circumspect fashion – the next chapter in what was obviously going to be a lifelong friendship. We had made some brave noises about staying in touch and remaining friends.

Naturally, we never saw each other again.

THREE

The hatch closes on Jim Lanyon's hand. He whips clear, catching his finger for a split-second between the hatch door and the sill. A dull compression pulses through the nail into the bone.

The tunnel lurches around him and his arm sweeps on a reflex, seeking something to cling to.

His hand finds something soft and lumpy and unmistakably alive. A face. His hand digs in, forefinger and bruised middle finger getting purchase around the arch of an eye even as he cries out in terror: he thought he was alone here.

The face joins in with Jim's screaming and swivels free of his grasp. His fingers trace thick, dense hair, a woman's hair, and his autonomous self, that diurnal part of him oblivious to events and circumstances, and which responds only to the routines and the givens of life, pulses out its interest.

The world lurches, throwing Jim and the face and a tangle of limbs and ducting into a new and radically different arrangement. It is as though they were the jumbled elements inside a kaleidoscope and someone is twisting the eyepiece, setting them to a new configuration.

The sound as it twists – this grinding, screaming corridor made kaleidoscope – fills Jim's head with metal, and he presses his hands against his ears and screams along to the buckling tube like a child on a fairground ride, screaming to take control, to rise to the fear, to perform it, anything so as not to be consumed by it, sensation piling up on sensation as the corridor buckles and twists, every failure a jagged edge, a spark, a scream, a puff of vapour.

He remembers the last time he was afraid like this, and screamed like this. He was a boy, strapped into a fairground ride with his dad. He and his dad had screamed together, surfing together the wave of their imminent destruction, and here, too, there is a second scream accompanying his own and the lights come on again. How long have the lights been out? Jim does not know. He had his eyes tight shut, the better to scream, but his eyes are open now and he sees the face, bare inches from his own, hurtling into him, into his face, filling his vision with shadow, a dark and heavy presence filling his field of view. Then the collision, forehead to forehead in classic silent-comedy symmetry to a soundtrack of mutual screaming, and the corridor thrusts itself straight again, a limb kicking itself back into shape, and the lights go out again.

They breathe together, suck air together, paired in the darkness, and in the eerie blast of cold that stops both their mouths, they are joined in the terror of decompression. But the chill dissipates and, released for a second, their rhythms come apart, each pants to their own beat. Jim is first to speak, if you can call it speaking, a wet swallowing that approximates his name.

The face beside him is a wet, hot presence at his left ear, and upside down – what quality of sound tells him the mouth is upside down he cannot say, but in the pitch dark he is certain that the face, just one inch from his ear, is now inverted. It *jabbers something, Venison or Tennyson or some other name he does not recognise. Not on his shift, not on his deck, not in his department. A stranger, even here, thinks Jim, and wants to cry. A dark unknown, suspended in a greater dark.*

Hands pat and palpate him, fumbling for purchase, and he feels her breath on his cheek, its hot, wet pulse as intimate and shocking as a tongue, and then it is gone as his hands and her hands find each other in the dark and her hand finds his bruised hand and he gasps with pain and pulls his hand away and the corridor rips along its length as sure and straight as if along a seam and flattens itself, showing them themselves against the stars, as in a vast and cinematic mirror. He loses purchase. She reaches for him, reaches up for him, to hold him fast, but she cannot reach him as he wheels above her, a new star, spread-eagled, Union Jack patch bright and primary against the welling Earthlight. The woman – Tenterden? Verizon? What's in a name? – turns to face that massive and appalling planet whose light and mass and heat they have so recently escaped. Jim, floating above her, waves desperately, while she clings to a stanchion in the unwound tunnel, her flesh gently swelling as though she were blooming in the light of Earth, and her outgoing breath is a puff of ice crystals that Jim, in his own anoxic, depressurised and surely dying state takes to be seeds or spores spilling from her puffball mouth. He fancies that she is shouting his name. But he knows he is only bootstrapping cold comfort for himself in these, his last seconds, and as the Earth rises over the metal ribbon in which they were wrapped, it comes to him that death is taking its own sweet time, and seems indeed to have forgotten him.

For the longest time he hangs there, spreadeagled British

star, contemplating, as he pulls away, the wreck of all personal and national hopes, and why can he not die?

Jim sees with a sinking heart that the ship has buckled, failing at the place, the joint, that even a child would have pointed to and said, The weak spot's here. *The giant shock absorbers have shivered and flung their sockets, sending engine and crew tumbling into different, equally unstable orbits.*

This undying man, this British astronaut called James Lanyon, does not understand his life, or why it should continue now that the face he clung to is gone. The face, the hair, her hands on him, her breath upon his cheek. This man turned dying star looks for the woman whose name he cannot figure and sees the corridor in which they were caught, spread wide and flattened like the tube from a roll of toilet paper. He sees her, tethered to a pipe by a yellow harness. She had been safe, he sees. She had been trying to save him. She had not careened into him. He had careened into her. She was the still point in that space: his anchor. And here she is, her breath a thousand spores scattering in barren space, her flesh blue and swollen, oedema puppying her, making a doll of her, a thing of fabric more than flesh, and he remembers her breath on his cheek. He feels tears, and how is it that his tears float liquid in his eyes, turning the wreckage before him into so many threads of light? How can his tears be wet, when her eyeballs are ice?

And thinking this, he lets his gaze drift away, which has been focused on the painfully fine grain of the stranger's body. His field of attention widens, threads clearing as he blinks, to take in more, and yet more, as he is led away (by whom? by what?), his field of view expanding with distance as he travels, faster and yet faster, from the scene of the disaster. He sees it whole now: the frigate-sized living quarters on whose behalf the Victory's great elastic heart once, and so very briefly, beat out a nuclear pulse. Where is that valiant engine now, its pneumatic legs spread and pulsing, appendages of an atomic space-jellyfish?

The ship's drive was a spinning disc of concrete, and through its centre, once every four seconds, nuclear devices were fed by a machine that, but for its size, would be familiar to any vending-machine engineer. When the ship buckled the living quarters, fighting free, limped off crippled, bent askew and barely space-worthy: certainly no match for the rigours of re-entry. In the tense hour following the accident, the crew held a silent vigil, all ears to the Tannoys on every deck and stair. Now all was being stored away again, as the doomed spacefarers set about softly tidying their tomb. With motive power gone, all was afloat. In silence, the crew moved listlessly, securing all the things they had already unstrapped, so cocksure, once the atomic engines had begun to pulse and the floors had begun, in jerks at first, and then with greater smoothness, to deliver the promised one-gravity.

With the drive gone, they knew they were doomed. Impossible to convince a crew so highly trained that a stable orbit was achievable now. Having flung itself from its broken but still-pumping drive, the accommodation module stood no chance of survival. They had only to look out of the frigate's many generously proportioned portholes, where the view was impossible to parse: a whirligig of stars and clouds as the ship tumbled around the Earth in an ever-tightening spiral.

The accommodation module had thrusters meant to orientate

it finely for docking with and undocking from its engine. Half these thrusters had been destroyed in the brutal act of separation, but the ones ranged forward remained and still held a little fuel. By line of sight, by trial and by error, the helmsman brought the ship about and steady on its axis. The awful Earth turned beneath and about them. The stars, doused by Earthlight, went out one by one. The crew waited for nightside, and a chance to hide in their minds from the planetary mass that would in a very little while embrace and consume them. But nightside did not come, and the Earth swung about them like a big, bright, smothering parent as if illuminated by its own light.

Of the sun, by some eccentricity of their turn and trajectory, there was no sign.

What further disaster has befallen the frigate, James cannot begin to guess, embroiled as he is in the event of it. He can only witness: a somehow undying eye.

Shocked out of the capacity for further shock, Jim watches with a feeling at once profound and nameless – a great annihilating wave of sensation – as the ship unfolds itself, an aluminium origami reversing itself into sheets of base metal. The flattened and unwoven plates of the ship turn on a mutual axis, plates striking plates without a sound, so that all are sent spinning on syncopated rhythms, turning to the light and knifing into the dark. A complex visual score, lacking all edge of violence, unfolds before his somehow still-working eyes. James grows drowsy. He closes his eyes.

And opens them, shaking, breath heaving, as the enormity of his state comes upon him. Where is everyone? How is it that he is *pulling away from all this? What explains his steady withdrawal? Refocusing, hunting for clues, he witnesses further mysteries. The wreck has begun to foam. White froth emerges from every intact hole in the dismantled craft. Once the foam has dribbled off, each hole yawns, a distorted, screaming mouth, folds open, turns inside out and unwinds into a kind of flower: its petals are metal surfaces, and a bouquet of tangled wires and mangled ducts serves for sexual parts. All these materials are sorted as he watches, bundled and batched; the flowers are picked and pulled apart – she loves me, she loves me not – and it comes to him that the* Victory *is being dismantled and sorted by agents which, at this distance, are too small for him to see.*

The froth, meanwhile, floating free of the ship, has formed lines, and these lines, like trails of spittle, like spawn, lead away from the ship; they are being pulled away from the ship, and it comes to him, in his strange, somnolent, undying calm, that this soft white stuff, these little beads strung on strings like fish eggs in a deep black stream, these bright things, these bubbles, are the crew.

He cries out, and hears his cry, and hearing it, the madness of it, the act of hearing in a vacuum that must by now have killed him, makes him scream the more, and since screaming is not enough, his hands begin to paddle, he scrabbles for purchase in the dark, and his left hand, the hurt hand, the bruised hand, catches against a film, an unseeable skin, and sticks there. Pain wells under his bruised and loosened fingernail and makes his hand a ball of hurt, and his gaze, drawn to that hurt, fixes on his hand, stuck there in a clear glue. A plate of his ship, turning to catch the light, appears as a sheet of light beyond his hand, and where his hand is stuck, there in the dark, the sheet twists, warps as through a lens, and it comes to him that he is in a bubble, breathing, screaming, that he is embraced within an egg, and sensing this, his bruised hand closes around the tissue it touched, and crumples it, and everything before him stretches and bends, the ship turns into streams of light, and above him the Earth itself vanishes in an ovoid blur.

Reaching with his other hand, his right hand, he grabs a fistful of that tegument and pulls himself forward, and the gluey stuff surrounding him folds itself upon his face and, screaming, he sees the material fog against his breath.

He is inside an egg. His tongue touches tasteless plastic stuff and he bites, desperate to be free, desperate to be dead, and something tears somewhere. He hears the air whine out and his ears pop and he begins to spin, tipping back into the violence of the world, a star no longer, but a lonely and unburdened man, riding a broken, bucking bubble in the dark.

The whining stops. The spinning world slows and steadies. The wreckage reappears, terrible in its tidiness: a palletised assortment of aluminium plates and drums of wire.

Jim breathes, and hears his breath. The bubble has mended itself. He reaches out again with both hands, steadier now, mystified by this bubble, and his hands meet gluey walls. He presses the walls wider: the egg gives a little, and the view before him wobbles. He lets go, and the world, or what there is of it – raw materials in space, turning in the light of Earth – recovers its shape.

He paddles around his little cocoon. He faces the sun, whose blaring light should blind and burn him, only to find that this quarter of his world is browned out. The material of his egg is responding to the sun's glare, protecting him.

He inverts himself, looking for an edge to his strange and sustaining prison. A door. A valve.

He sees another egg, and another man inside it. And below that another. And another. He stares, counting the stream of bubbles rising from the deep, each one holding a man or a woman. The man in the bubble nearest him has already seen him. He gesticulates wildly, mouth open against the wall of his egg. James, absurdly, waves.

The stream of bubbles weaves about, new bubbles coming visible then drifting into shadow. Beyond his own string, other strings grow nearer, all gathering together in a braid. We're saved, *he thinks,* we're being saved, *and the thought, which should comfort him, only fills him with a deeper fear. Saved how? And by whom?*

A skull's knowing rictus presses against the plastic just below Jim's nose, and as he cries out and bucks away, a second skull, armed like the first with hands clown-spread beneath its neck, seizes hold of his bubble, nudges the other, and makes eyes at its companion. And such eyes! James has never seen such eyes before: eyes like stumpy telescopes on the zooms of pocket cameras.

The skulls, appearing out of nowhere, adhere to the wall of his egg with long, spatulate fingers, human, yet threaded with black lines as though tattooed with a map of the vessels running beneath the skin. The skulls are not human, but they must have begun that way. Products of the Gurwitsch ray, is Jim's hysterical guess. An extreme fulfilment of Gurwitsch's promise to 'sculpt organic forms at will'. Their eyes shoot in and out and their necks, geared in ways that are not human, wobble their skulls about in strange and simple patterns, and it comes to Jim that the skulls are having a great time. That they are happy with their lot. That they are singing.

Jim backs away. The space outside his bubble is full of skulls suddenly, crowded with skulls, some adult, some belonging to children, some foetal and hardly formed at all, and as they swarm about his bubble, latching on with their big clown hands like so many putti, *it comes to him that he has had enough of this, that this is not a rescue, and he has had enough, more than enough. Pressing his face into the plastic wall, he hears their shanty, fudged and softened, through the gluey skin – 'Weigh, hey and up she rises' – and with a snarl of hate he lunges and bites and tears a great mouthful of egg wall free and spits it out and feels the air rush out and the cold rush in and his ears explode and he cannot hear his laughter.*

The skulls, bug-eyed and concerned, sew up the rent with dextrous fingers and invisible thread.

He bites again. They poke him with their fingers. He fights them off. They shuffle in. The egg is shreds. He tears and tears. The cold is everywhere and his blood fizzes like champagne. But still from somewhere comes the air to let him fill his lungs, and the skulls sing lullabies to him and paddle his flesh with big clown hands and absolutely will not let him die.

9

I spent two more days in London, 'clearing the flat'. I bought a rucksack and packed it with books and a few photographs. I left my drawing table behind, and ornaments I had bought for the flat at one time or another. Except for a denim jacket, I piled all my clothes into bin liners and carried them around to a nearby charity store. On the train, I treated myself to a sleeping compartment, and I was well rested by the time I reached the West Riding, at midday, not a week after I had left.

I wrote the whole adventure off as a mistake. I had let nostalgia creep up on me and I had got what I deserved. Fel was in the Smoke somewhere, very close, close enough to use the flat we had shared. She had a new life, a new lover, and she was at very least trying for a baby. She was living the life she had wanted and which I had not felt I could give her. I wondered if her boyfriend was unaccommodated, or a Bundist, like her. I had not stayed around to find out. I hadn't called Georgy, or even Stella – and by not calling her, I even passed up the chance to see my mother. I had run away from a place and time that had no room for me now. Perhaps "run away" is too strong. My quick departure did not feel like cowardice.

I stopped wondering. (Who is she seeing? What is she doing? Is she happy? Does she think about me?) I packed it all away. Some decisions cannot be revisited, even in the imagination. I was – I had to be – done.

The world had other ideas, naturally.

Bob welcomed me home with few words, and I could see he was sorry that I was not, after all, bringing back every stick and rag of my past life to fill his house. I told him about Fel, not because I thought it would help, but because I had no one else I could talk to. Bob's taciturnity normally drove me mad, but on this occasion it was a blessing. He did not tell me that all had turned out for the best. In my neurotic state, I thought I could see him thinking it. I should have found another woman, I suppose: some warm stranger with whom I could share, in complete confidence, my version of events. But I couldn't face it.

In November, a month after my homecoming, television signals penetrated the Calder Valley. The reception was surprisingly good for this foggy weather-trap. Nobody had a TV, not at first, and the first set we had access to was the one recently mounted over the counter of the fish-and-chip shop. It was a canny commercial move, but even a general curiosity could not explain the crowd Bob and I confronted one chilly

Friday. There were men and women milling outside on the pavement, taking turns, with their usual rough courtesy, to get inside and at the screen. I figured there was a rugby match on. I plucked Bob's sleeve. 'Let's try that new place by the canal.' I was oddly incurious, probably because I had found myself piecework with a local solicitor and was pulling regular hours again, sticking to regular mealtimes; I was famished. 'Come on.'

Why Bob, who was no lover of crowds, hung on, I cannot guess. He must have been visited by some fleeting sixth sense. He led me, his arm linked through mine, towards the door. The moment people saw us, they made room for us. Elbows nudged, shoulders were tapped. They made a path for us, all the way up to a spot under the blaring TV. It all happened so effortlessly, so smoothly, as in a nightmare. Standing there, surrounded by dozens of silent men, I wondered what had given us pride of place. Though it wasn't hard to guess: family of the first Yorkshireman to go into space.

The TV was not tuned to either of the familiar stations. I recognised it instantly: a Bund news channel. Why on earth were we receiving this? Come to think of it, *how* were we receiving this?

The Bund's peculiar style of news delivery – shaped to satisfy its people's vaunted appetite for information delivered logarithmically, always on a rising curve of complexity, difficulty, urgency – would have lent bombast and millenarian gloom to reportage from a village fete. The main story – the one the channel kept coming back to – was simply incomprehensible. The picture, slewing and cutting every which-way, was even more confused than its soundtrack.

There was a lot of repeated information, looping video and the same words uttered over and over. While these complex grammatical and visual syncopations were beyond me, I could not help but notice that very little news was being conveyed. Whatever this was – a close-up shot of a sheet of paper being screwed into a ball by invisible hands – the Bund's news anchors had yet to get a handle on it.

The balled paper blinked out, replaced by a channel ident whose swooping curves and rolling hills of Bayesian distribution unwrapped to reveal a studio – half-real, half-animated – in which two presenters were sitting opposite each other without a table between them, swinging idly in their padded chairs, and with a clipboard on each lap. The man leaned earnestly forwards as the woman, her too-tight skirt riding another inch above her knees, consulted her pad and recited an itemised list, turning this way and that on her chair as she read. The whole scene reminded me strongly of the white-coater pornography they screened at Bob's factory at Christmas, were it not that the backs of the presenters' heads were glass. Their brains, not so spongiform as usual, and animated – presumably by the same joke ingredient that had animated Windsor Castle's soup course – swam around on their cortical tethers, bashing the sides of their meningeal tanks like two angry fish.

A location shot: again we were confronted with what appeared to be a piece of crumpled paper. As I watched, it curled; ink burst from a tear, then bloomed into weird, globular flame. A blank, uncrumpled sheet filled the next shot. Then, crash-focusing, the camera revealed that the sheet was not blank at all. Indeed, it had ceased to be paper, become instead a solid surface: a door. The door opened and something knocked the camera aside. As the camera wheeled, it captured a pair of legs, knees bending frantically, frog-like, the legs caught at the ankles by a pair of thick white padded trousers. Then, kicking the trousers free, the legs shot out of view. The camera, untethered, rose with an undersea slowness after the legs and found them briefly, framed in the big round door. Not quite in focus, they gesticulated once, twice, then rose in a V against a wall of stars.

The studio reasserted itself and the news anchor's head wobbled slightly as she channelled the latest information, her brain buffeting the sides of her skull in a frantic bid at escape.

A sick vacuum opened in the pit of my stomach.

The camera wheeled.

The camera was weightless.

This was footage from outer space.

Paper became metal as creases rent and pulled away to reveal: duct-work, silvered padding and great handfuls of wire.

Stars hung in an empty sky. A cloudy mass, faintly edged with green, descended from the top of the screen: it was Earth seen from orbit. Flashing past – literally flashing, rhythmically reflecting the light of an unseen sun – came the wheeling parts of something: a flight of disassembled components flying together in close formation.

A Union Jack rippled by.

I realised at last that this was the *Victory*. Or rather, this was what was left of her. And that Jim, my brother, first Yorkshireman in space, had to be dead.

Betty, when I finally got her on the phone, wailed like a child, which, in an important sense, she still was. The grief of motherhood and the physiology of childhood are a heady mix.

'She's had to go and be sick.'

'Stella?'

'I'm so sorry, Stu.'

'I don't know what to think. I don't know what to feel. I don't suppose ... There's no way—? Christ, Stella.'

'Be kind to Bob.'

'Of course.'

'Hang on.' Stella left the phone. The pips sounded: I pushed in more coins. In a minute Stella was back, the tension high in her throat: 'Is Bob there?'

'He's in the pub. I can go and get him, it's just around the corner.'

'Betty says she wants to talk to him.'

I tried desperately to think of something to say.

'Stu.'

'I'll try,' I said.

I hung up, gathered my refunded pennies and went back to the pub. Bob was sitting in the lounge bar at a tucked-away table with Billy Marsden, his wife and daughter.

'Dad.' I beckoned him up. I didn't want Billy and the others to hear our conversation because I had no idea what Bob would say. For all I knew, it would be something terrible. 'It's Betty,' I said. I couldn't not tell him. I couldn't just send him out to the call box thinking he was going to speak to Stella.

Bob simply nodded. He headed for the door. Had he understood? He had never once spoken to his wife since her rebirth. I made to go after him, but stopped myself in time. I sat in his seat and the Marsden girl reached under the table and squeezed my knee.

Twenty minutes later, Bob was still not back, so I made my excuses and went around to the call box. It was empty. I walked home and heard Bob moving around upstairs.

'Dad?'

'Here,' he called, hearty enough. I climbed the stairs and looked in at his room: this room he had shared with Betty for years; the room in which Jim and I, I can only assume, had been conceived.

Bob was packing. 'I'm borrowing your case.'

'Dad.'

'Betty wants me with her. She wants me in Islington.'

I didn't know what to say. I wanted to be glad for him. I wanted to be glad for them both: Mum and Dad together again at last. But it was too much to process all at once. Had Bob forgotten what Betty was now? Had he forgotten what shape she was in? 'I'm catching the sleeper,' he said.

'The sleeper will have left. Dad, wait till morning.'

'I can get the last train to Leeds.'

'And then what?'

'I'll be all right.'

He was afraid to wait, I realised: afraid of second thoughts, afraid of his own fear. Inspired to action, he was having to commit to it, like a man on a high diving board. (The incongruity of that image was enough to make me smile.)

'Can I help, Dad?'

'Make me a tea.'

He asked me not to see him off. He shook my hand. He did not look like an old man who had just lost his eldest son. He looked like an old man on a date. I wished him luck. Perhaps it was the wrong thing to say.

Anyway, he never got as far as London, or anything like. Once again, his fear of the new bested him. The afternoon of the next day, Stella tracked me down by phone to the solicitor's office. She asked me when Bob would arrive. I told her I had no idea. Afterwards I was told off about receiving personal calls in the office. The next morning, early, a policeman banged on the front door, waking me. He told me I had to go and pick Bob up from Leeds. He was reasonably sober by then.

In the days that followed, Bob vanished into the knot of his workmates. They were bringing him home, paralytically drunk, each night. I didn't know whether that was a good thing for him, or whether he wanted it or not, but I knew better than to interfere. The factory was a community that, for better or worse, took pride in looking after its own.

On top of destroying the HMS *Victory*, the Bund had casually stolen our airwaves, the better to show us the futility of all our hopes of leaving the planet under our own steam. The first of these outrages was unconscionable; the other, infantile. Our response, as a government and a people, was immediate. King William was evacuated to Newfoundland. Bills were passed without debate through Parliament in a frantic attempt to contain Bundist communities in London, Birmingham and

Glasgow within their civic bounds. Chernoy's Process was challenged in the courts and class actions were organised. There were demonstrations. In London and in Bradford, riots. Leeds airport was overrun and a Bundist plane was set on fire.

Bob and I shared one more Christmas together, then I got my own room, and it was as well for him that I did. The locals saw my father as a man bereaved, but they very quickly developed a different opinion about me.

The room I rented was in a house by the railway: a garret space not very different from my old bedroom, but larger, with an impressive oak double bed with a frame too high for the room. On waking, I would look out through the window at the railway and feel caught in a dream of flying.

I was paying for my room out of piecework and favours, but in March a job came up that I could take a genuine interest in, working for the council in Bradford.

On the morning of my final interview, a rock flew in through my bedroom window. Straight through the gap between the top pane and the frame – it couldn't have been more than five inches wide – it landed on my bed.

I picked it up. A bit of clinker from the railway.

I went to the window and looked out. I couldn't see anyone.

It was a miracle the window wasn't broken. That had surely been the idea. If there was any trouble, the landlady was bound to ask me to leave. I didn't know where else I could go around here that was affordable and still near my father.

An hour later, stepping cautiously over the rails to the platform for an early train to Halifax, I turned up the collar of my only good suit, afraid of who might be taking aim at me. My feet wobbled on the stones: no shortage of ammunition around here.

What, I wondered, was my offence? That I had dated a Bundist? No one here knew about Fel. Was I being punished for Betty's choices? Even assuming word of her undertaking the Chernoy Process had got around, I'm still not convinced people here would have fully understood its transgressive implications. Which left the Smoke itself. Was my offence simply that I'd had the temerity to leave town in the first place, head for the capital, scholarship under my arm, to better myself?

That sounded more likely: the old tribal resentments given a fillip by recent headlines.

This was not a conclusion I found particularly reassuring. Petty fights are still fights. An old friend of mine lost an eye, the day before he matriculated from school, in a punch-up over a controversial goal in a friendly match between Todmorden and Littleborough. Littleborough! Pass by any factory gate in Hebden of a Monday morning and you would see them: the walking wounded of many a Saturday-night soccer battle. Shoe a town of stoppered men with steel-capped boots, add beer, and what else could you expect?

I sat counting the minutes while the train sat idle at the station and wondered what had happened to my old self – that rough-and-tumble kid who wanted to follow his brother into the army. The boy who set off stolen percussion caps to divert the course of streams. I felt as if, a long time ago, something had broken in me. I stood and pulled down the window and looked back up the wooded hillside to where, so long ago, I had watched a column of black smoke turn to white.

The flash seemed to take the whole left side of my head away. Something thorn-sharp entered my left eye. I fell back with a cry. I heard footsteps running along the platform. I cursed and turned over onto my hands and knees and tried to throw up. I stared at the grey-flecked linoleum of the carriage floor and was rewarded by the sight of two, three, four drops of blood.

Nothing was at scale. I couldn't even tell how close my head was to the floor. I was seeing out of my right eye, my left eye was glued shut, and when I looked up, I couldn't tell if the figure crouched in concern over me was very big or simply very near. For sure, it wasn't human.

'Ssh, sweet boy,' it crooned, through needle teeth. Its smile was sincere but its eyes were all black, no iris visible, and I read my terror in them. It put its hand against my wounded cheek. Instantly, I steadied. I took a breath. Another. I raised my hand to touch its hand and it was strange, bony, with wide, spatulate fingers. Gently, it withdrew, and I saw that it was hurt, or that it had been hurt sometime in the past: its nails had been pulled. And then I remembered.

'You,' I said.

'Of course, me. *Shush* ...'

More feet. More running. The guard had seen a boy throwing a stone. He tried to persuade me to leave the train and get someone to look at my eye. I made some feeble gestures at the figure opposite me but it had disappeared. The guard thought I was talking about my attacker. 'He's gone, sir. It's all right. You're safe.' I stayed where I was, made belligerent by pain, a handkerchief pressed to my face, and insisted I may as well go on to Halifax, since Halifax had a hospital with an A&E department 'who know what the hell they are doing'. Peremptory. Dissatisfied. Caustic. I had never sounded more like a Londoner, and after that people left me alone.

The chickie was gone. I couldn't work out how, and I was in too much shock to care. My handkerchief was all bloody and I still couldn't open my left eye, but in truth, given how hard I'd been hit, the pain was ridiculously little, as though the chickie, touching me, had salved the cut already.

Despite my appearance, I got the job. With a gauze patch over one eye, blood on the collar of my good suit and my voice pushed by shock into a strangled falsetto, I was, they said, exactly the man they were looking for: the very chap to draw up plans for retaining walls around their new coke plant. They even took the trouble to show me where I would be working. Above the council chamber were bright, glass-roofed offices, clean white work tables, and the air was bleachy with ink and paper and solvent. I felt immediately at home: looking around me, I recognised the appurtenances of my near-abandoned trade. Wet clay and scalpels and sacks full of balsa. Rolls of gridded blue paper. Stencils and slide-rules. The size of the room was bizarre, though perhaps I was seeing awry, still: getting the scale wrong.

The council's chief architect, a man with an improbably styled shock of white hair and a moustache clipped in the military style, shook some greens into the palm of his hand and offered me one. 'We'll show them, yes?'

'We surely will,' I said, and I hoped I sounded sincere. The War Ministry had already visited. Funds were even now being allocated. Emergency tax regulations were coming into force by Easter. The West Riding was building its own spaceship. Across the country, fully twenty ships had been ordered to avenge the death of the *Victory*.

I had expected to be kept waiting in a room full of other candidates, interrogated for at most twenty minutes, then sent home to await the bad news. But there hadn't appeared to be any other candidates, my interviewers kept me talking till noon, and they would have given me lunch if by then my face had not swelled up like a balloon. The chief architect insisted a chauffeur take me to a private clinic on the outskirts of the city, where they unbandaged me, tutted at the shoddy workmanship of the public service, and sewed up the corner of my eye with thread so thick and tough, it felt as though you could have mended a sail with it.

Feeling equal parts elated and nauseous, I swam more than walked out to the street, and a small figure barrelled towards me, like a boy but not, wearing a tasselled skirt, high heels and a feathered bolero shirt. As it flew past, it thrust into my hands a brown paper package the size and weight of a shoebox.

Fortune had been making such a plaything of me that day, I hardly dared open the package. I don't know what I expected. Sheep droppings. A severed rabbit's head. Used banknotes. Doubloons. I looked about me. The street was empty. If the box blew up in my hands, at least there were no passers-by to be injured. I opened it up.

Inside the box were six sheets of vacuum-moulded plastic parts, a paint chart and numbered assembly instructions.

I took the package home, laid out its contents on my bed, went around to Bob's that evening and, under the guise of telling him the good news about my job – 'an immediate start, and a month's pay in advance!' – fetched from my bedroom an unopened tube of modelling cement, a craft knife and my green vinyl cutting mat.

I hurried back to my rented room. It hardly registered with me that my window was still intact, that my landlady had not turned up at my door with a horror story of thugs lingering outside the building, or taken one look at my bandaged face and sent me packing, or, indeed, seen me at all. All the other events of the day were a grey blur to me as I tweezered and cut the grey plastic pieces from their frames and spread them on the mat. The instructions were clear, the pieces were few, but my hands were shaking so much I got glue all down the front of the figure's uniform. I had to wait for it to harden, then shaved it off with a scalpel. I didn't have any fine sandpaper and I was afraid that when the model was complete, the nubs that had attached each piece to its sheet would stop its joints from articulating properly. It never occurred to me that, once the model was done, it would be able to make its own repairs.

The jaw needed no glue. It just snapped into place. And then it was complete: a grey plastic miniature rendition of Jim, my dead brother.

Jim's jaw clicked up and down. The figure tried to stand. I scooped him up and laid him on my pillow, shushing him. 'You're still wet.'

I was so afraid of crushing him, I slept on the floor, the rug wrapped around me. Jim, in a voice squeaky from miniaturisation, insisted I at least take the pillow. Even so, by morning, I woke with the whole left side of my face aching as though it had been assaulted with hammers.

I don't think I even glanced at the bed as I stumbled out of the room. I had it in my head that I must have got drunk. That if I couldn't remember the pub, then I must have drunk enough to black out. That drinking enough to black out would at least explain the absurdity of my dreams.

I went downstairs to the bathroom and studied my face. The doctors had assured me that my scratched cornea would soon heal. My left eye looked like a raw egg in a dish of blood. My cheek was a perfect round purple lump, as though someone had stuck a piece of liver on my face. My landlady walked in, saw me and screamed.

I had forgotten to shut the bathroom door.

My Halifax job didn't impress my landlady much. She resented the insistent way I locked the door of my room each morning and pocketed the key. She resented my never letting her in to clean. Every so often, I'd find a reason to show her the room. That way I could demonstrate that nothing untoward was going on and that I was more than capable, thank you, of stripping and making my own bed. 'I have papers here,' I told her. 'Confidential papers. You understand.'

In truth, I did have such papers in the room, plans released to me on the strict condition that I hide them from casual view. But it was Jim I was most concerned about. Where he came from, I could not begin to guess. Jim himself did not know but, in that silly, squeaky voice of his, he speculated: 'I must be a Bundist thing, don't you think?'

I sat on the floor cross-legged before him. 'I suppose.'

'An earnest of their good faith.'

'Their good faith. The people who destroyed the *Victory*.'

'*If* they destroyed it. It could have been an accident. Maybe they saved us. Isn't that what they're saying?'

'It's what some of them are saying. The whole business is unclear.'

'And if they've done this –' he rapped on his hollow chest '– then I must still be alive. Yes? In any number of ways. In several editions!'

I had no answer for him. The destruction of the *Victory* had brought the unaccommodated world into a belligerent unity. Across Europe, our spaceships were proceeding ahead of schedule. But with the Bund it was a very different story. At the very moment when clarity might have been considered essential, for everyone's peace and security, the Bund had proved incapable of explaining itself.

The *Victory* had been attacked!

The *Victory* had suffered a fatal malfunction and been, so far as possible, saved.

The crew were dead.

The crew were alive!

The crew had been killed to serve as an example to others.

The crew had been restored using the latest medicine and would be returned home shortly.

The Bund welcomed guests to its new bases on the Moon's far side!

Any attempted incursion of lunar facilities would be met with overwhelming force.

There were no Bundist bases on the far side.

On and on like this. Was it possible the Bund itself was

splitting – even speciating? Might that explain those two TV news anchors we had seen, swinging back and forth, clipboards pressed to their groins, on the night of the *Victory*'s destruction? Their glass skulls? Their finned and spiny brains? I'd not seen the likes of them before, and no one had reported seeing them since.

'Fuck it,' said Jim, 'I'm going out.'

'Wait. Jim. I still don't understand.'

'Stu.' He sighed and ran plastic hands down his glue-spoiled front. 'You expect me to have answers? How do you think I feel? I don't even know what I am, let alone what I'm for.' He hefted up a sixpence and used it to turn the screw holding the wall vent in place.

Jim had been coming and going through the vent ever since I had managed to loosen it from the plaster partition at the back of my room. There was no way I could keep him sealed up in my bedroom all day. Jim, for his part, promised to conduct all his adventures well away from my landlady's house. How far afield he went, I am not sure. His stories were so highly coloured, it was obvious he was trying to get a rise out of me. Whatever the force animating him, modelling plastic has a tensile strength no magic can alter or improve. Were Jim ever to engage in hand-to-hand combat with one of the local mousers, as he claimed he did, I knew where I would put my money.

'Right through the *eye*, Stu!'

'Settle down.'

'It sneezed and some of its brains shot out through its nose. I took cover behind a cocktail umbrella.'

'Jim. Shut up.'

*

In retrospect, and with matters having reached such a head, it is easy to see all the things I should have done; easy to identify all my moments of funk and denial. But though I seem to have a talent for second-guessing myself, I cannot honestly say that I blame myself for the way I hid Jim in my bedroom.

What else could I have done? What authority was qualified to consider this grey plastic miracle that had been pressed into my hands? Jim wasn't some emissary. He wasn't asking to speak to my leader. He wasn't the scout of some alien army, poised to invade the Earth. He was my brother. Within the limitations set by his size and his simplicity, he was my family, returned to me. Of course I kept him safe with me.

Nor did I show him to my father. Bob had demons enough to contend with. His wife had been restored to him in a form he could not countenance; what would he have made of a son turned into a toy? I had it in mind to spare him, and even now, I think this was the right decision.

One thing I might have done differently: I might have taken Jim to London, to Stella's house in Islington, and showed him to Betty. Jim and I had even talked about it, or tried to, the pair of us hunting for vocabulary with which to discuss this bizarre eventuality: a resurrected child mother presented with a resurrected doll son. I have no doubt we would have visited eventually. But then, one day in early June, Betty was knocked down and killed by a hit-and-run driver on the road outside Stella's house.

The circumstances of the accident are still not clear. What was Betty doing, playing in the street? If she was playing. Perhaps she had seen something, heard something. Perhaps she had gone out to confront whoever was spraying threatening graffiti on Stella's garden wall. A strange sight that would have been: an old Yorkshirewoman's tirade spilling from the mouth of a child done up in this season's florals.

Perhaps they had been expecting her. Perhaps they had been baiting her. Whoever 'they' were. Perhaps they had been lying in wait. But what is the point of speculations like these? They don't do anyone any good. No one even saw the car. It was evening, and half-light, the time for stupid accidents. The doctors said Betty's injuries were total, that she wouldn't have felt anything, but I don't believe that. She died in hospital three hours after she was found, flung all haywire over the iron railings into Myddelton Square Gardens.

Because it was a police case, there was a delay releasing the body. This gave my father and Stella an opportunity to fall out over the funeral arrangements. Stella wanted her sister buried near her. Betty had been living with her for years. Stella had seen her through her first biopsy and every round of chemotherapy. It was Stella who had persuaded Betty to undergo the Process, and persuaded Georgy to offer her the Process in the first place. She'd brought her older sister up from birth, as though she were her own child. Whatever difficulties she and Georgy had experienced in their relationship, chances were they'd been started by Stella's preoccupation with little Betty. (Not every man wants a second family hot on the heels of the last, and for sure Georgy wasn't the type.)

None of which made a blind bit of difference to Bob. He was adamant. The plot in Hebden was paid for, and there the pair of them would be buried, husband and wife, with a view of chimneys and rain sweeping down the valley from Blackshaw Head. On the stone: 'Elizabeth Lanyon. Bob Lanyon.' Dates. A simple stone over a grave dug extra deep: when his time came, he'd be laid on top of her. 'It's all arranged.'

'You never even saw her!' The stage had given Stella lungs. I could hear her through the earpiece of the public telephone. She was so loud, Bob had to hold the receiver away from his ear, which made following the conversation even easier, though it was the last thing I wanted. 'You never even acknowledged that child was her!'

I could understand Stella being annoyed at Bob assuming responsibility for Betty's funeral arrangements. The sheer level of her rage was something else. I think it was a battle she needed, so that her grief had some way to express itself. Bob was tongue-tied but for once he did not cave in. He asked me to arrange transport for the coffin.

No one in my new job ever breathed down my neck, telling me who I could and could not speak to. From my boss's desk, I phoned Stella myself. 'I want to invite Fel to the funeral,' I said.

'That's a sweet idea.'

'She and Mum were so close.'

'Yes.'

'Have you seen her?'

'No,' Stella said. 'Not since you left London.'

'She's not been in touch?'

'No.'

'I thought maybe she'd been to see Betty.'

There was an awkward pause.

'It's all right, Stella,' I said. 'Has she been round?'

'A couple of times. But it was strange without you. I think Betty gave her a hard time.' She laughed.

'It was me that left,' I said.

'You don't say? Idiot.'

'Thanks, Stella.'

'Well.'

I asked Stella to call round at the flat in the Barbican, but there was never anyone in. 'You could always phone Georgy,' she said. She gave me his number.

So I called him, and what a weird conversation *that* was. No 'I'm sorry to hear about your mother.' No 'My commiserations for your loss.' I got the strongest impression that he was afraid of me. At any rate, afraid.

'So you can't help me.'

'I'm sorry, Stuart.'

By now, I was furious with him. 'You're telling me you don't know where your own daughter is.'

'I know exactly where she is. My problem is I cannot begin to tell you.'

'What? You think I would hurt her? Is that who you think I am?'

'I mean what I say, Stuart. Literally, I cannot begin to tell you. You would not understand.'

'Fuck you,' I said, and slammed down the receiver.

*

It was clear enough that Georgy was not going tell Fel about Betty's death. More: that Fel was in a place where she'd not hear the news from anyone else. What the hell was happening with her? This on top of everything else I was handling – the mourners, a sandwich supper in the Arms, my dad. All I wanted to do was think about my mum. But which mum? Even that had been made impossible for me. Was it the formidable and distant woman who had borne me I was supposed to mourn, or the charming and obstreperous child? The pattern of my feelings had been bent so out of true by Georgy's therapy, I could only keep returning to the one solid, material fact any of us had left to cling to – the horror of her unexpected and violent death. I had terrible, disgusting nightmares, perhaps because it was only in sleep that I was finding freedom enough to try and untangle my feelings. Spending time with Bob helped, I think. He showed me old photographs. My heart ached, but as it aches for someone very dear lost long ago. I began to understand that I had been mourning my mother for a very long time. Before her transformation. Even before her cancer. I began at last to accept the sorry fact that she had always been leaving me.

The coroner's office released Betty's body for burial in mid-July. The ceremony took place on a Wednesday afternoon. There were neighbours, and men from Bob's factory, and some of Betty's family had driven across from Wakefield. Stella had already said she would not come and there was no one turning up from the nursery in London. Not that anyone from Medicine City would have been made to feel at all welcome. Bob had even insisted that Betty be buried in an adult-size coffin. He was after an ordinary and present sadness, on this day of all days. Nothing remarkable. Nothing out of true. He had spent too many years trying and failing to accommodate the future.

The hearse crawled past us as we climbed the hill to the cemetery. Bob was ahead of me, walking arm in arm with Billy Marsden. I was making conversation with a Wakefield cousin whose name I had already forgotten. The road was muddy, slippery from recent rains, but the weather could not have been brighter. White shreds of cloud lay over Snay Booth while here, in the lee-side of the valley, the air was all mown grass and woodsmoke. The lane rose between high hedges and came to a plateau overlooking the southeast corner of the town. The hedges fell away and a low dry-stone wall marked the cemetery boundary. There was nothing special about the place, no planting, no effort at funerary architecture. The headstones, all of an equal height, suggested a bizarre crop left ignored in a field gone fallow. But smoke from the chimneys below the hill was filling and swilling the valley with washes of desaturated blues and pinks, and with such a view before me it was possible to feel attachment to this land. Even love.

The coffin was absurdly light, of course. How little Betty was secured in that great big black box I could not imagine. I took the head end, Bob beside me, some cousin of Stella's at the rear and Billy Marsden beside him, and it was no effort at all for the four of us to process across the damp, uneven ground to where the earth had been heaved up. I was afraid she'd shift, slumping to the foot of the box, or its head. But the weight, though absurdly little, stayed steady on my shoulder. What, I wonder, did the other bearers think? Down the coffin went, into its hole, and far too slowly. The weight of the box had the workmen confused.

And Betty's burial was only the beginning. There was tea to get through at the Arms, and seeing the Wakefield mob off at the station, and back to the Arms for a drink with the fellows at the factory.

By the time I'd tucked Bob in and set off for my own room, I was much too tired to deal with Jim. And Jim, of course, having spent the whole day stuck inside (I wasn't risking him being discovered on this day of all days) was just about ready to climb the walls. Failing them, the curtains.

'Come down. Now.'

Jim stuck his plastic tongue out at me.

'You'll get me into trouble.'

'Nah.' Jim swung from fold to fold, idly, experimenting. His whole environment was one giant climbing frame. He was only five inches high and can't have weighed much above a pound. This gave him a power-to-weight ratio even more monstrous than the one he'd expected to enjoy on Mars, gambolling about like a toddler in less than half Earth's gravity.

'We'll go to the cemetery together in a couple of days,' I promised him. 'You can say your proper goodbyes to Mum.'

Jim swung, missed and dropped onto the dressing table, knocking my wallet onto the floor.

'For heaven's sake.'

Jim sat on the edge of the table, swinging his legs as he watched me retrieve it. 'Sorry, Stu.'

'How are you feeling?' I asked him.

Jim's restitution was not total, and Jim himself was aware of the gaps. He frowned, struggling to assess this great imponderable: how *did* he feel?

'Sad,' he said. 'Angry, mostly. That she went through all that, only to die like ... that.'

Jim's sincerity shortfall was partly real (he was only a toy, after all), partly a problem of perception. However profoundly he might feel things in his plastic state, he could only ever express those feelings through a plastic mouth, and at a comically high pitch. How deeply can you rate the grief of someone who sounds like a cartoon mouse?

Jim sensed our conversation was going nowhere and, ignoring me, climbed up onto the shelf under the window. He traversed along my books, looking for something to read. I think he was after some inspiration for his storytelling because the volume he lit on was Betty's pocket hardback edition of the *Aeneid*. He grabbed the top of the spine and leaned back, angling it out from the shelf.

I stepped forward and rescued the book before its binding tore any further in Jim's tiny, crudely articulated hands. Jim, dangling one-handed off the spine, let go. He fell, picked himself up and ambled over to the fireplace, where he had his cushion. 'I could have got it.'

'You were breaking it.'

'I'm careful.'

'You're an idiot.'

'I'll be full-size again one day, so just you watch it.'

'And back in your right mind, I hope.' I laid the book out for him, not too near the fire, for fear his joints might soften, and while Jim read, scooping back the onion-skin pages as delicately as he could with mitten-fused fingers, I laid out the paints I had bought that day in Halifax. Humbrol's enamel range offered good approximations of the regulation colours of Jim's uniform. Jim's appearance seemed to have been based on his last moments aboard the *Victory*. His overall was of a piece with his flesh, his boots sealed seamlessly around his calves. His face, though rendered impassive, still carried – unless this was just my imagination – a faint ghost of my brother's death-terror.

I tested the brushes I had bought against my palm. Jim watched me, suspicious. 'If it tickles, I'm not doing it.'

'All right.'

'I don't know, Stu. Aren't all those colours going to mark me out?'

'Desaturated blues and black? This lot will camouflage you, if anything.'

'What colour are you going to paint my face?'

'I'm not going to paint your face.'

'I'm not having that flesh-pink stuff. I'll look like a Band-Aid.'

Downstairs, we heard movement. Other tenants, maybe, or the landlady herself. We sat in silence, waiting for the coast to clear.

'This is odd,' Jim murmured. I glanced over and saw he had worked his way through the book to the bookmark – Betty's appointment slip from the Gurwitsch Hospital. He had it spread out over the start of Book Six. I came over.

Easy is the descent to Avernus:
Night and day the door of gloomy Dis stands open.

But to recall one's steps, and pass out into the upper air,
That is the labour, that is the difficulty!

'Look at the date.' Kneeling on the paper, Jim reached and tapped its top right-hand corner.

'What?'

'Mum was already reborn by then, wasn't she?'

I looked at the date. 'So?'

'So she wasn't attending appointments at the Gurwitsch. She was well past all that.'

I made a face. 'Maybe.'

Jim was adamant. '"Maybe" nothing.' He stepped studiously over the paper, examining it. 'Her name's nowhere on it.'

'There's no name on it.'

'Isn't that odd?'

'I don't know.'

Jim stepped off the book onto the cushion and let it take his weight as he rolled backwards, head over heels, and onto his feet. At his size, it wasn't a particularly athletic gesture at all – just his natural way of moving. I thought of Mars and how Jim might once have gambolled there. I thought of the meal we had all eaten in the basement kitchen of Stella's house in Islington, and how Georgy had barracked Jim that night. He had been in a mood to make digs at everyone that night; even his own daughter. Even Fel.

Even Fel.

And then I knew. The truth came clear. It screamed at me, as surely as Fel had screamed at me on our last night.

There is no fucking time!

I remembered waking suddenly in the middle of the night. But the bedroom was not dark, there was a light on, and I turned over in the bed, and there was Fel, sitting up on pillows, the reading lamp on, poring over an old book. And when she saw that I was awake and felt me move against her, she grinned, the jewel shining in her tooth, and lifted the book for me to see – Betty's *Aeneid* – and said, 'The old stories are the best.'

And then she closed the book. The placemarker wasn't Betty's at all. It was Fel's.

The appointment had been Fel's, too.

I looked at my watch. I pulled my coat from its hook on the door. I checked I had my wallet. I snatched Jim up from the floor and crammed him protesting into my pocket. I hunted for my keys when all the time they were hanging from the keyhole in the door. I snatched them, left the room and locked the door behind me. My landlady looked out of the kitchen as I passed. I shouted some incoherent explanation as I barrelled past and toppled into the street.

I had ten minutes before the last London train.

10

'Eat your greens!' exhorts Hattie Jacques, from the poster on the tea-house wall. She has company now. Dirk Bogarde in Space Force blue: 'Together, We Can Build Tomorrow!' Underneath, a third poster. No photograph this time. Cheaply and hurriedly produced, with a War Ministry stamp. Absorbent paper: the ink's already begun to run from four block-printed words: TAKE BACK THE MOON.

Poster by poster, broadcast by broadcast, the world is rumbling towards another war. In the West Riding, the collapse of the old dispensation is expressed mostly through official directives. Posters on the tea-house wall. New projects announced, new targets set. Fatter pay packets and less time in which to drink them away.

In the Smoke, it's far more complicated. On the Thames, the ferries run empty that once carried unaccommodated guest workers to and from their menial jobs on Threadneedle Street and Bishopsgate. Someone built their own howitzer, if you can believe this, and shot out one of the Bund's bright civic 'moons', plunging late-returning workers into darkness: they had to navigate by the light from their own phones. And yet, as you come off the sleeper bleary-eyed – it's not much past six in the morning – you are confronted by protestors *defending* the Bund. They've gathered keen and early for the beginning of rush hour. They're a well-dressed lot: students. If all goes smoothly they can be in lectures by ten, nursing secret smiles and bruised knuckles and no professor the wiser. They're wielding banners sporting the entwined snakes of the Gurwitsch Hospital letterhead. They're fans of the Bund, cheerleaders of the posthuman future. Mortality's no friend of theirs; who wouldn't want to live for ever? The police are trying to corral the protestors out of the way of the escalators. You shimmy past, absurdly self-conscious, as if you might be recognised. As if your ambiguous and intagliated relationship with the Bund was something special, something unprecedented. Nonsense.

Down the escalator, the posters are stuck over with political symbols, the times and dates of marches and flags of several sorts, from the Union Jack to the Palestine tricolour; half-torn away, most of them, or obliterated with an angry pen. There are soldiers wearing the portcullis badge of the London Regiment waiting on the platform with you. You wonder whether they are peacekeeping now, in this city that is psychically coming apart. You wonder what the Bundists make of them.

The train arrives. The carriages aren't full, you board easily enough, and there's a seat for you. Someone has left their newspaper behind. You pick it up and refold it, beginning at the beginning. It's yesterday's late edition, and in the ticket office of the Underground you've already seen headlines that attempt to answer the bald question posed by the headline on the front page before you: WHAT'S WRONG WITH THE MOON?

Below the headline, a photograph of the full Moon is surrounded here and there (the areas helpfully circled by the paper's picture desk) by patches of blotchy light: a sort of ham-fisted corona.

Opposite you, a boy of about twelve leans in behind his mother's open paper. She's reading today's edition: on its front page, the picture is the same, or similar – the corona has become, or been made, more visible. The image has been moved to the top of the page and below it, the headline has been reduced to a single word: ATTACK.

Lost in the mystery and threat of that headline, you have lost your sense of time. Aware that the train is not moving, you experience a lurching moment of panic. After all this while, have you somehow missed your stop? No: the indicator at the end of the carriage still says Covent Garden. The train is being held in the tunnel. There are no announcements, yet nobody around you looks particularly put out. The carriage seats are all taken now and three people are standing by the doors through which you boarded.

The first is a young student, possibly a schoolgirl, wearing her backpack modishly low on her back; the second is an Indian businessman; the third an exhausted-looking young white man, his head shaved as though in preparation for a procedure. He's wearing plaster-spattered jeans and jumper, and he's holding on to a pole by the door, straddling a bag of tools. Perhaps you should offer your seat to this man: he looks so tired! He has rolled his sleeves up past his elbows and his arms – tanned, downed with blond hairs – tremble as if he has been lifting heavy burdens, or pulling himself repeatedly onto a ledge.

His fingers – do you see them? – are thick and worn and covered in white dust: powerful hands, the fingers held slightly apart. Imagine the muscles of his fingers, too, trembling, swollen with blood from some intense physical exertion!

Let your gaze move slowly, intensely, from the tips of the man's fingers, to his wrists, to the complex tattoo, already so old as to be blue and faded, that runs up his forearm: a set of cantilevered bars that stand in for the pumped musculature running beneath the man's honey-coloured skin.

The tattoo disappears under the man's jersey but don't let that stop you. Let your gaze continue to rise, as you speculatively sketch in the forms and images that lie under the fabric. You're up to the man's neck, now. See the stubble there? It's darker than the hairs on his arms. Keep going. That's it. Up, past the youth's strong chin, to his eyes and *there*: they lock tight on your own.

Your breath catches in your throat. Are you afraid? Why are you afraid? Look: the man is smiling. Such a burst of liquid warmth under your skin! You want to leave your seat, not to give it up for the man, but so that you can stand beside him, bathing in the light cast by his smile. To be any distance at all from that smile, even a few feet, is unbearable.

You're just in the act of rising when you notice the young girl, the student – perhaps she is still a schoolgirl – and she, too, has seen the young man's smile. She, too – it's obvious

– has seen the quality of it, the unusual intensity. Now she turns casually to see where that smile is directed, and as she turns, her backpack swings awkwardly against the small of her back and her shoulder performs a small, compensatory shimmy, keeping the straps in place. Gaze at her shoulders, her chest; measure the subtle acts of balance by which she turns yet keeps the bag on her back! The contrast between the subtle cybernetics and the frank invitation of her small, high breasts is heartbreaking, don't you think?

And, though he's paying no particular attention to anyone, something about this moment must be brushing the consciousness of the Indian businessman, whose closed eyes and flaring nostrils suggest that he is experiencing the onset of a spell of profound concentration. A beatific smile spreads slowly across his face, first as a pout, then a wave of relaxation that transforms his whole appearance, softening every wrinkle, every frown-line, before spreading to his shoulders, his back, even to the girdle of his hips, so that he seems without moving to grow, to unwind, his stoop and rounded posture gone, his belly not a burden but a part of him now, integral to this new shape as it emerges from its unathletic original.

Now the girl is watching the businessman very closely. Without even moving his head, the man opens his eyes, gazing deeply into the girl's eyes, so intensely that she blushes, the colour bringing life to her sallow cheeks before spreading prettily to her neck and even so far as her breastbone, and perhaps she feels the heat there, the power of that strong, involuntary flush, because she reaches a hand to her throat and her fingers linger there, and it seems in that instant as if she is caught between contrary impulses: to shield herself modestly from the businessman's smile, and at the same time to asphyxiate herself, stopping her breath so that her eyes might roll in ecstasy back into her head.

Sensing a crisis, the young builder shifts his weight onto one leg, his arms forming an encircling arc, as though to embrace the girl. This motion catches the eye of the businessman, whose admiring gaze explores the young man's face, and the three move towards each other in a single, sweeping embrace. You drop your newspaper between your feet. You have to join them. You have to. But you can't, the woman next to you has her hand on your thigh, her grip is like a vice, and her other hand is between her legs, lifting her skirts, revealing the smooth, full black flesh of her thighs, and even as you lean into her, toppling into her lap, the whole carriage gives a sickening lurch, and the blind black windows, caught in mid-tunnel, erupt suddenly with colour and motion.

Behind the mother and son sitting opposite you, entwined and kissing, something appears.

It is a mouth, pressed against the window, suckered there, its needle teeth tip-tapping on the glass.

A second later, it is torn away and a rain begins of limbs and eyes, the soles of feet, of scrabbling hands and spoon-shaped privates and grazed, bluish knees. *Excuse us! Coming through!*

All the chickies of the city are flooding past the carriage. There are thousands of them, piling one atop the other in the urgency of their passage. The horizontal rain hammers at the glass and keeps on hammering and hammering; there is no end of them. They're no threat, trust me, they're not trying to penetrate the carriage. They just need to get past.

But why?

The answer's there before you, quite literally in black and white. ATTACK.

The chickies know. They know what's coming. And they're afraid. Hell, they're terrified.

And it comes to you (though on a great calm wave of acceptance, so that it does not feel like a thought at all, but rather a change of perspective, a slight but significant shift in the meanings of things), that your own relaxed acceptance of this sight is of a piece with that peculiar, subaqueous episode just now with the student and the businessman and the builder.

And you wonder – without drawing any particular hard and fast conclusions – about the strange sexuality of these chickies, so abject in their self-abnegation, so strong in body, yet in mind, so weak!

And it comes to you – again, without the slightest trace of shock or fear – that this is bullshit. That we know exactly what we're doing, and that it's you, *you* who are being manipulated. And that it's not just you. It's everyone. And that this manipulation has been going on for some while – perhaps ever since that day, half a century ago, when chickies rose out from the dead and crawled their way up through the Somme's thick, stinking, bloodied mud, and saw the world, and saw inside the world, and saw inside the heads of everyone on Earth, and laughed their bright, needle-mouthed laughs, and said, as one,

LET'S HAVE SOME FUN!

, you have lost your sense of time. Aware that the train is not moving, you experience a lurching moment of panic. After all this while, have you somehow missed your stop? But no: the train is even now pulling into Holborn. You work your way as politely as you can out of the crowded carriage onto the platform, where colour-coded signage leads you to the far end of the platform, a flight of steps and a subterranean concourse ventilated by a large blue fan behind a grille.

Another corridor – the same white-painted tin, the same movie posters, Stanley Baxter, James Robertson Justice – and a spiral stair lead you to the Central Line and, after barely a minute's wait, an eastbound train arrives to carry you to Saint Paul's.

From here it's just a short walk to the Barbican.

At Moorgate Station, you find crowds gathering in silence. Moorgate itself, a road which meanders in and out of Bundist territory its whole length, has been closed to traffic. Today, though, it is anything but a no-man's-land. Quite the reverse: you see the ageless, bony-faced men and women of the Bund mixed in amid this crowd, who look as though they might have toppled out of the taproom of the Foresters. There's no argument. No jostling. No confrontation or muttering. There's nothing. People are moving *en masse* across the road towards Finsbury Circus, where the crush is less and the engineered baobab trees afford some screen against the sun. People are trying to see. People are trying to work out what is going on. They are looking up, all of them, in the same direction. They are looking at the Moon, pale in the bright and cloudless day, and circled – this is by now unmistakable – by a white sclerotic ring of stuff, like a wild and ancient eye.

You feel a weight shift in your coat, a tug at its lapel as Jim climbs onto your shoulder and perches there, unremarked.

He whispers in your ear: 'They're rocks. Big ones. Great hunks of regolith. Rail-gunned out of lunar orbit, set on course to hit the Earth. We knew of this in Woomera. Defences, the Bund told us. A last resort. A weapon to end war! The old story. I'm sorry, Stu. We weren't quick enough to stop it. We weren't strong enough. Hell, who am I kidding? We weren't clever enough.'

Gently, you pluck Jim off your shoulder and tuck him into your trouser pocket where he won't get away again and cause any more trouble. You blink to clear your eyes. You ease slowly through the crowd towards the Barbican.

This was the flat Fel used when she wanted to be alone. This was the place she came when she wanted to think about her time with you. This was where she stayed when she wanted to remember.

She came here when she was trying to get pregnant. You know that from the testing wand you found in the bin. What you didn't know, what you didn't guess, until Jim spotted the date on that appointment slip, was what her pregnancy was for.

You open the door. There's someone moving about in the bedroom and you think it might be her. There are heavy footsteps. Is she still pregnant? Are you in time? If you are, if she's still pregnant, if she's yet to go through with it, then maybe there's still hope. Maybe the Chernoy Process can be reversed. There may still be a way to save her.

The door comes open and you start to speak and into the

hall steps Georgy Chernoy, stark naked, his eyes gummed with sleep, one hand in his chest hair, the other scratching his balls. He stares at you.

You want to be sick.

'What the hell are you doing here?' he says.

You can't speak.

'This is my flat,' he says.

This, in all fairness, is true.

'Wait there,' he says. He goes back into the bedroom.

You lean against the wall, your hands over your face, and let gravity carry you down the wall to a sitting position. Something sharp stabs you in the thigh. Have you been stung? You stagger up, flicking at your trousers, and there is a dot of blood soaking through the khaki. Good God, you *have* been stung! Above the dot of blood there's a great bulge of stuff, jammed in your trouser pocket. The lining's got all twisted around. You dig your hand in to sort out your pocket and you prick your finger. You suck a bead of blood away and, shambling about the hall, you use both hands, tugging this way and that, to untangle the unholy mess stuffing your pocket.

Construction-kit Jim has vanished. Rule-bending sprite that he was. And it's a job of work, I can tell you, to bend your mind away from him. Jim, I don't mind saying, has been one of my finer creations. But what's happening here and now is more important. You need to concentrate. So, bit by bit, I scrub your plastic brother out of your head. He was only a bit of fun, after all. A bit of comfort, and you don't need him any more. In his place I've slipped the usual fetishes: an old straw doll and a picture of Jim in a pocket frame – only the glass has finally cracked and broken, and your pocket is full of shards.

Carefully you turn the mess out into your hand: shreds of stalk, ribbon and glass. Jim's picture looks okay. You palpate your thigh through the material of your chinos and wince: a splinter has lodged in the cut. You're taking your trousers down when Georgy reappears at the bedroom door, in slippers and dressing gown. 'What on earth are you doing?' he says.

You are sitting on the balcony, watching a daytime Moon set behind the blocks of the Barbican. The Moon's corona has evaporated, at least for daytime viewers. The rocks are separating, spreading out, each one individually targeted. And yet, with the corona evaporating, it is still possible to believe, in those few seconds of its setting, that the Moon now is as it always was, and that the shape of an ordinary, unaccommodated man is still imprinted on its surface.

Georgy brings out a tray with coffee and cups and a big plate of pastries and sets it on the green metal garden table you and Fel picked out one day, furnishing your first and only home. You hold the table steady for him as he presses the plunger of the cafetière. He sets out the cups and pours. You drink. You eat.

Georgy is a blowhard but he's not stupid. He knows why you are here. He knows the sort of explanation he owes you. He says: 'I come here often now. To this flat. To be among her things, you see. To remember her.'

'You put her through the Process.'

He does not look at you. He nods. 'Yes.'

'She wasn't ill. She wasn't old. Why?'

Georgy wipes the grease off his hands against the fabric of his dressing gown. 'I know what you think of me, Stuart.'

'Do you.'

'It's written all over your face. You think I'm prideful. A crackpot inventor only too happy to grandstand, and use my own daughter to do so.'

So now you know. 'She's on the Moon.'

Georgy smiles. 'Very good.'

'Is she alone?'

'No.' Georgy pours more coffee for you both. 'But she was the first.'

A sound comes out of your mouth. You're not sure whether it's a laugh or what. 'She beat my brother to the Moon.'

Georgy waits for you to calm a little. He says, 'You may think I have some sort of inside track on everything that's happening. Stuart, I don't. Most of what I know I get from the TV, same as you. But for what it's worth – and I can't promise – but for what it's worth, I think Jim is alive.'

A tricky moment for me, I can tell you, as suddenly your memory fills with the heavy solvent tang of modelling cement and enamel paint. You're on the very brink of remembering the toy I gave you, and that would not do *at all*. Scrub! Wipe! Delete! Erase! *Fuck*, but I'm cutting this fine . . .

'Alive.'

'Saved. Stored.' Georgy is in earnest: 'There was a genuine effort to save the *Victory*'s crew, Stuart. Give us a chance. This is a new world for us, too.'

A new world. Now there's a thought to conjure with. 'A second jar.'

'What?'

You push the plate away from you. 'At what time is the jar half-full? You told this story at Windsor Castle. The exponential function.'

'I did?'

'I was there. Stella was there. That was the evening I met Fel. You told us how long it takes a steadily growing thing to double in volume. At one minute to midnight, the jar is just half-full. The future looks rosy. At midnight, you realise you're going to need another jar.'

'Nicely put.'

'The Moon's your other jar.'

'A rather small jar.'

'And at one minute *past* midnight – what then? You're going to need two more jars. Then four. Then eight.'

Georgy watches you. He's trying to decide how much you've understood.

'But that first jar. It's consumed. It's done.'

'Not necessarily,' he says.

'Yes, necessarily. It's used up. It's done. And that's why you're cleaning it.'

'Cleaning it?'

'Bombing it.'

Georgy makes little brushing motions with his hands. 'No, Stuart. No, that's too much. The Bund is simply trying to defend itself—'

'I saw the corona around the Moon, George. I saw it even in daylight. You're trying to wipe us all out.'

Georgy's smile is, for once, not a mask. It is also, quite possibly, the saddest smile you have ever seen. 'And yet.' He fools with his empty cup. 'I'm still here. Aren't I? No room for an old man on the Moon. And what about all the others living here? These Bundists you're so afraid of, all of a sudden: do you see them leaving on spaceships?'

It comes to you that events have spiralled far out of everyone's control; that Georgy Chernoy, and many others, are even now being betrayed.

'I begged them to take her, Stuart. And I begged her to go. I told her more than I should have done, scared her as much as I could with what's about to happen here. The coming war. She absolutely ignored me, of course. Refused me. Of course. Any sane person would. She wasn't old. She wasn't sick. She was beautiful and happy and in love.'

He meets your eye. 'In love, Stuart.'

You see what he is doing. You see what this is. What he is trying to pull. 'No.'

'I couldn't have done it without you, Stuart.'

'No.'

Georgy's smile is still there, it is still real, and it is absolutely not a smile of victory. 'Don't feel bad, Stuart. What's coming is terrible. I thank God every minute that you turned her away. Don't feel bad. If you'd offered her a child, she'd have stayed here with you.'

'Stop it!'

'Don't you see? Stuart. My friend. I'm trying to thank you. You saved her life.'

*

The rest of the day you spend with Stella, trying to persuade her to come back to the West Riding with you.

Ridiculous, that Georgy and Stella should live such proximate lives and not be talking; that two people so in need of mutual comfort should be at hammer and tongs like this; Georgy sitting in an apartment on the eleventh floor of a tower block, missing his daughter, while deep in the basement of the same complex, Stella is slowly losing her mind among the props of her silly TV series, trying to rewind time to the day she was at home, working upstairs while Betty played in the living room and she thought she heard the front door clicking shut, and she paid the sound no mind.

'I didn't even hear the car!' she sobs.

You've found her deep in the basement workshops of the Barbican's theatre, at the heart of the world she has made. She's even sitting – see? – at the DARE commander's desk. Beside her, a small TV monitor is tuned to the BBC. Tears are rolling down her face. She has a look of such helplessness, you go down on your knees to hug her. She bends towards you, arms around your shoulders. You feel the tremor under her skin. Of course she is frightened.

Georgy has been no help. 'He told me it's a fight we should never have started!' Stella sobs. 'Orbital David and Goliath, he calls it. How can he be so callous!'

You don't want to get caught up in their war of words. Still, it occurs to you that Georgy probably feels entitled to be callous. The Bund has made its next and most dramatic play without him. There's been some split, some speciation. The confusion's not just on the TV. It's real. It's deep. Georgy told you the Bund means peace, that it acted in self-defence, and saved the crew of the *Victory*. He probably means it. He probably believes it. At any rate, he wishes it were so. But who does Georgy speak for now? For the Bundists who will be killed along with him in the coming bombardment?

'The Gurwitsch. Medicine City. All that work. It was supposed to be for everyone.'

'So what are you saying? That his own people have betrayed him?'

'Yes. Yes, Stella, that's exactly what I'm saying. Him and who knows how many thousand others. The people doing this probably don't even consider it a betrayal. Have you seen them on TV? The Bund's news anchors now? They're new. They're a new thing.'

Stella thinks about it. She sniffs. 'Typical,' she says.

'What?'

'Typical. The impatience. The Bund couldn't wait. Not even for itself. Who do we suppose is on the Moon now? A bunch of those fishbowl-headed types, I suppose.'

You tell her about Fel. She does not look surprised. 'She's Georgy Chernoy's daughter, Stuart. Think about that. It was a lovely dream you shared together. But she was always going to be among the first if the time came to advance.'

'She wanted a normal life.'

'She was barely into her twenties. She wanted out from under her dad. Don't be disheartened. She's up there. She's safe.' Then, in a much smaller voice, she asks you: 'Did Georgy say how long we've got?'

'A couple of days, he reckoned, before the rocks rain down. Thirty-six hours.'

'Can they be called off?'

'No.'

'So.' She stares at her hands. 'What are we now to the Bund, do you think? People like us. The unaccommodated. Work animals? An invasive species?'

Not even that, is your guess.

Every weapon the Earth wields weighs a ton. On the Moon, you can just lift a rock and hurl it. The Bund can throw rocks down Earth's gravity well till it run out of rocks. This is not going to be an ordinary war. This will be total. A fight to the finish.

Of course, you say nothing of this to Stella. What would be the point?

You look around the commander's office. A white desk, a Trimphone, a potted plant, a padded white chair and a large wall-mounted abstract that, come episode seven, turns out to conceal an escape route in the event of alien attack.

'I think I'll stay here,' Stella says. 'I'm near the Bundist half of the city. Why would they bomb their own buildings? Why would they destroy their own work? You should stay here with me. We're deep underground here. I can't imagine many places safer than this one.'

The truth is, the physical basements of the Barbican Centre are not nearly as protective, for Stella, as the psychic protections afforded by *DARE*, that far more removed world of her own devising. If these are to be her last days, she intends to spend them in a different, better world. A world without the Gurwitsch ray. A world unfractured by runaway speciation. A world of gold cars and skintight uniforms, glamour, secrecy and rigid, simple lines of authority.

Though, for some reason, her world is still – isn't it?

– menaced by aliens. Have you noticed that? It is almost as if aliens are necessary.

She won't be budged.

But then, neither will you. 'I have to go back home. Dad has no one. I have to go.'

'Factories like Bob's will be their first target!' Stella protests.

And she's not wrong. But there is no dissuading you.

She says, 'You know, war is mostly about lying. I don't believe the scare stories. I think we're going to be all right.'

'I'll come and find you,' you tell her.

She smiles a brave little smile, and leans back in her commander's chair, and reaches into a drawer of her desk, and brings out a paper bag. 'Have these.'

You take the package from her hand, mystified. 'What is it?'

'Sausage rolls.'

'Sausage . . . ?'

'For the journey. They're fresh today. Go on. I've got plenty.'

Why this absurd exchange, at the very last minute, should have such an effect on you, you do not know, but your eyes are filling with tears as you pick your way blindly through the prop shop.

What will Stella do when the rocks start to explode in Earth's atmosphere and the hydrostatic shock brings London down to rubble? You imagine her dispatching interceptors. You see her in close conference with DARE's forward stations at exotic beachfront locations across the globe. You hear her delivering inspirational speeches over the Tannoy system to the men and women of her secret subterranean headquarters, hidden under a film studio in Shepperton.

If you are not all right, if the Bund's threats turn out to be real and the destruction total, then this is how you will choose to remember your Aunt Stella.

Why should there only be one future, anyway?

You weave through the length of the prop shop, past the stuff from which the first season of *DARE* was made. A single line of workaday fluorescent strips lights this narrow space, robbing items of the solidity they would acquire under properly filtered film lighting. Here are the pilot's and co-pilot's seats for the Moon-based interceptor, itself dismantled into its constituent flats. These have been stacked carefully behind the chroma key-green cockpit hood of a submarine-launched fighter plane.

On the bridge of DARE's hunter-killer submarine, a raised ring of metal grilles forms a walkway for the operator of the periscope: a black, white and gold contraption that looks like (indeed, is) the barrel of a model rocket. Banks of switches and nested pipework (seconds, bought from Bob's factory) and consoles of no obvious utility, each console fitted with its integral plastic bucket chair, fill the narrow space. This can be accessed either through a small circular hatch or, when the cameras aren't running, through a cunningly concealed gap between two banks of controls, one armed with dangerous-looking red levers, the other dominated by a large, Perspex-covered Mercator projection of the world. The continents are white silhouettes while the ocean floors are shown in exquisite blue-and-brown topographical detail.

You edge around a table covered with scale-model trees and, beyond it, a tank of brackish green water. *DARE*'s big models, the vehicles, are packed in boxes full of wood shavings to protect their delicate parts: aerials and flip-up weapons arrays, wing mirrors, door handles. Fel's submarine, on the other hand, lives permanently submerged in its tank. Too heavy, too delicate and too waterlogged to lift out of the water, it would break in half if you tried. You hunker down, peering at it through the murk. You stir the water with your fingers – abruptly snatch them out. There's something moving in there. Something living.

It's emerging from one of the torpedo tubes. A white grub, much bigger than a fly larva. A tadpole-like thing. You stare at it, aghast. How is this even possible? How does it live? What does it eat? It wriggles free from the tube and as it swims, it acquires form. Arms and legs. At first transparent, it acquires pigment, texture. It is wearing a sturdy silver one-piece uniform. It is recognisably human.

Recognisably female.

Recognisably Fel.

She grips the edge of the tank and falls, panting and dripping, into your lap. She has been holding her breath a long time. You remember concrete walls and pipework; a floor with a drain. Water welling, and her unconcerned stare as the water rose to cover her face. You cry out. Blue as a berry, she laughs and reaches up and kisses you, hard, pressing her teeth against your teeth. You wrap your arms around her, run your fingers through her hair. Is it possible? Can it be that she has been returned to you?

Of course not. This is something else. Her hair comes

away, leaving only glass. Her skull trembles and rings in your hands. There's something thrashing around in there. You close your eyes, afraid to look.

'Too late.' She laughs into your ear, and licks your ear. 'Too late!'

Now what this all portends – Fel here and on the Moon at the same time; Fel small one moment, big the next and hot and in your arms; Fel returned and Fel naysaying her return, *Too late! Too late!* – you may suppose is my game. But you'd be wrong. This is none of my doing. This is something unexpected, and for that reason, frightening. This demands action, fast.

Flats topple. Boxes fall and lamps shatter. There's someone new entering this scene: you look up, wondering what on earth the next cruel surprise might be—

And here I am – *ta-da!* – arrived in the nick of time by the looks of things, all dolled up in red fishnets and glitter, a studded dog collar round my neck.

Fel lets go of you and turns. (If it is Fel. Of course it is Fel. You only have to look at her. You only have to hold her. But Fel, it appears, is multiple now.) What she intends, I can't imagine, and I'm not taking any chances, neither. I do my best to melt into the background, the way I disappeared in that train carriage the day you got hit in the face with that rock. But the trick that fooled you is having no effect on her. Fel's *looking at me*. She's *smiling at me*! She's not what she was, that's for sure. She's changed. She's something new and powerful and she's having none of my blarney.

For a horrible moment, I think she's about to go for me.

Her being a new type, I have no idea what would happen if she did.

Happily, neither does she. Discretion wins the day: laughing, she climbs off your lap, topples back into the water, shrinking as she falls so that when she hits the scummy surface, she's become no bigger than the toy Jim I fashioned for you; she makes hardly a splash.

I come over to the tank and together we stare into the mucky water. There she is: translucent, shedding limbs, retiring to her submarine. Grublike. Gummy. Gone. *How does she do that?*

I fix you with big, bottomless black eyes, reading you frantically. What did I interrupt? What did I miss? What did she want? What has she done to you?

She's put something inside you!

Keep still, let me see! What is it? A weapon? A bomb? KEEP STILL!

It's a delicate business, moving around inside a mind, dancing inside another's dance, it is so easy to ...

(10) Oh, bless my heart, (9) what have I done?

(8) I've tripped it! (7) Triggered it! (6) What can I do?

(5) Nothing. (4) The damage is done. (3) This thing she's put inside your mind, it's about to ... (2) what?

(1) The sets of *DARE* shift and reassemble to form—

A small apartment.

I am standing in the middle of a small apartment.

Well, this is new.

I can see a kitchen through a screen of beads. The bedroom's to the right. *The only other door is behind me and has a slot for letters. So this, I suppose, is it: a single room. Its furnishings are modest. Rugs. Pencil sketches in frames. Candlesticks over the fireplace. A bed, a bookshelf. The room's big, though. Well-lit. There are windows floor to ceiling all along one side, and wooden shutters. A narrow balcony beyond. Beyond that, woods roll down to the sea.*

There's even a piano in here. A grand. In gold leaf above the lid, catching the light: 'Bösendorfer'. A modest apartment. Not a cheap one. I wonder where (THE HELL!) I am?

Odessa, maybe? Is that the Black Sea down there? I suppose it could be Falmouth. Hell, it could be anywhere.

Or nowhere.

A modest apartment. Not cheap. Not tidy, neither: there are toys and baby books lying around on the floor. A toy xylophone with a missing bar. A panda. Some plastic building bricks. I wonder where our child is. (and all the while I'm thinking, WHAT CHILD? What is this? And why am I here? What am I supposed to do here? Who am I supposed to be?)

I peer around the room. Oh for goodness' sake what am I doing? *Do I imagine this mythical infant might be hiding under the floorboards, perhaps, or behind the lamps?*

And then I freeze, utterly transfixed. Because it has suddenly dawned on me, where I am.

Do you recognise this place? This place she's put inside you? You should.

This is the life you could have had.

Do you see? Fel, and a child. This is the future that you threw away.

Soon enough it is evening. Time is relative here, I've realised.

So is space. The room wobbles. The room has been changing as I've been moving through it. The windows are glassless now with wooden screens closed over them, carved into arabesques. The air outside is hot and spiced. In truth the flat's not changed much — the rugs are different, the sofa's vanished, there are cushions, and candles everywhere — but the real change lies outside. Which city is that out there? Tangiers? Istanbul? Some harmless, unquestionably patronising oriental fantasy.

And so to bed.

The Moon is out, and at an angle to send its radiance spilling over our room. We lie watching lines of pale light crawl across her floor like living things. We move against each other, softly, shh, don't wake the baby, and sometime in the heat of it all I murmur her name. 'Oh, Fel ...'

Well. It must have been something I said. Because all of a sudden this dream, or vision, or whatever you would call it: it is done with me. It spits me out and

(0) here I am again, among the toppled props of DARE. I hunker down beside you, squatting over a tank of brackish water, and lying on the bottom, the plastic model of a futuristic TV submarine.

It is not often I am at a loss for words. But if this transformed Fel is representative of what the Bund is becoming, I reckon I had better get used to this dumbfounded feeling. Logic dictates that there must always be a greater and a lesser than oneself, but Jesus, *how did Fel do all that?* How was she even here, never mind in that slippy, big/small form? And how did she leave *that* inside you? That dream? That room? That world?

It's no good; even if I wanted to, I couldn't rip her gift out of you. It's indelible; it's practically somatic. If you ever do have kids, they'll probably end up dreaming that very dream themselves.

'What are you talking about?'

It takes me a moment, bowled over as I am by what's just happened, to realise that you are speaking. Ah, so you *are* awake! And staring at me, what's more, as though *I* was the phenomenon that needed explaining! (What a joke.)

'What?'

My God, you remember none of it, do you?

'Do you want something?'

Not Fel in your arms. Not her mouth against yours. Not her heat in the bed. Not the room. Not the Moon. Not the music. None of it. Poor purblind boy, kneeling there, quite unaware that there are Gods going to war over you!

I imagine you will never really know her gift is there inside you. I imagine it will only ever visit you in dreams. I imagine that is why it is there: to sustain you. To remind you that the world is bigger than you are, and that love is possible.

For that gift to make you conscious of what you lost – no, that would be too cruel.

'What do you want?'

You cannot see how much people love you, can you? (Echoes of you and your mother, there.)

All right, then. One second. Deep breath. Regroup. Set Fel aside, and all these latest miracles: why *am* I here?

Oh yes. Idiot. Why do you think I'm here? I thought your silly life needed saving.

We stand and move away from the tank. I back off. For

a while, we watch each other. It is not a hostile moment. Eventually you buck up the courage to approach me. I'm short enough that you can look down on the top of my head. I'm going a little bald, do you see?

Now listen: if I were you – best guess – don't worry too much about your Aunt Stella. She's well underground where she is, and art centres will not be among the Bund's primary targets. Your instincts are right: look after your dad.

'You can talk.'

No, I can't. Look closely. My mouth is simply hanging open in a parody of speech. Is my mouth moving? It is not.

You gesture at me, then at your own neck. 'Do you want me to remove that thing?'

Well. I run a finger around my collar. Obviously not.

I realise this probably seems a bit trivial to you right now, but the grease is working its way through that paper bag of yours at quite a rate. In fact, I reckon it's going to tear any second – and I could kill for a sausage roll.

'Oh.' You open the bag and pull out a pastry and, timidly, remembering perhaps Wilkes's savaged face, you throw it at my feet.

Charming.

'What?'

Is this your idea of a serving suggestion?

'Sorry.'

But what the hell. I pick the roll up with my foot and, standing on one leg, lift it from my foot to my opposing hand to my mouth, into which the roll disappears in a single gulp.

'*Taaaaaaa.*'

(This much a chickie can vocalise.)

I have something for you, too. Since one good turn should always beget another.

Hold out your hands.

There.

It is a dolly.

Not much, by today's standards. Not much, compared to a selkie's gift of sustaining dreams. (And do I feel upstaged by Fel? I surely do. And does it rankle? Yes, it bloody does!)

But here: it is your dolly. I have refreshed it. I have cleaned and mended it. I have slipped ribbons through the torso at points to create the suggestion of arms, pressed to the sides of the figure as though it were standing at attention, like a soldier. Do you like it?

Really?

Your tears say you do, and this is good.

Now. Take my hand. That's it. And let's see if you can get it right this time.

'I knew you loved me,' you begin. The words are hard. The words are inadequate. Never mind. You are saying something, finally (and anyway, I can read your heart).

'I knew you loved me. I knew you meant the dolly for me. That it was a present. A love token? Is love even the right word?'

Yes. Love is the right word.

'I was so young. I didn't understand. If I ever could have understood. If I understand even now. What chickies seem to mean by love: it is so strange. Abject and—'

Go on. I can take it.

'Your love is terrible, somehow.'

There. Yes. You've understood something. It is.

'Funny and horrific and savage and self-destructive, all at once.'

Yes. Terrible. Terrible.

'Too much for me. I was afraid of it. Ashamed of it. And I so wanted to be like James. And James so wanted to be like his friends. And his friends so wanted to be like . . . I don't know. Like men they'd heard of, tough men, army men, maybe not real men at all, just the stories of men. Images of men. Men on a poster somewhere, or in the lyrics of a barracks-room song. So yes, I led them to that place on the moors. Where I found your doll. That earthen table. That knoll. Beered up and staggering, but I knew what it was. Those concealed holes. Your warren. I knew you were there. I brought them to that place, your home, so we could all be men together, rough and violent and to hell with the consequences. And, yes, it was me who struck the first match.'

There.

'It was me.'

Yes. It was you.

'Are you satisfied?'

Satisfied?

'Is this what you want? To hear that I'm sorry?'

Well—

'Is this why you haunt me? Oh, I know you. I see you. When you go, I forget. Then I see you again, and I remember. And I am so tired of it all. The game. A mouse being played with by a cat. That's what I am. And I am so very tired.'

Poor love.

'And I am sorry. I am sorry for what I did. But what

difference does that make? My being sorry?'

Difference?

'The match has never gone out. Has it? You've never let it go out. Have you? Now I understand. Smoke over the valley. The dolly always in my hand. You'll never let me go. You never will.'

Shush.

'You never will!'

I never will. But you don't understand.

'Please—'

Shush. Can't you understand even now?

Yes. Calm down. That's right.

Now. Look at me. Really *look* at me. My long, tiny teeth; my narrow tongue, working the crevices between them; my wide thighs and knock-knees and big feet. My outsize ears and enormous black eyes.

Can you not see? Can you *still* not see?

Can you not see how much I love you?

Your skin in the light, that day on the moors. So fresh. So young. That tiny little mind of yours, still growing. So serious and so uncomplicated. And so I fell in love with you. I fell in love with you the moment I saw you. I have never stopped loving you. Even in the moment you lit that match, I loved you. Yes. That's how terrible it is, my love.

So please. Just once. Hold me.

There.

Your lips on the top of my head.

Oh, my darling! Oh, my monster! Oh, my man!

This is the price we chickies pay, you see, for looking into other minds. Once we look, we cannot look away. The price for understanding all is that we must forgive all. We don't have a choice in the matter. Knowing all there is to know about another mind, how could we ever harm it, or wish it ill?

The most we would ever do is steer it to a better place.

Silly boy. Don't you see? *I'm here to help.*

We take carpeted stairs out of the Barbican Centre's basement levels and exit on a raised brick concourse.

'I saw you today. Lots of you. All of you. In the Underground.'

—Yes.

'You were running away.'

—Wouldn't you, if you could?

'You're fleeing the city?'

—Of course.

'But where can you go? Where are you going? Have you got some kind of . . . spaceship?'

—Ha! Nothing so fancy. We thought, the Thames Estuary. Serious. The water's going to be the safest place around here soon.

We come to an escalator leading down to street level. But that's your route, not mine.

—I go this way.

'I'm heading up to King's Cross,' you say. 'See if the trains are running.'

It's not my style to say goodbye. Easier just to turn my back. So I set off, following a line of yellow tape across the bricks of the highwalk. My steps are dainty and precise, as though the tape were a high wire. I follow the line around a corner, and—

You weave through the length of the prop shop, past the stuff from the first season of *DARE*. Here are the pilot's and co-pilot's seats for the Moon-based interceptor. On the bridge of DARE's hunter-killer submarine, a raised ring of metal grilles forms a walkway. Banks of switches and nested pipework and consoles of no obvious utility fill the narrow space. You edge around a table covered with scale-model trees and then a tank of brackish green water. Beyond it there is a door. Open it. Take carpeted stairs out of the Barbican Centre's basement levels and exit on a raised brick concourse. You will come to an escalator leading down to street level. Leave the Barbican.

It is later than you thought. The Foresters has already stopped serving. You walk by and see bar staff working under cold blue light, cleaning the bar, stacking glasses.

After a couple of minutes, you come to a bus stop that promises a night service to Euston. It will get you most of the way to where you're going, and this is good, because your feet in those ridiculous boots of yours are aching like a bastard.

You have already quite forgotten my existence, and in my place I shall put memories of the house you shared in Tooting, before you ever moved to the Barbican. Do you remember, two of your housemates had a stand-up act? They dressed as pirates. Their routine changed constantly but it never got any better. A warm sense of comradeship fills you, and memories of laughter, and faces you have not thought about for a long time, and how Fel visited and stayed with you sometimes, and how impossible it was to fall asleep together in that narrow bed of yours, and how it never mattered.

The bus arrives. It's late, and very full. You'll have to stand. The pole you hang from is cold against your forehead. You take deep breaths, trying to wake yourself. You're going to have to fill up on coffee as soon as you can, for there'll be no chance for you to sleep till you're on the train back north. At King's Cross, call Bob's usual pub and try and get through to him. It won't be easy, persuading him to flee his home. It's going to take more than one phone call. But you have to start somewhere.

The main thing is not to panic. You have all tomorrow to get home and begin the work. If you're lucky, and the milk train is running, then you'll be home by early afternoon. But even if you have to wait for the first regular train, that still gives you the evening with your dad, and by then there ought to be enough corroborating news on the radio to convince him to flee with you.

There's no telling the power of the coming impacts, and with more information, more people will be on the move. So if I were you, I would not delay. Get him moving that very night. Get far into the moors by morning, well up among the hills towards Walshaw, where there are (so far as you and I ever saw) no munitions, no radar arrays, no heavy industry, nothing for the Bund to target. Just sheep paths and peat and the wind blowing through meadows of sere grass and peat bogs you could lose a dog in, and subtle circles of long-since-vanished habitation.

You'll be glad of your sturdy boots by then.

But what if, after all your efforts, Bob will not be persuaded to leave? He may be too sceptical or too proud to abandon his station now that war is coming. All his life he has slogged out his weeks for hardly more than the promise of a weekend. Were all that to become suddenly meaningful – war work! The nation expecting! – it might tempt him to stay.

In that case: my last advice, before I let you go. Sweet boy. My darling unaccommodated man.

Stay with him. Stay by your father's side and watch the skies for daytime stars.

When they hit, the ground will heave. Stand by him.

The sky will fill with earth and leaves and the cries of men and bits of skin and foil and feathers. Hold fast, and take his arm.

The factory floor rises, the belts clatter and grow deranged, they flap uselessly, and soap and oil slop about the floor, and at last the great machines themselves, the lathes, topple and fall.

You may stagger. Your father may fall. But if he falls, you take him into your arms. Are you listening to me? Draw him up. He's dazed, his world is ending. But not yet. You turn and bend and reaching back you snare the old man's knees within the crooks of your elbows, and falling forward, your father wraps his arms around your neck, and so you'll rise, lifting him, and leaning forwards, staggering at first, but you'll find your pace. You run for the exit, past blazing pools of oil and burning men, upended tea trollies and clocks everywhere, crashing off the walls, and out into the yard, where pipes are rolling back and forth across the brick-paved yard, colliding with men and crushing them.

Pause. Observe. Bide your time. Then run, your father on your back, and—

—waking again, your forehead pressed to that cold steel pole, the bus rattling along now, making up for lost time on the wide, empty streets of Islington, I wondered where this plan of mine had sprung from.

—Do you remember the flat in the Barbican, your bed, and the cool of the sheets in the night?

Yes, I remember.

I remember waking suddenly in the middle of the night, convinced that there was a strange presence in the room. But the room was not dark, there was a light on, and I turned over in the bed, and there was Fel, sitting up on pillows, the reading lamp on, poring over an old book. And when she saw that I was awake and felt me move against her, she grinned, the jewel shining in her tooth, and lifted the book for me to see – Mum's *Aeneid* – and said, 'The old stories are the best.'

ACKNOWLEDGEMENTS

Thanks go to my agent Peter Tallack, and to my editors Simon Spanton and Rachel Winterbottom.

The workings of the HMS *Victory* are loosely based on designs developed at General Atomics during the late 1950s, discussed in George Dyson's *Project Orion: The True Story of the Atomic Spaceship* (Henry Holt & Co, 2002).

DARE is a loose homage to *UFO*, a TV series created by Gerry and Sylvia Anderson which ran from 1970 to 1973.

Simon Ings is the author of eight previous novels (some science fiction, some not) and two works of non-fiction, including the Baillie Gifford longlisted *Stalin And The Scientists*. His debut novel *Hot Head* was widely acclaimed. He is the arts editor of *New Scientist* magazine and splits his time between a sweltering penthouse in Dubai (not his) and possibly the coldest flat in London.

THE RIG
ROGER LEVY

Humanity has spread across the depths of space but is connected by AfterLife – a vote made by every member of humanity on the worth of a life. Bale, a disillusioned policeman on the planet Bleak, is brutally attacked, leading writer Raisa on to a story spanning centuries of corruption. On Gehenna, the last religious planet, a hyperintelligent boy, Alef, meets psychopath Pellon Hoq, and so begins a rivalry and friendship to last an epoch.

So many Lives, forever interlinked, and one structure at the center of it all: the rig.

"A triumph that is guaranteed to blow your mind."
Lavie Tidhar, author of *A Man Lies Dreaming*

"Roger Levy is SF's best kept secret, and *The Rig* is a tour de force: a darkly brilliant epic of life, death and huge drilling platforms. Read it and discover what you've been missing."
Adam Roberts

EMBERS OF WAR
GARETH L. POWELL

The sentient warship *Trouble Dog* was built for violence,
yet following a brutal war, she is disgusted by her role
in a genocide. Stripped of her weaponry and seeking to
atone, she joins the House of Reclamation, an organization
dedicated to rescuing ships in distress. When a civilian ship
goes missing in a disputed system, *Trouble Dog* and her
new crew of loners, captained by Sal Konstanz, are sent on
a rescue mission.

Trouble Dog, Konstanz and Childe find themselves at the
center of a conflict that could engulf the entire galaxy. If
she is to save her crew, *Trouble Dog* is going to have to
remember how to fight…

"It's a smart, funny, tragic, galloping space opera that
showcases Powell's wit, affection for his characters, world-
building skills and unpredictable narrative inventions."
Locus

"An emotionally wrenching take on
life in a war-torn far future."
Publishers Weekly

TITANBOOKS.COM

ZERO BOMB
M.T. HILL

The near future. Following the death of his daughter
Martha, Remi flees the north of England for London. Here
he tries to rebuild his life as a cycle courier, delivering
subversive documents under the nose of an all-seeing state.

But when a driverless car attempts to run him over, Remi
soon discovers that his old life will not let him move on so
easily. Someone is leaving coded messages for Remi across the
city, and they seem to suggest that Martha is not dead at all.
Unsure what to believe, and increasingly unable to trust his
memory, Remi is slowly drawn into the web of a dangerous
radical whose '70s sci-fi novel is now a manifesto for direct
action against automation, technology, and England itself.

The deal? Remi can see Martha again – if he joins the cause.

"One of the most innovative and outspoken new writers of
British science fiction."
Nina Allan, author of *The Rift*

"Intense and well observed, *Zero Bomb* delves into our fears
and distrust of technology."
Anne Charnock, author of *Dreams Before the Start of Time*

For more fantastic fiction, author events, competitions,
limited editions and more

VISIT OUR WEBSITE
titanbooks.com

LIKE US ON FACEBOOK
facebook.com/titanbooks

FOLLOW US ON TWITTER
@TitanBooks

EMAIL US
readerfeedback@@titanemail.com